THE NIGHTMARE TREE

PAUL O'NEILL

THE NIGHTMARE TREE

Paul O'Neill

First edition – September 2021

Cover art by Fantastical-Ink.com

For Zoe, Bodhi and Avery.
May we never find the Nightmare Tree.

CONTENTS

THE GREAT SLIME KINGS

Arlys watched her little brother kneel in the crackling underbrush by the swamp. A slimy frog hopped into his cupped hands. The green air billowed in her lungs, making her cough as Zack brought the frog slowly to his face. His eyes lit up like he wanted to lick the slimy thing.

Zack sighed and his thin legs wobbled.

She leapt forward, laying a hand on his shoulder, steadying him. A warm smile played on her lips as she pictured him splatting face-first into the thick goop of the swamp. She patted his shoulder, the bony ridge hard on her palm – she always kept him at arm's length.

Wet twigs snapped under her boots as she turned to face him, his pale skin reflecting the brilliant green bouncing up at him from the pond. She could see the bones of his ribs even through his baggy Legend of Zelda t-shirt.

His severe anaemia had made a guardian of her. It made outcasts of them both and she had no problem getting into a scrap whenever anyone at school picked on him. She swallowed the rising acid in her throat, the acrid air stinging her eyes.

"I'm leaving," said Arlys.

Flies danced frantic squares above the surface of the water as a cloud of leaves above them rustled, shielding them from the brightness of the September sun.

They'd stumbled upon the swamp years ago. No matter how often they came, she still couldn't get used to the mossy stench that wound its way round her tongue.

She leaned over, staring at her brother's chest, making sure he was still breathing. It was like he was made of jelly, always at risk of keeling over, his skin forever clammy, almost see-through. He stared at the frog with dream-hazed eyes, not blinking. The thing looked up at him like it beamed some psychic message at him.

"Did you hear me? Zack? I said I'm leaving, I—"

"They say you can tell what weather they've experienced just by their colour. This one's been in the rain recently. Look, it's brown. Not surprising really, it is Scotland after all." He snorted, then stretched his hands out to show her the frog. "They turn a yucky shade of yellow when they hit the sun."

The frog opened its gaping mouth and rolled its pale pink tongue at her. She averted her eyes, staring at the moss and mud on her brother's knees, knowing their dad would go through her again for letting him get dirty. She inhaled a lungful of cloying air. That was the least of her problems.

"You listening to me? I'm moving out. I'm..."

Last night, she'd waited in their warm living room, the old paper smell of a hundred books lining the wall wrapping its way around her heart as she wondered where her dad had got to. He wasn't one for staying out late. She'd helped Zack to bed, ready to call for help after a bad coughing fit. Her heart was thumping in her throat as he hacked up a clot of bloody mucus. Luckily, it passed, and he collapsed into fitful sleep.

She kept the TV off and the living room door open. The only sound was the chirping and buzzing of Kazooie, her blue budgie.

Her dad crashed through the door, stumbling about in the dark, trying his best to be quiet and failing miserably. She chuckled, put down her copy of Skagboys by Irvine Welsh, and walked to the hall. The warmth fled out her face when she saw his ashen expression – it was like he'd aged twenty years since he stepped out the door. The wine rolled off him in waves and his knuckles were bloodied, as was his shirt.

"Rough night?" asked Arlys.

Her dad scowled down at her, a look she'd never seen on his normally open, bookish face. "Get away from me."

"What's gotten into you?"

"Turns out your mother was a whore. I did everything for that woman. Thought the sun shone out of her..." He coughed into a balled fist and turned away. "You're not mine's. Found out yesterday. Had myself a little drink to come to terms with it. That so bad?"

"Da—"

"You do not call me that!" He covered his mouth with a trembling hand. "Don't call me that anymore."

He stumbled past her, evading her confused gaze, stottering off the doorway and into the living room. He paced back and forth in front of the bookcase that took up an entire wall.

She followed him, feeling like someone had just smacked her in the chops and did a runner. "Just how pished are you? What's going on?"

He thumbed the spine of a book, then shook his head, his curly hair bouncing from side to side as he marched to Kazooie's cage. The bird chirped at him as he opened its door. A metal *ting* sounded through the room. He snapped his hand around the budgie who let out a pained screech that made Arlys step forward, holding her palms up.

"A few weeks ago," he said, "wee Darby mentioned something that got me thinking. I laughed it off at first, but it rung too close to the truth."

She moved closer, watching her dad squeeze Kazooie, its tiny beak pecking at the hands that had always been so gentle with her. The soup of a bad nightmare made her skin clammy. "Put him down. You're hurting him."

"Normally Darby talks a lot of crap, but it gnawed at me. I sent away some samples to this place, and what do you know, he was right. Looks like your mother played the field." The budgie pecked and clawed his tight fist. "You're not mine's."

He scowled down at the bird, tears flowing down his cheeks.

Kazooie's little head rocked back and forth, bouncing off his fingers as he squeezed tighter still.

"Stop it!" Arlys stepped forward, pulling at his forearm.

A sharp cry of anguish burst from his mouth and he stomped to the window, opened it, and threw the budgie out. Arlys's heart pounded as the bird tumbled to the ground, but it unfurled its wings and flapped into the night.

He turned, absently running his thumb along his pierced skin. "Get your stuff packed. I want you out of here. To think, the one I was actually proud of isn't mine's. Ain't that a kick in the teeth."

A slime bubble plopped in the pond and she stared down at her brother, her pain binding her throat, stifling her voice. "I'm moving to Linwood Home. Just for a wee bit." *With all the other waifs and strays,* she thought. "Zack? Say something. Please?"

Zack stared deep into the frog's eyes as they both breathed a slow rhythm. The frog's transparent membrane under its neck expanded, and a gentle croak bounced around the shelter of trees. It opened its large mouth, a shriek growing in pitch, making her close her eyes. It was a sound somewhere between standing on a cat's tale and a balloon deflating out a tiny hole.

She shook her head and looked around the swamp, focusing on the blackened, split-open trunk of a huge tree. They'd huddled together inside its broken trunk, protected from downpours when the rain sluiced off the leaves above like a hundred waterfalls. They'd spent countless days laughing and joking around inside that dark place.

"Maybe I'll just move in here," she joked, then coughed when she got no reaction. "I'll still come hang around with you, alright? You ain't getting rid of me that easy."

Little flowers of red anger glowed on his shiny cheeks. He juggled the frog onto one outstretched palm, whipped something out of his pocket that glinted, then sliced it along his thumb. She gasped as runnels of blood flowed down his wrist. Lost blood normally meant hours spent pacing in hospital waiting rooms, holding her dad's hand as they prayed.

He dropped the knife and held the bloody thumb toward the frog. It flowered open its huge slit of a mouth, enveloped the thumb, and suckled on it like a new-born baby. The wet smacking and slurping noises made Arlys's stomach flip.

"No," whispered Zack. "You're not allowed to leave me."

TWO DAYS LATER, she stuck a photo of her and Zack in the centre of a bare wall, then threw herself on the single bed in her new room. She lay with her chin on her forearms, staring at the rain pelting off the window. Tree tops blustered about in the gale-force wind.

She'd walked into the mansion, head down, evading the narrow glares of the residents lining up to take shots at the new girl. The huge doors and darkened spaces seemed to weigh on her shoulders whenever she went anywhere. It hadn't taken long for her to get into her first fight. She'd lived through enough to know that to roll over in this place would cast her as the weakling.

Yesterday, she'd raced home, her heart breaking to see Zack, but her dad, her former dad, stood in the doorway, refusing to let her in, telling her to go back to where she belonged. She'd turned, eyes full of tears, seeing her brother at the window. He'd placed his palm against the glass, a blue plaster over his thumb. He looked so pale. She walked the five miles back to the Home in the drenching rain.

She didn't deserve all this – her mum dead when she brought Zack into the world, and now stripped of her brother and her dad, stuck inside this prison of thick concrete and echoey halls.

"I'm getting out of here," she whispered.

"I like what you've done with the place."

She spun round, almost tipping out the bed. Her brother stood in the doorway. A goofy grin spread up his face.

"How in the hell are you supposed to change that lightbulb?" he said, craning his neck. "Highest ceiling I've ever seen."

"Zack!"

Tears pricked the corners of her eyes as she raced toward him, arms stretched wide. He stepped back, holding a palm up, stopping her in her tracks. She squinted at him, then patted his arm. A croak bounced off the walls.

"Tell me you didn't bring a frog with you, dork-face."

Zack puffed out his meagre chest. "You mean my wee pal, here? Came home with me after we found him the other day. He's been living in the stream next to our house."

"Your house, you mean."

"No." Zack's chest deflated. "It's our house, and you need to come back. Dad sucks at Mario Kart."

"Sorry, I'm stuck here in Linwood. A dreamy, castle getaway full of all the lock-in fights and chunky stovies you can ever handle."

From his bony shoulder, the frog stared into her, light creeping around its large, orb-like eyes. She'd never seen a ruby coloured frog before. When its throat ballooned, she took a quick step back. Swirling liquid billowed in its transparent skin like blood dripping in water.

"Just... come back, alright?" said Zack.

"You think I like it here?" She took his wrist and turned his hand over, seeing splotches of purple bruises dotted up his arms. "He's not been hurting you since I left, has he?"

"You know Dad. He wouldn't kick a magpie. I, ehm, had a stumble in the woods, that's all."

He turned his back on her, stepping into the hallway. "I'll be at the swamp tomorrow. I have something to show you. Something to help bring you home."

HER SKIN TINGLED as she fled down the massive steps outside the Home, stepping out of its clinging shadow and into sunshine. The sun fought for one final summer's day before autumn flooded the sky. Stone lions perched at the bottom of the steps, and she turned to look at them over her shoulder as she hurried through the iron gates and out onto the street.

She ran her tongue over her swollen lip – the aftermath of another tussle with Pamela, a runaway who acted like she ruled the roost, picking on Arlys on account of her newish clothes. There were no teachers to stop the fights, and Arlys refused to be the one to give in first.

She stuffed her hands in the pockets of her army camouflage jacket, staring down at the boots that had delivered damage she hadn't thought herself capable of. The Home was dragging her down into a life of zero promises and crime – a fate most of the residents had consigned themselves to long ago it seemed.

Branches and weeds smacked her calves as she rounded the small dirt path that led to the swamp. She walked up a small incline before reaching a wall of trees that circled the town of Kirkness. She turned, looking down at the sprawling town. From here, it looked like the remains of a squished bug, its streets the zigzag patterns of broken limbs.

Following the edge of the trees, she stopped beside a cracked tree stump. It marked the point where they marched into the density of trees and into their swampy little world. She closed her eyes, took in a steadying breath, then walked through the trees, the air around her becoming wetter and sludgier as she moved deeper into the forest.

Standing at each side of the path, rows of croaking frogs glared up at her like sentinels on watch. They were the colour of purple bruises. Their wet skin glimmered as she passed them. One muscled frog whipped out a barbed tongue in front of her foot, then licked its own eye. It gave a little jerk of its head and a sharp hiss as creamy puss dribbled down its face. She shuddered and marched under a tree limb.

Zack faced the pond, a pulsing frog on each shoulder. "They showed me how to fix everything..."

Sweat rose in a cold wave across her forehead as she stepped closer to her brother. Stifling air made her lungs work harder. Her eyes ached, adjusting to the bright green of the swamp.

"You can join me, here," said Zack, his voice hoarse.

"Quit it, dork-o," said Arlys. "You're creeping me out."

A frog landed by her feet, its thick body slapping moist leaves. It studied her with its buzzy eyes as she stepped back, slipping on slimy ground, almost falling over. She exhaled a sharp note of disbelief when the frog turned and hopped away, looking back over its shoulder, bobbing its head as if beckoning her to follow.

"Aye, Lassie, lead the way," she said under her breath.

"Frogs swallow their food whole, kinda like a snake does," said Zack.

She followed the bouncing frog as it leapt about, its meaty hind legs kicking up sodden leaves and twigs. They stopped at the edge of the brilliant green water. The reek of sewage caught the back of her throat. The frog bent, then sailed into the air, landing on a large boot bobbing in the pond.

A joke about a man having sex and forgetting his boot dissolved in her brain as she followed the boot up to the slimed carcass of what used to be a man. Its mouth screamed open. Mossy tendrils swayed from yellowed teeth.

"Jesus!" Arlys stumbled back. Her butt hit the wet ground.

Zack turned to face her, his pupils like moons. "You always protected me when I needed it, so now it's my turn. Now that he's dead, maybe Dad will take you back in. Let us be a family again. No reason not to, now. It's not home without you there annoying the crap out of me everyday."

She scrambled to her feet, wiping her palms on her jeans. "Zack, what happened here? Talk to me."

"I suppose you won't recognise him, now that my friends have finished with him. That's Mr. Arnold. Remember? Darby said he was the one that had gotten too close to Mum. That was before me." He stared down at the ground. "Before I killed her."

"You didn't kill her, you dweeb."

Arlys stared into the pond, at the creamy green circles outlining the man's floating body. Three more frogs hopped on to the carcass. A rising chorus of happy croaks filled the air, echoing all around them under the dome of shaking leaves.

"Zack?" She stared at her brother. "Did you do this?"

He looked steady, his hands folded behind his back. A smile creased the rosy spots of colour in his cheeks. "They eat their own skin. Did you know that?"

It was all too much. She spun and dashed through the trees, branches whipping at her face. Behind her, the forest erupted in a song of frog noise. A crescendo of shrieking wails deafened her as she pumped her arms, sprinting as fast as she could.

. . .

Back in her cell at the Home, her clothes still holding the tang of green swamp, she stared out the window trying to piece it all together. What was her brother becoming? Her fingertips itched, longing to be back in their living room. To clutch a controller playing endless rounds of Mario Kart or Crash Bandicoot with Zack.

Something smacked the window, making her sit up. She yelped as a frog pounded the glass. It made a sound like a mushy tomato, its arms and legs splayed. It left a pink streak as it slid down.

Her upper lip creased as she strode over, seeing a dark figure hunched among the trees in the Home's garden below. She'd recognise those bony, slumping shoulders anywhere. Zack stared up at her, then turned and ran. She grabbed her jacket and tiptoed into the hall, sneaking out into the evening's dying light.

Cold nerves swam in her stomach as she reached her old house, going over and over the things she'd say to her dad. She didn't care what any test said – he raised them both, and she needed her dad back in her life. They needed to help Zack before it was too late.

She marched to the open front door that swayed in the breeze. "Dad? You there?"

Smashed photos and tipped over tables greeted her as she stepped inside. Her boot squealed as she stepped on a wet patch, her heart booming in her chest. Wet splotches marked the hardwood floor. She checked every room, but no one was home, just more wet marks like some swamp monster had stomped through their house knocking everything over.

"Zack? You here?"

Her foot zipped forward as she entered the kitchen, sending her crashing to one knee. A puddle of thick, dark liquid surrounded her hand like black ink.

A bloody trail was smeared over the floor, leading out the back door.

. . .

Arlys ran to the trees lining the sorry looking town. The threat of autumn rain was on the air as she watched the sun climb down the sky, hanging over the forest. An image of the dead body in the swamp buzzed around her mind.

She found the large stump and burst into the trees, and into an eery, silent world. The sun was dimmed by the curtain of shifting leaves above. The thought of being stuck in here at night with those red, unnatural frogs made stomach acid burn up her gullet.

They watched her as she walked deeper into the trees. Sitting on a felled tree by the side of the path, five sets of eyes glared at her, blinking in unison, their transparent eyelids making wet sucking sounds. She slowed her step. This close, she could see the layer of slime on them, shuddering at the thought of running her fingertip along their wet, pulsing bodies.

She leaned back, turning away from them as she walked past, not daring to take her eyes from them. One let out a burbling croak, its tongue shooting out its mouth. Arlys felt the air shift as the pink tongue sailed by her cheek. All five frogs opened their mouths wide. Rows of silver fangs gleamed. A high wail rose like a cat defending its territory. The sound grew and pierced her brain.

Acid crawled up her throat. Her face flushed in the humid heat as she tumbled onwards. Bright red flashes burst from the trees. The frogs landed with wet thuds all around her.

Pain sliced her calf. Hot blood trickled down her shin, staining her jeans as she stared down at the frog that had sunk its tiny teeth into her flesh. She stomped on it. Pink and yellow entrails popped under her boot. A stench of iron wafted up to her, making her gag.

She ran on. An army of frogs exploded all around her. The drone of their screams robbed her of the ability to think straight. Her foot splashed the swamp. A wave of turgid green mess sloshed over the toe of her boot as she stumbled to a halt.

Her ears rung as the world went silent. More bodies lay in the swamp. Heavy droplets of sludge swayed off bone as they floated in the water, bumping into one another. She coughed up a mouthful of yellow bile.

Behind her, the swarm of frogs waited.

"Arlys..." a hollow voice rung in the green silence.

"Zack? Zack, where are you?"

The frogs pounced on her, tearing gashes in her arms and legs. She frantically batted them away. One sunk its needle teeth into her thigh, making her fall into the pond. A wave of oily, mould-layered water swam over her legs. The frogs were on her, sinking their tiny fangs into her skin, painting the green swamp red around her. She leapt to her feet, roaring in agony, slapping the slimy creatures away.

"Sis..."

The voice came from the old tree that lay split open – where they'd spent so much time over the years huddled together. She kicked a frog, sending it flying through the air, and raced toward the tree.

She slid at the entrance of the tree, seeing the words 'Zack and Arlys were here' carved into its base.

The frogs stopped their assault. They gathered around the foot of the tree, studying her. Some whipped their pale tongues at the air as she crept forward. Blood seeped from a hundred small wounds.

A rustling noise came from inside the tree. She squinted her eyes, trying to see into its cave-like darkness.

"Zack? You have to stop this. Are you controlling them? It's not a game."

She recoiled at the broken quality of her voice. The muscles on her face scrunched up. Tears streamed down her cheeks as she tiptoed forward. The crowd of eager frogs watched her every move.

She took a deep breath. "If you don't come out here, I'm gonna drag you out by the ear. Y-you hear me?"

There was more movement, and a figure stepped forward. Its thin, emaciated form swayed side to side.

Her legs wobbled and she fell to the ground, staring up at a face distorted by bulging, shining eyes. Its webbed hands had dirty, gunmetal claws on the ends of long, alien fingers. The skin on its face was pallid, coated under a layer of dripping slime. A warbling voice steamed out of its wide mouth.

"Welcome home, sis."

Moist branches whipped her face as she flew through the trees, willing her stumbling legs to carry her away from this place. Away from the slime-skinned thing her brother had become.

A cacophony of piercing screeches exploded around the forest as frogs slapped the ground behind her.

THREE'S A CROWD

Irvin hauled the bundled cargo across the dusty concrete floor toward his small boat, the last rays of the sun beating into his garage that reeked of salt, and wood, and iron. Footsteps sounded from the path outside, making his heart pound in his ears. He hauled the heavy shape over his shoulder, the wheels of the skiff's trailer creaking as it thudded onto the wooden deck.

"Is that," said Jamie, his shadow spilling onto the boat's white hull, "is she dead?"

His friends Jamie and Harry stood in the doorway. Jamie's mouth bobbed up and down as he searched for words, worry sprayed across his sun-worn features. Harry chewed gum, hands stuffed in the pockets of his puffy jacket like he waited for a bus that was running late.

Sunlight glistened off a hammer on the floor as Irvin stared at the limp leg hanging over the side of his boat, thankful for the brown throw rug that covered the rest of her.

"Irv, man," whispered Jamie, "what did you do?"

Harry blew a pink bubble and popped it. "What you getting het up about?"

"Ya donut, you not see? He killed her."

Harry gazed at the leg, eyeballing jeans that met felt boots dotted with spots of red. "Oh, right." He continued chomping at his gum.

"Why'd you do it, Irv?"

"You whack her with that thing?" Harry pointed at the hammer with a meaty finger.

Irvin took in a deep breath and picked the hammer up. He still smelled her lemony perfume, still tasted their heated, rushed kisses on his sensitive lips. She'd threatened to tell. Then one screaming thing led to another and—

"I didn't mean for it to happen," blurted Irvin. "I swear, I..."

"Poor Michaela," said Jamie.

"Aye." Irvin stared at his skiff, watery eyes settling on the scrawled *The Michaela* written up its side. He'd never taken her out on his boat before. "Michaela."

"She ain't going fishing anymore," said Harry. "That's for certain."

Jamie slapped the back of Harry's bald head, the sound ricocheting off the low ceiling. "You're not helping."

"I can't go to jail." Irvin strode forward, the sunlight beaming up his legs, the hammer loose in his grip.

"Woah, woah." Jamie held his palms up. "Just calm it, man. I knew you were always radge, always a bit mental, but this..."

"Aye," said Harry, hands still in his pockets, eyes glazed like he watched the telly.

"We're still mates here, alright? We got your back."

Jamie's face creased as he wrestled with something, turning it over in his mind. He straightened, peering over Irvin, trying to catch a glimpse of the leg hung over the hull like a doll thrown away.

Irvin shoved the leg over the gunwale, the dead weight thudding off the deck. He pulled the throw rug over her, catching a glimpse of her dead eyes that made the blood rush down his neck. He tensed his fingers around the warm leather of the hammer's handle, stepping toward his two friends.

"Hey, hey, man," said Jamie, backing off. "We knew she was sleeping about, alright? Guess you found out and—"

Harry clucked a loud *tut-tut* like a horse clopping and mimed a hammer blow.

"If you ask me," said Jamie, "she got what was coming to her."

"You what?" said Irvin, trainers scuffing the dusty floor as he stopped.

Jamie scratched his head, panic in his eyes. "I was the one warned you off her when you first started seeing her, mind. I told you she was trouble."

"Out with it."

"She was a bit loose."

"A bit?" Harry snorted.

"Bobby, you know Bobby, worked at the garage a wee while. Well, he sends the lads a message with a photo of her. All dolled up. Pure glam, like in those pics you used to get in magazines."

"No one buys magazines these days," said Harry.

"Would you shut it? Anyways, these messages go on and on, until he starts bragging about banging her in his van a few times a week. I warned him off it, but I figure you gotta give her most of the blame, you know? Putting it about like that."

"Sent me a picture once." Harry scratched his nose, the sound of skin under nail loud in the small space. "Real nice, likes. Want to see it?"

"No, he doesn't want to see, ya nugget."

Irvin tapped the hammer against his thigh, the cold metal seeping through his jeans, the blood in his temples throbbing with each heart-beat. "How long's this been going on for?"

"Couple of weeks," said Harry.

"Months at least," said Jamie. "We won't tell anyone you offed her, alright? Here's the plan. Me and dummy here, we head down to the Harbour Inn. Get us a few pints. You clean up and join us. We'll say you were with us the whole time."

"Alibi. Boom!" Harry clapped his thick hands.

"Sound like a plan?" Jamie waited, head craning forward, his long neck straining.

"That would be sound," said Irvin. "Cheers."

"Right, then." Jamie's shoulders dropped, tension melting away. He let out a mirthless laugh. "Know what, for someone who just killed their bird, you seem awfully cold about it. Me, I'd be freaking by now. Brain all over the shop."

Irvin watched his friends leave, levelling his best, promising glare at both of them. They turned and walked out into the sunset's rays, away from his house – the house he and Michaela had bought together only a year ago.

He looked at his beloved boat, at the scuff mark the boot had made against the perfect white hull. His mum had always berated him for not proposing to Michaela, for not 'strapping her down', as she'd say.

"Too late for that now," said Irvin. "Too late."

He closed his eyes, dreamt of floating on the sea all by himself. Just his boat and the sparkling sun pinging off the salty, majestic ocean.

The sound of boot heels echoed, snatching him from the fantasy, his skin turning winter cold. A shadow spilled from the dying afternoon into the garage.

"Shopping all day sure makes you feel all dirty and stuff," said Michaela. "Gonna take a quick shower. Wash the stink off. Babe? You hear me, aye?"

Irvin turned to face her, the ruffles of her fluffy jacket making it look like she wore a lion's mane. The hammer lay heavy against his thigh.

"Did you see Jamie and Harry on your way home?" said Irvin.

"Nope. Took the long walk back. Just wanted to, ehm, clear my head."

"Where's your shopping bags?"

Michaela's large eyes widened, red quickening up her neck. She stared down at the space by her leather boots. "Didn't see anything I wanted. Babe, you alright? Look like you're about to pop a blood vessel in your eye."

The leather of the hammer's handle creaked in his palm.

"Come in here a sec." He tucked his hand behind his back. "Got something I need to show you."

THE SUMMER BULLET

All I wanted was to see someone else's face, to look another human in the eye, to know I wasn't the only one left. I guess you don't realise what true loneliness is until it's too late.

Outside my living room window, the quiet sky burned a deep, angry orange. The whiskey distillery in the next town over had turned into a ball of flame. I could taste the burning malt of it seeping through the window frame.

I used to think of myself as a lone wolf, not needing anyone or anything – typical teenage chest-thumping. Mum used to say in her quiet but firm voice, *Jude Guthrie, one of these days you'll realise how much you need me and I hope it smacks you across the face like a wet fish*. Well, she was right about that.

She left the house two, maybe three days ago. It was hard to tell. All the days blended into one big vortex of swirling nerves as I resisted the urge to bludgeon my head off the walls until I became numb. No radio, no internet, no more YouTube readings of Charles Bukowski or those compilations of cat videos I'd never admit to watching – just me and my soaring panic. I gasped at shadows and flinched like a nervous cat whenever I heard someone talking, only to realise it had been me.

Before the great shut down, there'd been reports of massive, alien-like blob things swallowing cities across the world. We'd all laughed it off, thinking it was some stunt like that War of the Worlds radio show that made everyone go nuts, thinking the world was going to end back in the 30s.

When the blob came to Balekerin I was in my room, sunshine prickling my forearm as it beamed through my bedroom window. School had finally ended for the summer, and my head was abuzz like a kid on Christmas Eve. Weeks of freedom lay ahead, hanging loose on street corners with my mates, raising hell, maybe we'd even sneak in some booze. My daydreams of blue skies and laughter burst away when Mum screamed into the house, slamming doors.

"Jude? Shut all the windows. Now!"

The torn note in her strangled yell killed the question inside me. I leapt up and slammed my window shut, then bolted through to the other rooms to make sure all the windows were closed upstairs. I opened my mouth to shout, to ask what the heck was going on, but my jawbone hung loose like it detached from muscle.

A rolling, oily blackness slimed its way over the window. The wooden frame of our house cracked under the immense weight of the lava-like sludge that slowly shut out the sun. My legs gave in and I slumped to my knees, my insides turning January cold. A smell like burning tar and soggy mushrooms floated through the walls as the thing engulfed the window, smothering the house, locking me in a darkness so deep I couldn't tell if my eyes were open or not.

It trapped us for six days. Mum and I huddled together, leaving all the lights on as the air grew stale and thin. There was nothing to do but go crazy with worry.

I was staring off into space, dreaming of the summer wind whipping through my tangle of brown hair, a sob baking inside me at the thought of never feeling free again. The blob unstuck itself from our house with an ear-rending noise like a million suckers ripping away all at once. The house cracked, settling into place as I rushed to the window, almost blinded by the beaming, glorious sun.

To my right, I saw the rows of houses that marked the start of our long street. Past our neighbours on the left, a black tide engulfed everything. It was massive, moving with slug-like muscles, pulsing itself onward.

Mum and I argued about whether to stay inside or go hunt for food, for help, for Dad. He was still out there somewhere. We had to find him, but we had no idea when or if the blob would be back, and what would happen to us if it sucked us into its black mass.

When I took the first step outside into clean air after six days inside, the oxygen whooshed straight to my brain like the whiskey Dad sometimes let me drink with him when he got home from the pub. I stifled a silly giggle and batted away a tear. The sun shone hard on my skin, urging me outside.

By the time we stepped through Mr. Kellerman's open front door, the fuzziness wore off. Our old neighbour's skeleton lay in the middle of his living room floor as if he'd fallen off the couch, a clawed hand stretched toward something no longer there. His bones had been stripped so clean they were shiny.

We took his food and I nabbed myself a few books, hoping the old guy wouldn't mind. The collection of beat-up Michael Connelly books came in handy when the thing consumed our house again the next day like a nightmarish wave. It went on this way, covering our house and then moving off days later only to come slithering back, swallowing everything.

When we ventured outside those first few weeks, anyone we passed looked at us in horror, like I was the blob, ready to steal their life away. They'd jump to the other side of the road, refusing to look us in the eye. I wanted to shout at them to grow up, that we could help each other, that the government would be here soon to nuke the black thing into oblivion. I'd always thought that when the world ended, we'd all band together, but that wasn't the case at all. Humans suck, big time.

The thick, orange sky was enough to make the base of my stomach quiver. I tiptoed closer to the window. It was one in the afternoon and the sun tried to burn through the orange haze while I went out of my mind, wondering where Mum had got to and whether or not to go after her.

Being inside all the time withered my soul – I was made for the outside. Growing up, Mum and Dad knew grounding me was the only thing that would get through. They could take my toys, but when they forced me to stay indoors, something would stir inside me, demanding to be set free. I was born to scrape my knees, to swing high, to feel the wind push and tug at me as I sped downhill.

I pressed my palm against the cold window. Were Mum and Dad laying somewhere like the countless, pristine skeletons I'd seen? Was anyone out there fighting this damned thing? Was I the only one left?

Remembering the last thing I'd said to Dad spiked me in the gut. I told him he could go to hell. I guess, in a way, he did. He'd walked out the door, a hurt look in his eyes. I watched him kick stones up the path, his head down as he rushed away. Soon after that, the blob came to swallow reality as we knew it.

He binned my bike – my beautiful Summer Bullet. I used to ride that thing until my legs couldn't keep up with the pedals and then *whoosh*. With the wind pressing at my back, I'd close my eyes, a bullet shot from a barrel, tunnelling through the warm, summer air.

I didn't ride it enough, he'd said. He looked hopeful when he said that, like a kid who'd just been told Santa wasn't real, pleading for a grownup to take it all back. The lads at school teased me rotten about going 'riding' with my dad, so I let the Summer Bullet rot, and our relationship along with it, I guess.

What I wouldn't give to stand on that red bike's peddles, the bumpy pavement rumbling up the handlebars and my forearms, wind catching and whipping my hair as I flew down the street, the bright sun sizzling my back. All thoughts and cares blurred when I rode my Summer Bullet. I'd whip round corners, crunch over stone, slice through grass, the rubber tyres churning and zipping over hot concrete. Dad would be with me, hunched over his bike, spinning his long, dangly legs, the years thawing off his face.

My stomach roared at me, snapping me out of my happy place. It wasn't just a subtle hint for food, either, but a long rumble like it growled at me. The last of our food – a tin of hot dogs – sat lonely on the kitchen counter. The orange light that buzzed through the window made it look like I stood in the centre of some ancient, sepia-toned photo. It made everything feel fake, like I was watching a film – a film about a boy, a blob, and the end of the world. Man, I was so close to losing it. I closed my eyes and my stomach screamed at me again.

No. I needed to wait on Mum. I couldn't trust myself not to wolf down all the hot dogs once I got started. She had to come back soon, before the thing returned to blot out the world again.

HOT BLOOD THUNDERED around my ears as I opened the front door. A whoosh of muggy air flowed over my face. For a brief, childish second, I thought a ghost leapt at me. I stumbled back into the house, nearly falling on my butt. I exhaled a meek laugh and stepped outside, shaking my head. I needed to find Mum before the blob returned.

The baking heat made a sheen of sweat prickle my forehead before I reached the end of the path. The taste of cloying ozone held the promise of a thunderstorm as I stared up at the glowering orange sky.

I closed my eyes, recalling frantic neighbours shooing kids to school, straightening their ties before fleeing to work in the morning bustle. It was nice here – the kind of street you could belt up and down on your bike all day long and no one would give you any bother.

I slunk into Mrs. Peterson's house, the remains of her front window twinkling on her lawn, courtesy of yours truly. The cold kitchen tiles welcomed me when I broke down, sobbing hard. What sort of dirty rat sneaks into a nice lady's home and raids her cupboards?

I threw the bag of tinned food inside my house then walked down the silent street, trying a few doors, shouting my loudest but friendliest hellos. No one answered. How long could we survive like this? What happened when the food ran out?

I slumped down on someone's doormat, back against a sun warmed door, resting my arms on my knees. I didn't even know who lived in this house just a few doors up from ours. Crazy how you can live your life so close to someone and know nothing about them.

On the path, tiny black slugs crept, their oily skin glittering under the dull orange sky. It was as if the big blob left little parts of itself behind. My shoulders rattled against the door as a shudder rolled over me, and I inhaled a sharp lungful of the fire-dead air. A small slug reared up like it stood on hind legs, sniffing at me. Its shunting movements made cold ants swarm underneath my skin.

A wet, slopping noise like rising surf broke the silence. I leapt to my feet, bounding across the road to my house, looking over my shoulder. A mass of black tar sloshed its way around the corner and into my street. It slithered over garden walls, cars, fences, trees, until there was nothing but a black tide rolling toward me, consuming everything.

This close, greens and blues swirled off its surface like oil in a puddle. My legs turned to gum under me as it folded itself forward. Tips of houses vanished slowly under the blob's dark depths. The air shifted my hair as a string of blackness shot past me. It slapped the pavement with a sucking noise that made my insides shudder, then the black mass hauled itself towards me like it gave chase.

I nearly made it to my house when the darkness swirled around me, splatting against the front door. It toyed with me, ready to slurp me into its flowing, glistening dark. I ran in the only direction I could – through my gate and into my back garden.

The gate swung open and without thinking, I sprinted to the shed, jangling at the padlock, a bubbling moan wailing up my throat as the tidal wave of nightmare blotted out the sun, turning my skin cold. The padlock clanged loose to the ground. I opened the door and leapt into darkness, rattling it closed behind me.

I gasped in ragged breaths, old books, paint and wood mingling inside the muggy air of the dark, spacious shed. The thing thumped against the door, making me fall backwards over a plastic bag full of hard, plastic junk.

Sweat tumbled down my temples as my scrambled nerves settled. Dad must've been in here before he left, forgetting to lock up. The wood above me groaned and splintered. My mind wobbled at the thought of that darkness engulfing the world above me, like I was a submarine lost at the bottom of the deep ocean.

I slid along the wall, tracing my fingers over the rough wood, reaching for a light switch like a man walking on the ledge of a tall building. I hit the switch, and two fluorescent tubes pinged to life, sharp light shooting along the length of the shed.

. . .

DAD CAME through for me again, big time. In the corner, in the largest shopping bag I'd ever seen, was a supply of tinned food. Fair enough, it was the food from the back of the cupboard that no one ever wants to eat, but beggars can't be choosers, right? He must've emptied our cupboards to donate to the food bank. He was always doing stuff like that.

My surge of elation turned to mushy desperation as I hunted for something to open the tins with. Hunger howled at me, clawing me down as I sat with a heavy tin of beans and pork sausages in my hand. I managed to pry the tins open with a pair of pliers, slicing up my lips as I shoved the contents down my throat.

I'd no idea if Mum made it back, Dad vanished the day the blob showed up, and I couldn't tell if it still engulfed the shed. It was just me, the tins, and the huge spiders that claimed the shed as their home.

My Summer Bullet was in the shed, all sleek and red and wonderful. Maybe Dad couldn't bring himself to bin it after all. I wiped a tear from my cheek and lifted the back wheel off the floor and gave the wheel a spin. Its *tic, tic, tic* lifted me back to days spent peddling, weaving, popping wheelies, hopping over kerbs and zooming through my childhood. Ah, to feel that light again, like air, like freedom.

"Fly, Bullet, fly," my croaky voice echoed off the walls as the wheel gave its final *tic*.

I closed my eyes. I was with Dad, flying down the street, my Summer Bullet wheeling under me, the uneven path rumbling up the handlebars and through my wrists as I channelled through the warm air. Dad was behind me on his bike, a smile stretched across his face. It was as if he turned back into a kid when we cycled together, and I could imagine that kid being my best friend.

The memory socked me in the gut as I traced my fingers along the brilliant red of my bike's frame. Why couldn't I have swallowed my damn pride? I let my 'mates' mock me into ruining something special. It was only sitting alone amongst the junk and the spiders in the shed that I realised Dad needed those bike rides as much as I did.

My supply of tinned goods wouldn't last much longer, especially since I couldn't stop eating once I begun. It was the only comfort I had in the four days I'd spent crammed in here amongst the junk. The sane part of my brain screamed at me to ration, but once I started one tin, I found myself ripping open another, and a wave of self-hate would take over.

I needed to find out if the thing still consumed our street. A sizzling fire zapped its way up my fingertips when I touched my Summer Bullet. It missed the wind, the speed, the jealous wonder on blurred faces.

"I can't go on like this."

My hands quivered as I leaned over, grabbing a handlebar in each hand. The rubber creaked in my palms as I pulled the bike off the wall and walked toward the door, the *tic, tic* of the spokes singing to me.

"What you say, Bullet?" I said. "Time to fly."

I leaned my hand against the door, images of the black, swirling blob shooting into the shed, smothering me into its darkness, ending everything. I pressed the door gently with a finger and it flew open, swinging out, slamming against the side of the shed. A smile stretched up my cheeks as the sun warmed my skin. The light made my Summer Bullet pulse with red fire. The burning orange sky had been replaced by a wondrous, unbroken blue.

I threw my leg over my bike and onto the leather seat. Something melted inside me as I rode out onto the empty street, slowly at first. The blob was nowhere to be seen. Just me, a beautiful day and my Summer Bullet under me, ready to fly.

The chain clunked as I changed gears, then pushed down with all my might, my unused thigh muscles aching with pleasure. The wind shoved at my back, willing me forever onward.

A vision of my dad appeared, roaring with silent laughter as he cycled behind me, a boyish smile plastered on his face, willing me to go faster, faster. I obliged. I whisked round a corner, Dad's image flickering in and out as I gave my tears to the cooling wind.

A mass of blackness engulfed the bottom of the long, winding road, eating up houses, the bright sun glittering off its oily surface like a distant, tar-filled sea.

My fingers hovered over the brake. The song of rubber mowing over hot concrete, the tunnel of blowing wind, and the whirring of pedals clutched at my soul.

I dropped my fingers from the brake, and pushed down hard on the pedals, zipping down the street, screaming at the sky until my throat cracked.

As I whizzed downhill, closer to the blob, it smelled like a campfire gone cold. I pushed until the pedals went loose and free under my feet.

I closed my eyes, holding on tight to the handlebars, holding on tight to my Summer Bullet.

THE ONLY EMPEROR

Across the silence of the slush-covered road, the snowy field pulled at Cain, begging him to go dance through its unbroken crust. Hurrying flakes of snow held him captive as alcohol lit its embers within him. A slow buzz began to creep through his stomach, easing the knot of guilt that had been building there since the first snowfall two nights ago. He shoved his numb, red fingers into the pockets of his large coat, watching the snowflakes swarm across the night sky like a plague of white locusts.

"I love you pricks," said Marko, shattering the silence. "Nobody I'd rather spend Christmas Eve with, honest. You alright there, Cain?"

Air plumed out of Cain's mouth like white fire as he looked back at the bus shelter where Marko and Barry huddled on a plastic ledge, passing a bottle of red Aftershock between them. He caught the bitter cinnamon scent of the liquor as the chill wind snapped at his cheeks.

He'd lived in some bleak towns, but Pitlair was the worst yet. He felt something was always watching him, beaming its hateful stare between his shoulder blades. A shiver lanced through him, and he let out a heavy sigh, an aftertaste of aniseed clawing the back of his throat.

"Hey, skinhead," called Barry, his neck tucked into his puffed-out chest. "What's your problem, you mopey arsehole. Put a smile on that face or I'll punch you so hard you'll not wake up till New Year."

Cain turned his attention back to the snowy field. He'd never seen snow lie so still, so perfect. A small mound marked the lip of a hill that dipped sharply – a perfect place to sled down, he mused, though none of his previous four families had ever owned a sled.

"Cut him a break, Baz," Marco hissed. "Sounds like he's getting the boot from his foster family."

The mixture of street dirt and snowmelt reached his nostrils as he stared at the shifting, dancing snow shapes in the sky, feeling his balance waver. A dark shape caught his eye. A boy stumbled through the white field, reaching the crest of the hill. Cain blinked and shook his head – the boy left no trail of snow in his wake. The figure spread its thin arms wide, bent its knees, and leapt down the hill and out of sight. Cain's right trainer squelched as he stepped onto the road.

"Where you going?" shouted Barry. "You not talking to us, princess? I tell you what, for somebody about to be turfed out on the street, you've got an entitled way about you."

A familiar white blaze of anger pulsed in Cain's temples, and he ran his tongue along the vertical scar inside his cheek where a former father had slit him with a Stanley knife. He stepped back onto the path. "I'll do whatever it takes to make sure I'm not sleeping on the street. And would you get your chin out your neck? You're not intimidating anybody looking like a jacked-up frog."

"You wee—"

"Easy, Baz. Calm down, big man," said Marko.

Barry snorted, then yanked the bottle from Marko and downed three large gulps, all the while glaring at Cain. When he was done, he wiped the sticky red liquid dribbling down his chin. "Oh, I know what's got your knickers in a twist. It's your pal, ain't it? You're thinking about what happened to that specky prick. He's probably lying down the bottom of that field there, under all that snow."

The bottle shook in Marko's hand as he lifted it to his lips like he had some kind of wasting disease, and he spilled more down the front of his jacket than he drank. "What was it he did just before we broke off school last Christmas? Talking some pish about ice cream."

Cain stared down at the snow-spattered path and whispered part of the poem he remembered little Donnie reciting so passionately. "Let the lamp affix its beam. The only emperor is the emperor of ice cream."

The poem had given him the shivers for days, and he couldn't keep it out of his head. It had repeated itself over and over until the day Donnie vanished. He tried to swallow the rising guilt in his throat, but it wouldn't shift, so he turned his attention to the field again.

Cain...

The faintest whisper carried his name on the winter wind, and he swung his head in every direction, looking for its source. He shook his head, then laughter exploded from the bus shelter, the noise amplified by the enclosed space.

"You're a regular Rabbie Burns, Cain," hollered Marko. "Didn't know you had it in you."

"Always did wonder why you hung about with that Donnie," said Barry. "Did you write each other love notes and read them out loud?"

Cain turned, his jaw muscles clenching. "Shut it, Barry."

"Or what?" Barry stood, bottle of liquor clutched like a weapon. "If I mind right, you laughed just as loud as the rest of us at that nerdy prick."

He was right. Donnie had looked Cain right in the eye when the class erupted during his impromptu recital, and a something passed between them. Donnie had learned how to deal with the constant jibes thrown his way, but the disappointment in Donnie's eyes when Cain cackled alongside his hooting classmates still haunted his sleep.

Cain, a small, cold voice called again.

He stepped toward the bus shelter and stood eye-to-eye with a red-faced Barry. They stared at each other, and Cain smelled the foul mix of aniseed and cigarettes on Barry's breath. Cain grabbed the bottle, making Barry flinch. He took four long gulps and handed it back, sucking in freezing air through his teeth. A great cloud of angry gnats buzzed inside Cain's skull.

Last December, when he'd heard Donnie had gone missing after a long walk to 'clear his head', Cain ran around Pitlair desperately calling his friend's name into the empty air.

When he reached the snow-covered grounds of an abandoned church, he tripped over the root of an oak tree, and came face-to-face with his friend's small, twisted body. The cracked lenses of his thick-rimmed glasses lay crooked on his face, and his taut skin was mottled with shades of custard-yellow and blue-purple that Cain hoped never to see again. He'd bolted home to call for help, but when the cops eventually showed up, the body was gone. No one believed him, and he'd spent a night in the cells for wasting police time, hearing Donnie's recital of the Wallace Stevens poem cycle round and round in his brain as he stared endlessly at the grey walls.

Alcohol blew numbing fire through his veins as he stared into Barry's menacing eyes. "Donnie was going places. He'd have made more of himself than any one of us."

"You, maybe, ya worthless rat. I'll tell you—"

Cain leaned back, then head-butted Barry square in the nose. Barry toppled sideways like a felled tree, landing in a heap inside the bus shelter.

Cain booted a plexiglass window and kept on kicking until a long, thin rectangle of clear plastic came away from its fixings. He grabbed it in two hands and crossed the road, looking back at Marko and Barry, who started brawling inside the shelter.

His trainers crunched across the snowy field, and he crested the small rise, looking down the steep hill onto a plain of unbroken white. The wind picked up, sending wisps of misty snow into the air like sand in a storm.

I've been waiting for you, Cain...

He dropped the clear plexiglass on the snow and threw himself on it. Splashes of white plumed up from both sides of his makeshift sled as he sped down the hill.

THE GROUND LEVELLED out to a vast white nothingness as he slid to a stop, wiping hot tears from his cheeks. On his way down, the snow had whipped up into a blizzard, flying into his face like he was in a spaceship streaking past the stars.

He stepped off his makeshift sled and the snow swallowed his trainers, coming halfway up his calves. Cold seeped through his puffy coat as he hugged himself, trying to rub some warmth into him.

"Cain, what the hell you doing down here, pal?" he said, seeing nothing but misty white all around. His words bounced around as though he was standing in a dark cave and not an open field where cows once roamed.

He leaned into the howling wind as it blew its sharp chill into his eyes. A layer of crisp, sparkling snow crackled underfoot. He punched his feet through it, reaching the compact ground beneath. The scent of earth and grass floated up to his nostrils as he trundled on.

Just before he'd vanished, Donnie had come to Cain's home, sneaking into his room to avoid his foster folks and their awkward, stilted way of talking to kids. Cain had gone to steal some cans of juice from the kitchen. When he returned, Donnie was sitting cross-legged on the floor beside a small box that Cain kept under his bed. His friend flicked through a small, worn journal. Cain dropped the cans of juice and yanked the book from Donnie's hands.

"What do you think you're doing?" Cain exploded.

"I thought I'd find me some naked lassies under there," said Donnie, gazing at Cain in that open way he had. "How long you been writing poems?"

"Poems? They're not poems, they're just — If you tell anyone, I'll smash your specks off your face, got that?"

"Cain, they're good, I swear. I mean, your writing's so wobbly it looks like you did it sitting on a washing machine, but they're so raw."

Cain pressed a balled-up fist against his forehead. "How many did you read?"

"Just a couple. You've never said how it felt getting carted about so many foster carers. 'This Family is Forever' really stung. You know you can talk to me about stuff like that, eh? You don't need to go bottling it up."

"Tell anyone and you'll be sorry."

Donnie stood. "Why? You think writing a poem makes you queer or something?"

Cain scowled and a vein pulsed in the centre of his forehead. The journal was a place where he tried to expel his angry demons. When he wrote, he pressed the nib into the paper so hard nearly every page was ripped. "It's not that, it's just... just..."

Donnie pushed his large glasses up his nose. "I get it, I get it. Heaven forbid you actually try at something and get caught doing it. Cain, you've got something here, trust me. You deserve better than the hand God dealt you."

"God?" Cain threw the book at Donnie. The spine bounced off his freckly cheek and pages fluttered as the book struck the floor. "You think God gives a shit about forgotten people like me? Get out before I do something I regret."

That had been the last time he'd seen Donnie alive. He'd blown up, like he always did when things got too tough or too close, and pushed away the only person who'd ever encouraged him to be better.

His feet looked like white cinder blocks covered in compact snow as he crunched on. The wind whistled as though someone blew through a glass bottle as snow latched itself onto every surface of his clothes like a new skin. He looked about for any landmarks, but all he saw was nothing in every direction. It seemed he wasn't moving at all.

He thought about how many times he'd 'lost it' over the years, blasting through foster families in countless screaming matches.

I'm down here. Hurry.

"Donnie? Donnie, that you?"

Donnie's whisper turned into a screech that rung in his ears. *They've almost got me, Cain. Help!*

When Cain removed his hands from his throbbing ears, a shadow blurred across the snowy surface. It stumbled toward a drift of snow that rose up, circling into the air like a small tornado. The wind almost knocked Cain over, sending needles of ice pinging against his face.

He stood outside the spinning, misty vortex, squinting his eyes, seeing Donnie's shadow vanish inside. He reached a hand in and jerked it back when ice sliced his palm, making blood drip into the snow.

Silence billowed around him as the winter wind stilled, and the cyclone of snow crumbled like a wall of dry sand.

A scorched, wooden door stood where the swirling snow had begun. There was nothing on either side of it. Written in claw marks scratched across the wood were the words, *Your forever family awaits.*

Cain stepped toward it and reached out a hand to turn its golden doorknob. His hand stopped as ice fizzed up from the ground, covering the wood like a colony of ants devouring it. When the popping, crackling sounds stopped, Cain saw that the door had been engulfed, turning it into a misshapen lump of white-blue crystal.

He placed a fingertip on the door and scalding cold seared up his hand. When he pulled it away, small pieces of his skin remained on the door.

Help me.

Cain's shaking hand moved toward the handle that was now laced with shards of jagged ice. "I've finally cracked, I'm making this all up in my head. It can't possibly be you. I saw you, dead in the snow."

Don't leave me in here alone, Donnie's small voice echoed.

He closed his eyes, recalling the mottled, ice-burnt face of the only boy he'd known as a true friend.

Cain set his hand on the doorknob, and ice sliced his palm, sending tendrils of blood onto the door. Where it hit the ice, the crimson smoked, then turned solid.

He turned the handle, pulled the door open and jumped inside.

As Cain stepped into a picturesque winter wonderland, his foot fell through inches of fluffy powder. The night's bitterness stung his cheeks as the door slammed shut behind him. It melted away, leaving a deep hole that was soon covered by the constant dusting of white that spun all around him.

The snowy landscape was postcard perfect. Looming large were rows of huge, snow-sculpted creatures. Cain walked over to a giant crow that stood four times his height. It gazed down at him like he was a worm, its feathers carved in such intricate detail he almost expected it to take flight.

The statues stood in two rows facing each other, inviting him to walk down the middle of them. He shielded his eyes, gazing into the distance. The sculptures stretched on as far as he could see.

A dark figure ran out from behind a raging dragon, and down the middle of the countless sculptures.

"Donnie, wait!"

The snow deepened as Cain lumbered after him – it was like wading through water. The cold misted in his chest and he wheezed for air. He willed his legs to power through the packed snow and go after Donnie who didn't leave a trail. His burning lungs forced him to stop, and he leaned on the thighs of his white-powdered jeans, catching his breath.

"Donnie? Stop. Let me help you!"

The blustering wind stung as it hit the sweat on his forehead. He felt it chill the tears that streaked down his face.

This was all his fault. He'd blown up at Donnie, and for what? For encouraging him? If he'd kept his cool that day, Donnie wouldn't have gone for a walk alone at night, disappearing forever.

"Donnie!" His shout was whipped away by the fierce wind.

Cain stared up and snowflakes brushed his face. A massive owl statue held him in its all-knowing gaze. Cain thought if he turned his back, the owl would swoop down, tearing into him with sharp talons before ripping him to shreds with its beak that glinted like glass.

He walked on, looking behind him every other minute, sensing cold, preying eyes examining him. Only the army of animals stood, their eyes tracking him as he stepped onward.

Something blurred by his cheek, leaving a disturbance of cold air in its wake. A snowball rolled to a stop in front of him, making a little comet streak on the ground.

Howling laughter broke the silence. He looked in the direction of the loud cackling and rubbed his eyes, waiting for them to refocus.

In the distance, a jaunty snowman with a huge striped top hat stood hunched in the middle of the field. Its hysterical laughter rose and rose, though it didn't move. Cain caught a glimmer bouncing off its face, like sunlight reflecting off a mirror.

He stepped backward a few paces, spun, then ran. Donnie appeared in front of him, pointing a finger toward a large gateway that appeared on the white horizon.

A snowball pelted Cain's shoulder, sending spray into his eyes, and cackling exploded from behind him. He turned to see the snowman just twenty paces away, gazing at him with its black stone eyes.

His muscles went shaky and useless as he beheld the impossible vision, listening to its clown-like laughter climb octaves. He shoved his hands over his ears, but the noise was coming from inside his head. It made his stomach heave, and his legs gave in, sending him flopping onto his knees.

Don't let it suck you up, Donnie's voice called. *Get on your feet, Cain! This way.*

The snowman's laughter fizzled out, and a booming voice rang inside Cain's head. "Oh, this way indeed. Step right up, Cain, step right up. Admission is free for street dirt like you. Donnie paid the full price – such a talented boy, that one. But you pushed him right into our hands, didn't you? Come, the Christmas adventure of a lifetime awaits!"

Cain gazed into the thing's unmoving face. Its sharp twig arms were frozen in place as if reaching out to him. It looked like a typical snowman, though its head was tilted as if it were giving him a stern talking to, and ice-blue bristles grew below its nose and chin.

He took two slow steps backward, then fled toward the distant gate, his legs burning as he chopped through the heavy snow. A noise like a boat speeding through water roared behind him, then a ball of ice flew past his face, tearing a gash along his cheek.

He stumbled to the ground and turned just as the demon halted right in front of him, its top hat wobbling as it stopped, as though Cain's gaze had frozen it in place.

Cain wiped his cheek, flicking spots of blood onto the pristine snow around his feet. "You can't have Donnie. He's... family. I—"

The thing's mouth opened wide, revealing thousands of needle teeth that glinted blue in the moonlight. It launched itself forward and he caught a glimpse of a hideous bloodshot eyeball in its gullet. It glared at him, threatening to turn the contents of his stomach to water.

Cain sidestepped and slapped the side of the snowman's head. One of its needle teeth lanced through his shoulder, spilling hot blood that mingled with the cold air in a fusion of pain. He clutched his arm as he lay in the white powder, staring up at the huge flakes that streamed in the air. Against the white of the clouds in the sky, the flakes looked like thousands of grey, flocking bats.

"You'll make such a nice addition to the festival of winter wonders we have here," said the snowman. "We're your family now, Cain. And isn't that all you've ever wanted? A family who'll take you in and actually want to keep you?"

Cain stood, still clutching his bleeding shoulder. He clenched his jaw, and a cold shudder ran through him as he stepped backwards, away from the evil thing before him. The frozen demon hopped forward, its mass of three large snowballs coming apart and then snapping back together as it moved through the snow.

"You're not getting to keep us. I'll find Donnie, and we'll..." In his mind, he saw Donnie's eyes light up that day when he'd read Cain's hidden poems. "Donnie?" he shouted in a hoarse voice. "You hear me? I'm sorry for pushing you away. Come help me fight this lopsided freak."

The thing paused, cocking its head, a huge smile growing upon its jolly face, revealing rows of glinting teeth. "Oh, but you will push him away again. That's what you do, isn't it, Cain? You hide whatever makes you sing inside, as singing in this town is forbidden. Come with me, we can sing forever. You should listen to the poems Donnie writes now. They're rather... *dark*."

Cain walked forward, stopping an arm's length from the waiting snowman, and stared into its black marbled eyes. "You think you can just steal my best pal and get away with it, aye?"

The demon's sharp, grotesque smile fell, turning into a scowl. It leaned back and let out a sky-splitting roar, then darted forward, opening its mouth wide enough to swallow Cain whole. Cain stepped back, seeing the metallic spines coming for him, then lunged forward, cramming his hand down the thing's throat, wrapping his fingers around the waxy eyeball inside.

It gurgled, and closed its teeth around his forearm, slicing and tearing its way through his coat and into his flesh. He tried to scream but all that came out was a hushed wail, and he pulled on the arm, trying to free it. As he tugged, peels of his skin scraped off, and agony exploded through him. He placed a foot on the snowman's face and yanked as he squeezed the moist, pulsing eyeball in his hand.

The thing let out a burbling cough and Cain's arm came loose, sending him crashing to the ground. The fresh cold lit up his arm in agony. The snow around him soaked up the crimson that flowed from criss-cross slits in his flesh.

In his hand, the eyeball darted its gaze about in alarm, wrapping its tentacle-like nerve around Cain's bloodied forearm. He got to his feet, threw the ball-shaped thing out in front of him, and kicked it as far as he could, leaving a yellow, curdled smear of milky pus on his trainer.

The snowman rose, and Cain's world turned into slow-moving nightmare as he watched a river of red pour from its mouth full of razor teeth. A trembling weakness made his muscles useless, and he stumbled backward, seeing every minute spark of light that ran along each length of deadly metal in the snowman's mouth.

With its black twig hands, it tore a handful of spikes from its mouth and cocked its arm back, ready to throw them at Cain, but then something black streamed through the demon, making it explode in a puff of powdery snow that fell to the ground.

"Donnie!" yelled Cain, and he sprinted after Donnie.

If he collapsed now, he knew he'd stay here forever, leaking all his life into the welcoming white. He willed his feet to slice through the tall snow, and the agony in his arm ascended to levels that made his vision pulse in and out.

He puffed out clouds of shaky, cold air, following a trail of balled-up paper.

THE FREEZING WIND snapped around him as he stumbled under an archway built of solid, twinkling ice. He leaned against its slick surface, a cloud of cold vapour building in his lungs, making him splutter and wheeze. His tattered arm sang a faraway note of agony as numbness took it.

He squeezed his eyes shut, then dragged his feet through the snow, following the trail of paper.

On top of the massive arch, a white crow cawed, the sound echoing through the silent wasteland. Cain's heart galloped in weak, uneven beats, and his legs crumpled beneath him.

A rivulet of blood he hacked up was swallowed by the snow where he lay. The chilly softness bade him stay as flakes fluttered around his face. He fumbled with the zip of his jacket, feeling as if he were burning up inside, desperate for cool air. He groaned in anguish when his numb fingers wouldn't do as he asked.

He had to get up. Not close his heavy eyes or else he'd freeze to death in this cushion of snow. He pulled himself up and managed to unfurl one of the balls of paper. It was a scrawled line from one of his poems.

A street-dirt boy deep in the Never,

He awaits a dawn that never will be.

The wind snatched the yellowed paper from his hand.

He smelled the pines of two massive evergreen trees that grew out of the ground in a garden filled with icy flowers, and fountains that had spewed water into the air now frozen into jagged, alien formations. A figure stood at the end of the garden between the trees, its back turned as it read something in its hands.

"Donnie, I came, I'm..." Cain called, but the sound was carried off by the wind.

He dragged himself forward. The icy powder caked his knees. His injured arm dangled loose from his shoulder like it didn't belong to him. White static fizzled around the edges of his vision, and the next thing he knew he was lying face down in the snow.

He clawed at the sudden, engulfing dark. When he broke the surface, the breath he sucked in burned his throat with cold. His muscles refused to obey when he tried to stand, so he crawled towards Donnie. The frigid air clamped his lungs as he fought to keep his head above the snow.

"Donnie!" yelled Cain, yards from his friend's turned back. "Donnie, it's me." His world spun as he battled to his feet, blinking the clumps of snow from his eyelashes. "Donnie, come on, let's get out of here."

He heard a constant high-pitched note in his ears as the blustering wind eased to silence. He stepped forward. "D-Donnie?"

Spots of colour exploded in his vision, and he felt his brain begin to short out again. He knelt in the snow, closing his eyes, tethering himself to the solid ground. He tried to rub the bridge of his nose, but his fingers wouldn't bend, so he ran a freezing hand along his forehead instead.

"Donnie," he croaked. "It's all my fault. If I'd just kept my cool, you'd not be in this place. You've helped me more than I can ever tell you. Let's go before we freeze forever, alright? Donnie?"

Cain tried to stand, fell into the snow, then tried again, feeling his heart thump in his chest. He willed himself on, finding the last of his energy, and he reached Donnie and put a hand on his friend's bony shoulder.

The hand sizzled like he'd placed it on a hot iron. Donnie let out a throaty, growing laugh that made his small shoulders bounce up and down.

Cain fell back into the snow.

Donnie's little frame turned. His eyes blazed with pale, blinding light, and long needles protruded from his mouth.

Cain's friend smiled, then stepped toward him, opening its mouth until Cain heard the dislodging of its jawbone.

DOWN BELOW IS SILENCE AND DARKNESS

Gillian sprinted through the house, chased by her galloping siblings. The scent of dusty towels hit her as she opened the linen closet. She closed the door and cool darkness enveloped her. All she longed for was a moment's silence.

Her army of brothers and sisters hooted as they thundered past. With her head in her hands, she waited. Soon, they would find her and drag her out into their noisy world.

In her best dreams, there was no sound. Fantasy to her was floaty nothingness. She often dreamed of walking a silent beach, utterly alone.

She had nine brothers and three sisters. She had nine sets of aunties and uncles who brought their own kids to their large house most nights. The loudest family in Pitlair and possibly all of Scotland – that's what Gillian had been born into. A girl who'd love nothing more than to finish a book in sweet silence. The house clattered with noise at all hours.

The back of her head tapped against wood as she blew out a long breath. Footsteps pounded outside, breaking the line of light at the bottom of the door. She braced herself, ready to be dragged downstairs where the karaoke machine was already in full swing, and the parents glugged their drinks, shouting over the music to be heard.

Something rustled. The noise came from the corner of the luscious darkness. She leaned forward, straining her eyes.

A boy peered back at her.

She flinched, her elbow knocking into a pile of towels that tumbled over her.

The boy looked about eight, just like her. By the thin light that buzzed from under the door, she saw his cold, black eyes. His skin was dusted with something like grey ash. Atop his nest of hair, horn-like curls flicked at the air.

Gillian held her hand over her chest. Her heart pumped against her palm. "Who—"

"Shh," the boy said, raising a finger over his mouth.

She wracked her brain. Was this some distant cousin she'd yet to meet? There were so many, it was hard to keep track.

"Who are you?" said Gillian, whispering. "Are you a... a bad thing?"

The boy's voice was high and innocent, but laced with the buzz of an angry wasp. "We are all a little bit bad, aren't we, Gillian?"

"I guess so."

When she was frazzled, she often slapped or kicked her brothers and sisters, screaming at them to just leave her the flip alone. They swarmed around her every second of every day. She eyed the door, waiting for them to come find her.

"Silence awaits," said the boy. "Just take my hand. Come down below."

"B-below?"

"Down below is silence and darkness."

"Silence..."

She breathed the word, tasting it. She had never experienced true silence before. Sitting here in this moth encased space was the most silence she'd enjoyed in months.

"I can take you with me," said the boy.

"How do I get there?" she asked. "Quick, quick. Tell me."

"You must do something bad."

"Like, how bad we talking?"

"Bad enough to get *his* attention."

"I—"

The door swept open. A lance of bright light stung her eyes as her brothers grabbed her. Bob and Albie wrestled her out into the light, yanking her by the pigtails. Through her flower-dotted leggings, the rough carpet burned her knees.

She pushed one of the laughing boys off and glanced to the closet.

It was empty.

THE CONSTANT NOISE made her feel hollow. Her house, in the middle of their sad, broken street, teemed with bodies. It was a wonder no one went missing.

Saturday came and that meant one thing – another party. Even more people would cram the halls with their chattering and their booze.

She sucked it up the best she could, running and playing with her siblings until her forehead was all sweaty, hoping they wouldn't hunt her down when she tried to sneak away later.

Had she dreamed up that ashen boy who hunkered among the clean towels? He hadn't appeared to her since.

Do something bad, he'd said. But what to do? If she did something mega bad, she'd get a hiding. But the lure of peace sang within her.

She hid in the upstairs toilet, drawing a breath. She didn't need to pee, but it's how she recharged, if only for a moment or two. Already the tunes were pumping down the stairs and the doorbell ding-donged every five minutes letting in new partygoers. It was no use staying in here. A penny was all you needed to unlock it from the other side.

She'd never felt so alien. Her family were people people, and she thought life was hell. She couldn't keep up.

"Hey, Gilly poop-poop," called Albie, knocking on the bathroom door. "You taking a massive dump in there? Ha!"

She sighed, then flushed the toilet and joined the throng of people and rampaging kids downstairs.

Bodies crowded the hallway, cackling and roaring with laughter. The false smile she'd stuck on her lips took everything from her. It took twenty minutes before she felt the walls closing in, zapped of all energy.

"Take me away from here," she said to herself as she walked into the wall of noise that was the living room.

She could feel the blare of the music through the karaoke machine, the dead notes rattling her eardrums.

She bolted up the stairs. Someone grabbed her by the ankle. Her teeth clattered when her chin hit the step.

"Ow, watch where you're going," said Joy, the oldest sister.

"Off me!" said Gillian, kicking her ankle loose.

"Or what, bookworm?"

Gillian stood. She glared at her bigger, broader sister, then shoved her in the chest and ran upstairs, taking them two at a time.

Pamela, ten, was waiting at the top of the stairs, a waiting smile on her face. "Where you headed, Wordzilla? We not cool enough to hang out with?"

Gillian ran past her, heading towards their bedroom, knowing they wouldn't leave her alone now until they got bored of teasing her or slapping her around.

Joy tackled her from behind. The air whooshed out of Gillian as they hit the floor. Joy flipped her over, driving her bony knees into her shoulders, pinning her arms to the floor.

"You like books, eh? How about I write one now?" Joy stabbed at her chest with pointy fingers, pretending she was pressing keys on a typewriter. "Blah, blah, blah. Boring words, blah." Joy slapped her face. "Ding!"

Pamela stood on one of her pigtails. A rip of pain blazed along her scalp.

"I'll tell Mum!" said Gillian.

"Ha," said Joy, typing away. "Gotta find her first."

Gillian squirmed under her sister. She brought her knees up, thudding them into Joy's back.

"Right, you wicked trollops," said Granny Lottie. "Get off that poor lassie."

Joy gave her one last vicious poke in the chest before getting off her. Pamela giggled by Joy's side and they both went thundering down the stairs, toward the noise.

"Thanks, Gran," said Gillian, getting to her feet.

"Don't you sweat it, dearie. Quiet wee girl like you in this house of ruffians. Must be terrible."

"Aye, it is. I just want peace and—"

"But you've just got to get on with it. Grow a pair. Life's gonna pass you by if you don't dive in headfirst. Come back down the stairs like a good wee lassie. Face the music."

"Suppose so."

"That's my girl. Why you so quiet all the time? Like you don't even like us."

"It's not that. I just... you wouldn't understand."

"No need to be quiet when you've got all this family around you. Life is people. I wish you'd just learn that, okay? Come on down with me and we'll sing us a tune on the karaoke."

Her gran shuffled her foot over the first step, her weighty flesh overhanging her ankles. The stairs protested under her as she stepped down.

Gillian watched her gran's bulky form wobble back and forth as she struggled. One push. That would be enough of a bad thing, surely? That would buy her a one-way ticket to sweet, sweet silence.

"Down below is silence and darkness," whispered Gillian.

"Eh?" Her gran turned, mid-step. She tried to grab the bannister and missed. "Woah, woah!"

Gillian shot forward and grabbed her arm, saving her from tumbling down the steps.

"Thank you, dearie," said her gran. "Let's get our sweet arses back to the party."

GILLIAN STOOD in the apex of noise. In the living room, the party went full tilt. Every inch of space taken up by drinking adults or the kids zipping among them. The tangy smell of beer seemed to seep up from the carpet.

Auntie Bets leaned over and handed her a warm microphone. "Give us your usual."

Gillian's cheeks went red with fright. "Oh, no. Not—"

Countless eyes turned toward her. The track started its pedantic beat. She was trapped. She held the microphone so close to her mouth that her lips touched the cold, silver surface.

"One man went to mow, went to mow a meadow," she started.

The crowd roared as she sang the song, clapping along. Never mind that she sounded like a squealing guinea pig, they loved when each of the kids performed.

When she was done, she felt dead inside. Energy used up. Cream-crackered to her soul.

"Ha, ha," said Albie, pointing at her, "ya total singing fanny."

Their dad slapped him across the ear. "Stop that, you. She gave it a good pelt." He turned his slurred attention on her. "Well done, Pamela."

"I..." Her dad forgetting which one she was hit her like a physical blow. The edges of her vision fizzled. She suddenly felt far away from herself.

"Dance time," said Gran. "Time for some boogie arses. I'll show you how I used to make the boys crow."

The room sprung back to life. Adults and kids bumped into her, almost knocking her over. A gap appeared at the centre of the room.

The boy stood. The last of the day's light shone in through the window. His skin had looked grey in the closet, but now she saw it was tinged with blue.

Gillian's stomach nearly came out of her arse. He coiled a smile at her. Everyone danced around them as she stared at the boy. Despite there not being enough room to sling a cat, they avoided him like a stink.

He raised his hand and snapped his bony fingers.

"What are—" said Gillian.

Everyone froze like statues.

It was quiet.

Her skin tingled with it. Something in her soul seemed to turn inside out. She basked in it.

"Down below is silence and—"

"Down where?" she said. "Take me. Please? I can't take it here anymore."

All around her were the people she loved most, but she felt like an island here. A book lover. A library seeker. A silence craver.

"*He* needs you to do something bad," he said again.

"How bad?"

"Bad enough."

"Show me."

A smile broadened on his smooth face. It slithered across his cheeks like blue plasticine. "Kitchen."

"Are you the de—"

"Kitchen."

She manoeuvred her way through the busy hallway, past the frozen statues, careful not to touch any of them. Her aunt Cathy stood against the wall, looking down at her drink while her uncle Bert whispered in her ear. Her youngest brother Andy leaned into a corner, his eyes frozen wide, his hands covering his legs like he was about to pee his pants.

The party was in the kitchen. Smells of cigarettes and fruit punch filled the room as she tiptoed around the throng of people.

The boy with the plasticine face stood at the end of the counter, next to a glass punch bowl. Her socks stuck to the linoleum floor where the red punch had spilled over. She recognised the high smell of vodka and rum and opened spirits.

"Spike it," said the boy.

"Spike it? Smells like it has all the booze in it already."

He pointed to the cupboard beneath the sink. She went over and opened it, bringing out a large, plastic container. Liquid sloshed around inside visible behind the red warning crosses.

"This?" she said.

"Something to really get this party where it needs to be."

"Won't that hurt them?"

"A bit."

"I don't want to hurt anyone."

"I can give you what you want. Silence. Darkness."

She closed her eyes. In the quiet, she could hear herself think. It was bliss. The knot of tension that forever squirmed in her mind dislodged itself. Her skin prickled with relief.

"I don't want to hurt them, though," she said.

"*He* needs a bad thing or *he* won't let you in. Come on. It won't hurt much. Just a tummy ache is all. Why don't you take some first? That way you'll see it'll be fine."

"Oh, alright, then."

The bright cap didn't want to budge. Eventually, she wrestled it off. The pungent chemical smell hit her, catching her throat. It reminded her of day trips to the swimming pool where the whole family would seem to take over the building.

"Ugh," she said. "If I put that in the bowl, they'll notice for sure."

He pointed to the glass bottles beside the large bowl. "Mix in our special ingredient. They'll never know. Come on. It won't hurt too bad. Then we can go to the down below."

"Down below is silence and darkness."

She poured in the liquid. It glugged into the bowl, thinning the bright red colour.

"More," he said.

She emptied the bottle into the punch, then grabbed a random assortment of spirits and mixed them in. The red of the fruit juice brought the bowl to the brim.

"You first," he said, handing her the ladle.

"Promise it won't hurt them?"

"It won't. Go on. Down that cup. Do it in one." His lips cracked as the edges of his mouth formed into the shape of a smile. "Quicker that way."

"Alright, then. Here goes."

The taste throttled her. Her face went red as it burned its way down. She held on to the thought of sweet silence that he'd promised. Stabbing pains in her stomach brought her to her knees.

She coughed up a line of blood that splattered the floor. A twisting heat gripped her brain. Her limbs gave up and she fell forward.

His gleaming eyes were the last thing she saw.

. . .

THE DARK SEEPED into her like a cold mist, settling about her shoulders. It was sweet and quiet and heaven. She felt no pain, no fire in her stomach. She stood in darkness – weightless, dreamy and utterly alone. Bliss.

It felt as if she walked through space, some ghostly being with nothing weighing her to the ground. The darkness seemed to breathe around her.

She cast her mind back to the bad thing she'd just done, praying that no one drank as much of that poison punch as she had.

"Hello?" shouted Gillian. "Is anyone there?"

Her screechy voice echoed back to her.

The silence washed over her, claiming her.

A man's voice broke her peace. "Ehm, hello?"

"Uncle Bert?"

Another voice. "That punch sure packed a punch, ha, ha."

More voices joined her, filling up the dark world.

"No! It's not fair. You're not supposed to be here," screamed Gillian, clamping hands over her ears.

The party continued down in the dark.

GUARDIANS

"That you playing with your dolls again, aye?" asked Dexter's dad, mumbling over syllables like his tongue was too big. "You need to learn you can live without them. You're seventeen, for Christ's sake."

Dexter sat cross-legged on his bedroom floor, lost within the twisting, roiling fog of his mind. He scrambled about himself in a mad circle like a dog chasing its tail, patting about the crumby carpet in the dark room. He needed to find them.

"Aw, don't give me that clueless puppy look. You can hear me just fine. Summer's about here. What you going to do when you finish school, eh? Think you're living here the rest of your life?"

Dexter searched desperately around the room, then scuttled to his bed by the wall, snatching Hood, one of his plastic action figures from atop the covers. As soon as his fingers touched the plastic, his father's earthy scent filled the confined space. Scattery fear gained a hold of Dexter's gullet as he stretched a thin, ropey arm under his bed, grabbing Max Altitude, his mountain climber figure.

He sat up, feeling the plastic of the two toys start to warm in his palms. The small room slowly crystallised into reality. Since his head injury, the dolls were the only things that let him feel the world around him. Without them, he was lost.

His father drew a long, harsh toke of a half-smoked joint, then took it out his mouth, holding it between his middle finger and thumb like it was the world's biggest and most precious cigar. His slack eyes vanished behind a cloud of lazy, thick smoke.

"Well?" said his dad.

Dexter shuffled back, bumping into the wall where a streak of orange light shone from the street below his fourth-floor window. "W-well, what?"

His father let out an agonised groan, his face reappearing from the smoke. "Don't give me that. You can hear me just fine. A knock on the head years ago doesn't mean you get to go about playing with toys all your life."

"Do you think I chose to be like this?" said Dexter. "I-I'm useless without them."

"You're nearly finished high school. What you—"

"Would you leave him alone, Rab," Dexter's mum called from the kitchen of their two-bedroom council flat, the noise ricocheting off the close walls. Just hearing her made a warm, familiar glow sizzle in his belly.

"I just want my wee sherpa-dude back." His dad took a long, trembling draw of his joint, gazing at the floor between them. "Before your accident up Ben Lomond, you mind that time we bagged Schiehallion? We trekked up that damn mountain so fast we hardly paused for breath. We were a good wee team back then. I almost lost you in that dense fog near Schiehallion's summit. I turned round and you were nowhere. Gone. It was like some white beast just come by and swallowed you up. My heart nearly sunk into the splodgey ground, so it did. That fog though... it hung in curtains like something alive, something breathing. That's what I see when I look at you." His dad looked up. "It's like that fog got inside your head somehow, and no one can get it out."

"D..." started Dexter, but it was too late. His dad marched out of his bedroom and he was left clutching his action figures alone in the dark.

He waited until sharp conversation echoed from the living room across the hall, then closed his door as lightly as he could.

On his way back to his bed, he scooped up his wrestler, Claymore – the last of his plastic triad.

"Yer auld man's gonnae get a Celtic Chop ti the heed if he doesn't stop it wi aw that chitter-chatter," said Claymore in his shaky wrestler voice. The lips behind the marred blue and white face paint never moved.

"A true mountaineer never leaves someone stranded," said Max Altitude, bare-chested, draped in climbing ropes and pick-axes. "I grow concerned that your father will cut the rope loose one day."

"Listen ti me, Dex. I'll skelp yer da 'til he's black and blue. He's nothing but a bone-heeded—"

"Claymore, easy," said Hood in his hushed, melodious voice.

"Shut it, ya faceless, druid bastard."

Dexter couldn't help but snicker, looking down at his trio of guardians as they stared blankly up at him, arguing inside his mind.

In the months after his fall, he'd been bed-bound, staring unblinkingly up at the spider-smeared ceiling. Max had been the first of his figures to awaken. His brain fizzled when his mum placed the toy in his loose hand one cold and dull February morning. It felt like the clouds parted, letting the blazing sunshine dazzle him with understanding.

"I'll be your guardian," Max had said, shocking Dexter. "You will see the mountain tops again, but we have a long and arduous journey ahead."

Whenever he held Max, detail poured in around Dexter like rippling, bubbling juice filling an empty glass. It gave him reason and knowledge but gripping the plastic doll didn't help him comprehend the words people said.

A year later, when he wrapped his thin fingers around Hood, his murky-green druid whose face was hidden inside a cowl, it felt like his head broke through the surface of icy water. Syllables no longer came to him in muffled, gargling nonsense but began to piece themselves together between his ears, granting him the power to speak.

On his fifteenth birthday, as he watched the autumn rain pelt his window, thinking how easy it would be to stride into the river that flowed on the outskirts of Pitlair, Claymore spoke to him.

The wrestling figure had long, rubbery black hair, and the Scottish flag painted on his scowling face, though some of it had chipped away long ago, in a time when Dexter played with his toys without a care in the world.

"Right, you," Claymore had barked. "Nae mare sulking aboot, or I'll give ye the Celtic Chop."

Holding Claymore caused a swirling energy to burn through him. It made him want to grab their tattered old football and kick it against a wall for hours. On lazy summer afternoons, he and his dad used to play one-touch, taking turns to hit the wall next to the 'no ball games' sign.

Now, back in his sparse bedroom, Claymore stared up at him, the snarling head set squarely atop two bulging rocks of shoulder muscle. "How's oor Dex supposed ti get anywhere in life wi those knuckle-heeds fir parents?"

"Anger is not the righteous path," said Hood.

"The problem is not insurmountable," said Max. "We will overcome it as a team, or not at all."

"I've had it wi you, and yer speeches," said Claymore. "It's time fir some action."

"Would you just stop it?" Dexter heard the angry tears in his voice. "How do you think it makes me feel, eh? My brain doesn't work unless I'm holding... dolls." He stared down at the three lumps of plastic that had become his guides, his way out the fog. "I'm starting to wish you never came for me. What good has it done?"

Dexter threw himself back on his bed and stared up at the ceiling, remembering what it was like to be sucked down into the mattress a little more each day in a murky haze.

"Your brain is getting stronger," said Max. "You're healing, you're within reach of a bright future."

"Bright future?" Dexter chuckled, a warm tear sluicing down his cheek. "What future is that, exactly? Summiting K2 holding on to you three?"

"Be still, my boy. Peace," whispered Hood. "Perhaps a new dream is what you need."

"A new dream? I don't know how to dream about anything else." He absently traced fingers along the ridges on the side of his head where his black hair no longer grew. "I don't *want* to dream about anything else."

"Let's start wi that eejit father o' yours," rumbled Claymore. "He needs a frying pan ti the heed."

"I just need to sleep." Dexter rolled over, holding his guardians beside his face, breathing in their oily, plastic scent.

"I'm gonnae give his dad the beat-doon of his mopey, pathetic life," said Claymore. "He needs ti be taught a lesson."

There was a small vibration in the centre of Dexter's palm. Claymore's head had twisted. The wrestler aimed a rageful glare in the direction of his parents' muffled argument.

Dexter turned the figure back around, and settled onto his pillow, imagining a cold wind bite into him as he surveyed the joyous sights from atop the summit of a huge mountain.

He shut his heavy eyes and drifted off.

HIS DAD nearly kicked his bedroom door off its hinges. Dexter shot up, his brain mushy as a marshmallow, no toys in his hands. Something hurtled toward him and he cried out as hard plastic bounced off his cheek bone. Dexter blinked, feeling a pinch of pain where he'd been hit. He scooped up Hood and Max from under his covers, feeling the world and the pain become more solid.

"What's that stupid thing doing in the hall, you buckle-headed prick?" his dad screamed, voice straining.

Dexter peered over the side of his bed, letting out a gasp when he saw Claymore's leg bent the wrong way. He reached to pick up the broken toy, when his dad stepped over and shoved him back with all his might, sending his head clashing off the wall.

"I know you're just faking it. You don't need them," said his dad.

A shiver ran over Dexter and his mouth went all watery. He clung to Hood and Max, staring up at his father.

"Oh Christ, I'm sorry." His dad clawed at his cheeks, fingers pulling his sallow skin, elongating his face. "Just keep them away for me, alright? I see another doll in my way again, I'll snap your neck. You got that?"

His father stared down at Dexter, clenching and unclenching his fists, waiting for a response. When he didn't get one, he fled the room, slamming the door closed.

Dexter leaned on his elbows and heaved himself up. It felt like he'd run up a mountain too quickly and his head went all dreamy. He reached down and picked up Claymore, hugging the three figurines close to his chest.

"Look at what that prick did ti ma leg," said Claymore.

Dexter's heart shuddered at the sight. "W-what happened? How did you? Did I—"

"Your father," said Max. "Trod on our muscled friend."

"I see that. But how did he get there?"

Dexter stared down at his dolls, a buzzing, empty static filling his head. He closed his eyes. A burst of agony fired along his brain. When the hot pain passed, he opened his eyes and mused that Claymore's angered expression had turned into a pained one. He blinked, and the angry scowl was back.

"Is your head okay, my boy?" asked Hood.

Dexter switched Max to the same hand as Hood, and dropped Claymore, feeling the fire melt out of himself as soon as he let go. He ran his spare hand over the back of his head. A lump was starting to grow, giving off a sickly heat.

His mind flashed back to the top of Ben Lomond. He and his dad had hopped around in glee as they bagged another Munro, adding it to the others they'd scaled over the years.

He could still taste the heavenly, buttery ham roll they ate as they looked upon the wondrous panorama from the summit. He remembered dusting the flour off his black and blue insulated gloves as the sun vanished behind an angry, heavy cloud, and soon the rain splatted on warm stone, filling his nostrils as the ground cooled.

The smooth slice of rock that led to the summit was a flowing river by the time they got their hoods up and began their descent. He chuckled as he heard his dad slip. The smile fell from his face as the foot that held his weight slid and he, too, rolled down the wet stone, clawing frantically for a hold as the rocky bumps burned his stomach. He tumbled over the lip of the summit.

He landed head-first on a small ledge that saved him from certain death.

All he remembered from that point was his dad's desperate screams as he reached out a useless hand, calling his name over and over.

"You've said you're my guardians." Dexter scooped up Claymore again, feeling a river of energy creep up his arm. "But what are you, really? Am I just making you up?"

"We are the souls of the lost," hissed Hood, "who only sought to help in life."

"You're, like, reincarnated ghosts, then? You had your own lives before you woke up as chunks of plastic?"

"Does it matter our previous deeds? How we came to be? Our past means naught. We are here for you, my boy."

"We've come to an impasse," said Max. "A decision must be made. Will you let us help you?"

"Help?" said Dexter. "Help how?"

"By stomping yer auld man's face into the mud," said Claymore.

"That's hardly what we'd—" started Hood.

"You'd hurt my dad?" Dexter asked.

"Only if we exhaust all other paths," said Max. "We must plan how we rid ourselves of—"

"No, I won't hear of it."

"Come on," yelled Claymore. "Let's dial it up a notch, let's get cookin'. Yer dad crippled me, and I'm gonnae pummel his face in."

"No."

"I'll snap his—"

"But he's my dad."

They used to be inseparable, with ambitions of scaling K2 someday. Now all he knew was his dad's happiness had evaporated on the summit of Ben Lomond, and he was to blame for the sickly evergreen odour that burned through the house.

Dexter grit his teeth, trying to stop the agonising flood within him that begged him to go do something, anything, to get out of this box of a room and live.

He hurled the three toys across the room, and felt his world go hollow.

LATER THAT AFTERNOON, holding Max and Hood while staring at the perfect, windless day outside his window, Dexter longed to lace up his walking shoes and find his trekking poles. His mum called to his dad that she was just popping out, and a warm glow rushed over him at the sound of her voice, quelling his sadness.

"Hey sweetie." She strained as she gently guided a large holdall to the floor. The bed bowed ever so slightly as she lowered herself beside him. "I-I can stop by the library on my way home, and get you more books about mountains, if you like?"

He was about to say yes when the words jarred in his throat. For the first time, he noticed the lines on her face, her drawn in cheeks. She wore a blue summer dress speckled with white lilies, ready to be whisked away on some adventure. She wrung her hands near her stomach like she was missing a fancy, frilly hat.

She sighed, then took Max and Hood away from him. His skin turned cold and he felt his jaw muscles slacken as dullness smothered his senses.

"My wee guy, how did we ever get to this?" She traced a dainty finger over Hood's cowl. "I had such high hopes for you, but then your father took you up that mountain, and nothing was ever the same. I always told him to be careful, but no." She blew shaky air out of her parted lips like she was going to be sick. "You've got nothing, Dex. I can't take it anymore. I can't."

She laid the figurines down beside her leg and tidied a strand of her jet-black hair, tucking it behind an elf-like ear. Her words hovered and buzzed around him – they were so close, closer than they'd ever been.

"I saw Mrs. Devlin at the shop. I tried to avoid her, but you know what she's like. Proper eagle-eyed headmaster, that one." He felt her tremble when she took his hand, and tears started running down her pale, heart-shaped face. "She told me not to give in. That you're still in there, somewhere. I don't know why I'm telling you this. You can't even understand me. It's just, I guess that makes it easier."

Dexter saw the tears tumble out her eyes as she looked at him. She laid a warm hand against his cheek. She tried to talk but her face screwed up into a mask of grief.

"God forgive me for what I'm about to do," she said. "You see, Dex, my wee guy, I can't do it anymore. No matter how much I try to help you or your drugged-up father, it makes no difference." She stared deep into his eyes. "It's awful, but I wish you'd died up that mountain."

She wrapped her arms around him, holding him tight. He leaned his head on her frail, cold shoulder, catching the bitter smell of red wine on her breath.

She gently shoved him away and opened her mouth to speak but jerked instead like a wasp stung her leg. Her lithe hands covered her mouth. "No. No, it can't. How?"

Dexter grabbed his three toys. They were still warm, and as meaning flooded back into his world, he saw his mum staring at the figures with wide eyes.

"Mum?" said Dexter. "Mum, what is it?"

"I have to go." She grabbed her heavy bag, and stepped backwards. Her eyes darted around like a caged animal. "Get a hold of yourself, Lizzie." She sighed. "I'm a failure. I can't go on watching you like this. I love you."

"I'm getting better, I swear."

"I wish I could believe that." She leaned forward, studying his eyes. "Could you still be locked in there, somewhere?"

She spun, her dress swishing behind her as she stepped out to the hall, the large bag making her lopsided. Dexter ran a hand through his hair that stuck up on ends like a thicket of grass.

"Tell me what she said when she took you off me. What made her cry?" he asked his figures.

There was a long pause before Hood's mellow voice sounded in his mind. "She was saying how much she wishes for you and your father to be happy again. How much she longs for the old you."

"Tell me what she said. I've never seen her so down before."

"It is a mighty weight for her soul to bear. She—"

"Needs a punch in the puss," said Claymore. "Is what she needs. The boot."

"Be calm," said Max.

"Ye really no gonnae tell 'em what she—"

"Claymore, please," Hood snapped.

Dexter turned the toys over in his hands, feeling the plastic squeak against his thumb. "She's ashamed of me. That's what's breaking her."

A tear ran off his nose and landed on Max's rugged face. Dexter stared at the chiselled mountain-climber, whose determined expression softened like it had soaked up his sadness.

"The bag." Dexter raced down the hall clutching his three toys.

Moving his dolls to one hand, Dexter opened the front door and stepped out to the vestibule they shared with the other residents in the block of flats. A deep, fishy odour assaulted his nostrils as his trainers squeaked loudly in the dim, cave-like space.

He leaned over the rusted railing outside their door, his stomach squeezing tight as he stared down the stairwells of all four floors. The metal slam of the heavy communal door shuddered through the bars beneath him. He heard a gang of young boys whistle at his mum as she disappeared from view.

He looked down. Musty yellow light shone in Max's twinkling irises.

"She is gone," said Max. "We should not follow. It would be brave, but the risk is too great."

"Aye," grumbled Claymore. "Those wee erseholes oot there might try ti steal us again."

"I can't live like this. Something needs to change," said Dexter.

"Aye!" shouted Claymore in his mind. "That's mare like it. Time fir some action. Who's gettin' it?"

"We must plan and chart the correct course," said Max. "We must be careful with whatever steps we take."

"I can't go on like this, taking the blame for what happened. It wasn't my fault, but it wasn't my dad's, either."

"The drugs. They cloud his understanding," hissed Hood.

"The drugs."

Dexter marched back through the front door, following the thick, leafy smell of his parents' bedroom. The closed blinds swung in the breeze that crept in from the open window. His dad lay on his back like someone had sucker-punched him and that was how he landed. He was out for the count, his body at crooked, unnatural angles. His dad's hands trembled as they hovered above his chest like they'd gone rigid and he couldn't lower them to the bed.

A small square packet caught his attention, and he leaned down and picked up the gold sachet. The word 'Spice' was scrawled under a drawing of a leering eye. On the bedside table were smaller, see-through packets that contained dustings of white powder.

"Take the tin," said Max.

"Aye, chuck it oot," said Claymore.

He leaned over and tweezed a lit cigarette from his dad's unmoving grip. The tense fingers stayed locked in place. Dexter stoked out the cigarette on the ash tray next to his dad's chest that emitted shallow, ragged breaths. A dented metal box lay open on the covers, spilling out clumps of dusty green swirls like something regurgitated by a hoover.

Shifting his three dolls to his other hand, he picked up the tin, marvelling at the overflowing drugs. His dad spluttered a weak cough and Dexter flinched, making him drop all three figures onto the bed. They clattered off each other as they landed on their backs.

The room turned into a soft blur. He stared at the open tin until his eyes went dry. His heart thudded so hard it felt like it might climb up his throat, but he couldn't tear his gaze away from the collection of weed and pills.

Dexter's mid-riff jerked forward like he was tugged by a support rope. Max stood on the bed, his plastic arms held up toward him. He stared at the action figure as a muffled sound of someone shouting at him rang through the musty room. He picked up Max, then suddenly became aware and panicked as his dad let out a nightmarish groan. His eyes were open, glaring at Dexter. "Don't..." The bloodshot eyes closed again.

"Dae it," said Claymore.

Dexter scooped up the tin and snapped the lid shut, crept over to the window, and lifted the blind. Outside, the spring sunshine had just been cancelled, and a torrent of rain bounced off the cars below. The smell of hot, wet pavement drifted up to him. He tossed the tin out. It clattered off the concrete below.

He stared down at his father, lying half-naked in a drugged stupor, and resolved that no matter how bad it got, he'd find a way out of this house, and back to a life filled with views that made a man believe God existed.

"Noo we've binned that arsehole's stash," Claymore said as Dexter closed his bedroom door behind him. "What we gonnae dae next?"

"Let's all calm down," said Hood.

"Aw, just you go and knit a sweater wi someone's granny, eh? That pot-heed needs bashing aboot."

"I don't want my dad getting hurt," said Dexter. "Maybe this will make him notice me. See that I'm getting better. Maybe he'll spend some time with me again."

He swallowed a knot of rage that billowed up his throat seeing Claymore's buckled leg pointing the wrong way. "It's me he needs to escape, isn't it? It's never going back to how it was."

"It's us against the world, champ," said Max.

Dexter climbed into bed and lay on his side, hugging all three of his dolls close to his chest, giving them his tears.

HE PUNCHED the end of his trekking pole into dry rubble, and hauled a heavy foot forward, hearing the crunch of white ice under his crampons. He took a deep breath of the glorious, freezing air and lifted his head to take in the view. The villages and other distant mountains were so far away they looked fake. He held no toys in his shivering, gloved hands, and he turned, a smile beaming across his face despite the cold clamping his jaw.

Behind him, his dad puffed great clouds of air, and leaned on his poles, defeated. His dad groaned as he removed his hat, throwing it to the ground. "I can't do this anymore."

His father turned, spread his arms like an angel, and sailed off the mountain and into a cloud.

Dexter screamed awake, feeling the sweat cling to him and his drenched covers. He absently padded around his bed for his figures, still able to feel the cold from his dream.

As if he was wearing boots of lead, he shambled over to his desk, where his toys stood facing each other. He lifted a numb hand he swore was frostbitten and scooped up his three toys. The world fizzed and coloured around him.

"But how to get rid of them both?" said Max. "They deserve cruel ends, but—"

"What?" said Dexter.

"It is nothing, young one," hissed Hood.

"Were you just talking without me? How?"

"Naw, that was aw in yer heed," said Claymore. "Talkin' of such, ye look like ye got dragged through a hedge backwards. Bad dream?"

"It's the first dream I remember having since Ben Lomond."

"That means you're on the mend," said Max.

A touch of sun bleached his window, and heat prickled his bare arm. "I was sleeping, and you were talking on your own. What were you saying about my mum and dad?"

"They need—" started Claymore.

"We only want what's best for you," said Hood. "That's what Claymore was about to say."

Dexter rubbed his eyes, and a frustrated groan rumbled up his throat. "Claymore, your leg. It's fixed."

The bedroom door flew open, denting the wall opposite. "Where is it?" his dad shouted. He wore a few days worth of stubble and the same tattered clothes he'd had on yesterday.

Dexter gripped all three figures. "What?"

"You think I was born yesterday, ya wee bastard?"

A fireball of emotion erupted from the pit of Dexter's stomach to his mouth. "How many nights have you smoked your brain away instead of coming to talk to me, eh?"

"You think spending time with you and your precious dolls would do any good?"

"How would you know? You've never tried."

"It's not like that. It's hard seeing you like this when it was me who..." His dad's voice turned sour. "Gimme the stupid toys, alright?"

His father held his hand out and walked forward, but Dexter slapped it away. This close, Dexter saw the bloodshot lightning bolts in the whites of his dad's angry eyes.

"Why, ya wee—"

"Just leave," said Dexter. "You should've left me up Ben Lomond. Maybe if I'd died, I'd still remember what having a good father felt like."

An open palm belted his face, and tendrils of flashy, hot pain spread over his cheek. His dad stepped forwards, fist cocked back and ready to strike again.

"I'll knock his heed clean aff his ugly shoulders," shouted Claymore.

His dad froze in place, staring down at the wrestler like a sneering, petulant child.

"Ye heard me. Come closer and I'll chop ye up," said Claymore.

His father shook his head and took a step back. Dexter lifted the fist that held the wrestler and rammed it into his dad's face with all his might. He bolted into the corridor clutching his guardians.

Dexter threw open the front door, and ran into the damp hallway, stumbling and catching himself by clutching the rusty bannister. He looked down the four flights of stairs, his world doing a little spin like he was back up Ben Lomond tumbling end over end. He shook the vertigo off and turned.

The air was punched out of Dexter's lungs as his father tackled him. All three toys scattered across the cold linoleum floor. Meaningless grey shimmered in all corners of his vision.

His dad straddled him, holding a fistful of t-shirt, and punched his jaw. Dexter felt far away as each blow landed, and something coppery trickled into his open mouth.

Everything seemed to slow, but before his father could wind up another blow, something blurry thudded off his dad's shoulder, knocking him off.

Dexter slowly got to his feet, turning his dimmed attention to his dad, who looked up, flinched, and fell back onto his hands, crawling until he reached the top of the stairwell.

Something crumbled in Dexter's mind as his toys bounced about, hopping in front of his dad like a gang of monkeys spoiling for trouble. Hood knelt, his plastic joints creaking, then jumped, landing an uppercut to his dad's solar plexus that sent him stumbling back, choking for breath.

His dad stood, wiping his mouth with the back of his hand, leaving a dark red smudge up his face. "What is this? Y-you're not real, you can't be."

The words were a jumble as always when Dexter didn't hold his plastic figures, but when he concentrated, he caught a fully formed word here and there. He fought through the sludge, forcing his legs forward.

Max unfurled a small red rope, slinging it around Dexter's dad's calf and yanking it taut. Claymore ran and sprung into the air, spinning his arms round and round. He collided into Dexter's dad's stunned face, sending him flying back and tripping over Max's rope.

Dexter heard himself call out as his father fell. His head bounced off the third step down, but he managed to grab a metal bar on the bannister to keep from falling any further.

A yellow tooth landed next to Dexter's foot, and he stared at it, gleaming in the hall's fluorescent lights. He felt his brain cramping, like all his synapses were ablaze. Colour crept into the edges of his vision.

A memory surfaced. He was on his way up Schiehallion with his fresh-faced dad watching a field of purple heather swaying like waves in the strong wind.

"Dig in, son, that's all I ask," his dad had said. "If you want something, dig in and go get it. No matter how hard life gets. And don't you ever forget days like today with your old man. I love you, my wee sherpa-dude."

Claymore swaggered past, staring up at Dexter with his angry, beady eyes. "Time fir the Celtic Chop."

Dexter looked at his dad, who leaned against the bannister catching his breath. Max and Hood stomped their little plastic feet and clapped their hands in unison, urging Claymore on.

A glowing tingle rose up the back of Dexter's neck, shooting all over his brain like a thousand tiny lightning bolts.

"No," whispered Dexter.

"Ye've hurt oor wee lad enough," said Claymore. "Time ti go night-night."

Claymore knelt like a sprinter and began a twisting, exaggerated run towards his dad. Dexter felt his own muscles jerk to life, sprinting to his father, pumping his arms.

Dexter got there first. He wrapped his arms around his father and shoved him aside, turning just in time to see Claymore flying toward him, pin-wheeling his plastic arms. The figure crashed into his chest and it felt like a rope tugged him backward, sending him soaring.

His hip hit the railing, and he tumbled end over end, the hallway spiralling wildly around him as he fell.

"Dex, no!" His dad leaned over the bannister, his face floating further and further away. "Nooo!"

Dexter's body crumpled and bones snapped, but he felt only a dull, distant ache as he lay in a heap on the bottom floor, a kaleidoscope of colour floating in his vision.

Everything was clear to him.

He closed his eyes and dreamed of basking in the crisp sun atop a cloudless summit.

DARKNESS PRESSED IN ON HIM, though he saw slithers of light shining through gaps in what felt like some giant coffin. To each side and below him, he felt hard and soft objects press against him.

He remembered saving his dad from his out-of-control toys, and ricocheting down to the cold, hard floor in a crumpled mess at the bottom.

A door slammed from outside the great box. There was a wooden thumping above, then bright light flared into the box. A huge face loomed above Dexter, tears streaking down his puffy cheeks. A giant stared down at him, sobbing hard as only a child knows how.

In Dexter's field of vision, he saw the vacant stares of a hundred plastic, beady eyes.

Dexter felt the giant's tears splash against his face. A large hand reached down into the box, blotting out the light, then Dexter felt himself lifted up, seeing the toy chest below.

The kid continued to sob like the pain vibrated from some primal part deep inside him.

Dexter spoke, though his molded lips didn't move.

"Hey, kid, it's going to be okay. I'll be your guardian."

IN A JAR OF SPIDERS

Jack Sinnard tasted the earthy autumn breeze as his friend gently guided a thick black spider into a jam jar. Tam stuck out his tongue and closed his eyes like he prayed that God himself would guide the big-arsed thing into the jar along with the others they'd collected from the street's ragged, unkempt hedges.

"Easy does it now." Tam gave the spider one last gentle tap with the lid then screwed it on tight.

A thin wind rustled the hedge as Tam held the big jar up to his broad, joyous face. The lazy, cloudless afternoon held the last dreams of summer. After this, it would be six months of rain, snow, and bluster.

"Just like old times, eh?" said Tam.

Jack leaned in, watching the chunky spider land on its back, clawing its pointy legs at the air. The other spiders, tiny red ones, long-limbed gangly ones, and jumpy brown ones, all squirmed away from it as it managed to flip itself over.

"You've not lost your knack for finding the wee things, I see," said Jack.

Tam chuckled, his nest of shiny blond hair bouncing with every word. "Mind that time one got out and crawled right up your arm?"

"Och, spiders ain't scary."

"Nothing much ever scares you though. Jack the fearless, ha. That must've been, what, five years ago? We'd have been eleven. Right before you went and got too cool for the likes of me."

Jack ran a hand along his fuzzy, freshly cut hair, feeling the bumps of the lightning bolt the hairdresser had shaved on both sides of his head. A knot of guilt rose up his throat. "Look, it's just—"

"I know, man. It's cool. Your races and all that kept you well busy. No time to scoop up eight-legged beasties with your old best pal. That and what happened to your dad."

Jack bit his lip and held out his hand. "I'm sorry, dude. Forgive me?"

"Forget it. Ain't nothing to forgive."

Jack felt the cool, bumpy jar in his palm as Tam handed it over. The clutter of spiders jostled for space inside. As Jack put his eye to the glass. The new spider skewered a small brown one, shoving it into its mouth with its spindly front legs. Seeing its fangs sent a trickle of ice down Jack's neck.

"Where's your biker buddies now though, eh?" asked Tam.

Jack glanced down at his worn red hi-tops, then strode down the street. Kirkness was a town of boarded windows, keyed cars, overgrown gardens, spray-painted walls and angry, frothing dogs.

"I want to find one of those huge, hairy bastards you get in those horror films," said Jack, tucking the jar into the crook of his arm.

A dirt bike blared behind them. Its *braaap* noise destroyed the stillness. The bike hurtled towards them on the path, forcing them to step onto the road to avoid getting pancaked. Jack watched the idiot pin the throttle on the purple mud-covered bike, and he filled his lungs with the strong, sweet petrol smell.

Tam snapped his fingers. "Jack? You there? Hello? Let's get home. If you think I'm dipping about in hedges for spiders in the dark you're two sandwiches short of a picnic."

Something glinted at the corner of Jack's vision. He marched towards a tall hedge. Its branches hung over the path like hundreds of tiny hands clawing at passersby.

Jack stuck his hand into the hedge, hauling branches aside, feeling twigs snap as he leaned into it. He peered into the cool, dark of the hedge, breathing in its damp green scent. The world wobbled beneath him as a thin beam of sunlight struck a solitary leaf inches from his face. A tiny spider lit gold by the sun fixed Jack with its rows of black, black eyes. He yearned to hold it in his palm, to make sure nothing would ever hurt it.

"That's the weirdest looking thing I've ever seen," said Tam, huddling close to Jack's side. "I didn't know you got gold ones."

Jack unscrewed the lid on the jar. A long-limbed spider made a break for it, skittering up the back of his hand. He barely noticed the tingling track it made. "Me neither."

"You're not going to put it in with that lot, are you?" Tam pinged the jar with a chubby finger.

"It'll be alright."

"You can't possibly know that."

"A wee bit of faith is..."

Jack coughed, ran a hand through his hair, stopping himself from regurgitating one of his dad's rambling lectures about faith from the Big Book.

He inched closer, directing his breath away from the spider that stared innocently up at him. He proffered the jar. The golden spider zipped into it, and he screwed the lid on tight.

As he held the jar up to his face, he saw the spider was brown with patches of gold and cream that zigzagged along its hairy body. It raised one front leg and tapped the glass as if using Morse-code.

They raced home. Jack cradled the jar, cushioning the spider as much as possible. Tam lived upstairs from him in one of the many two-storey, semi-detached council houses that dominated their street.

Tam scuffed a foot on the first step leading to his front door. The cheery light in his eyes flickered out. "Well, let me know how you get on with the spider."

Jack held the jar up to his face. The new spider was circled by the others, as if mesmerised by its brilliant colours. He fought the urge to open the jar and take it out to make sure it wouldn't come to harm.

"Here, you look after it." Jack held the jar out, offering it to his old best friend.

Tam took the jar. Jack stuck his hands in the pockets of his faded jeans.

"You sure?" said Tam.

"Aye, my dad needs me to—"

"Woah!"

They huddled over the jar. The new spider stood in the centre of a mass of eight-legged creatures. It thumped its forelegs and spun like it was holding court. Jack thought of how Father Brown liked to descend from his altar to come face-to-face with his flock as he bellowed out the Lord's word. The priest had fled faster than a Scottish summer after the incident.

The large black spider moved closer and closer toward the gesticulating gold one as if it were eyeing up its next meal. Jack's breath misted on the glass. He saw the little one had no chance in hell against the lumbering, stalking thing that promised its death.

Jack went to open the lid, but Tam laid a hand on his and shook his head. When Jack looked back into the jar, he thought he'd see the little one being torn asunder. The big one folded its legs under its body as if it were kneeling.

The golden spider plinked a slow rhythm on the glass. The enthralled gathering of spiders watched as it turned to face the large, black spider and placed a tiny leg on its head.

It rammed its tiny fangs into the big spider's eyes. It tore and slashed at the big spider that put up no fight. The glinting fangs and lightning quick bites made bile creep up Jack's throat.

THE IMAGE OF TINY, devouring fangs spun in Jack's mind as he stuck his hands into lukewarm dishwater, sponging sticky bean stains off a pot. The spider had seemed so unreal, swallowing great chunks until there was nothing left. It was like the big one had made a sacrifice of itself. As he washed the dishes, he fought the urge to bolt to Tam's house to check in on the spider.

He turned to his mum to say he'd be right back, but the words stalled in his throat. In the dim light of the kitchen, her skull seemed to press its way through her skin. Her once flowing blond hair sat like a dead bundle of straw on her head. She wiped at the counter in small, frantic circles, her thin wrists poking out her pink marigolds like brittle twigs.

"Don't worry about that, Mum." Jack dried his hands. "You go have a rest."

He tried not to stare at her scar. It ran diagonally from above one eye in a jagged, criss-cross line down her nose, stopping at her jaw.

She let out a sad, soft chuckle. "I've still got the looks, I see. Least you can stand to look at me. Your old man's barely acknowledged me these last six months."

In the dark living room, his dad sat in his wheelchair, crying anguish into the velvet cover of his favourite Bible.

Jack closed his eyes tight, hearing the screams and the falling, splintering wood that fell all around them on the day of the incident.

On that last walk to St. Michael's six months ago, his dad had looked at him with his jolly grey eyes, breathing deeply of the fresh spring mist that hung in the air.

"Breathe it in, my wee Daredevil," said his father. "*He* gives us such days to look back on when life gets tough. Believe in *Him*, son, and everyday can be just like this."

His dad would churn out Bible passages, seeming at such peace inside that palace of stained-glass windows among the deep leathery scent of teak pews. Jack denied his faith whenever his old man questioned him about it, but he couldn't deny the peace inside when he knelt on the church's benches. His friends had teased him relentlessly, but the truth was he liked going.

Jack remembered opening his mouth to hum the first note of a hymn when a thundering crack reverberated above. Beams of wood crashed all about them.

His mum got her face nearly ripped off by a beam that had shattered in front of her, sending its splinters into her face. He saw the white of her nose as she wailed in agony, holding her face together in her bloodied hands.

Miraculously, no-one died, but his dad got it worst. Crushed by God's own ceiling. Jack had hauled at his dad's limp form, screaming for help, unable to budge the pieces of wood that pinned his dad from the waist down.

His mum still held it against him. It was in her eyes. They seemed to say he had no right to come away without so much as a scratch.

"I don't know what to do." Her scarred face contorted, and she sobbed into her palms.

"No need for that." Jack whisked a plastic seat from under their small dining table and gently guided her onto it. He swung his legs around another chair, sitting on it back-to-front. "It'll get better. You'll see."

"No, it won't. They're going to kick us out if I can't magic up rent money. Unless we find a pot of gold, we're out on our arses."

"I can leave school. Get a job. I'll help out."

"You've already done enough, selling that bike of yours. I can't have you giving up on your education as well."

He stared at a cobweb that swayed back and forth in the breeze that sighed in through the window. The image of the wondrous spider tearing into the big black one crept into his mind. It was like he could hear those minuscule needle teeth ripping into flesh. A shiver ran through him.

"Sod it. It's not like my grades will get me anywhere. I can get a job no bother. Honest."

She laid a hand on top of his and gave it a gentle squeeze. "I don't know what we did to deserve a son like you."

THE CRISP MORNING air melted Jack's weariness away as he pushed his dejected dad to the shop. The chair creaked as Jack manoeuvred it around a blob of dog shit.

"Next time I see somebody leaving their dog's mess on the path like that I'm going to pick it up and throw it at them," his old man said.

"Just be thankful I'm the one in control this morning. Mum would've rolled you right into it."

His dad sat up straighter. "You mind when you first learned how to ride a bike? I remember setting you on it and you were off like a rocket. Fell off and jumped straight back on again like you didn't even feel the blood dripping down your knee."

"I guess we're both made of tough stuff."

"If I fell off this thing, I'd flail on the ground like a useless turtle until somebody scooped me up."

"Dad—"

"Stop here."

"What?"

"I said stop this abomination right now."

The chair squealed as Jack jammed his foot on the brake.

"Father Brown said something once." His dad balled up a tartan blanket that covered his dead legs and threw it on the path. His voice was tinged with fire. "'A man lives by his own limitations. Cast the impossible aside, and you can achieve anything your heart desires.' Well, today, I'm casting." He slapped two hands on the chair's plastic armrests.

"Woah, Dad, what the—"

Jack shot forward and placed his hands under the wobbling, straining arms of his dad as he tried to haul himself to his feet. His dad's ancient aftershave reminded him of time spent shoulder to shoulder with him on the church's benches.

His old man closed his eyes. "Let me go."

"You wanna crack your skull off the ground?"

"Cast the impossible aside."

"Alright." Jack took a step back, palms up. "If you want a sore face, then fine. You go for it."

"Watch that tongue of yours. I'm still your father."

His dad's arms still shook as he leaned on the plastic armrests. He stared along the path as if it were some great mountain to conquer. Jack supposed that was exactly what it must've felt like. He resisted the urge to pounce forward as his dad removed his hands and balanced on his own.

His heart thumped in his throat as his old man shuffled forward, scraping stones under his slippers. His father let out a laugh so joyous it pricked tears in his eyes.

"See?" said his father. "A wee bit faith can get you through anything."

Jack wrestled the voice inside his head that kept his muscles primed to dart forward and lend a hand. His dad was moving under his own power, shuffling forward like a man reborn. He'd never seen such a childish glee in his father's eyes before. It was like he was taking a new bike out for a spin at Christmas.

"You're doing it," said Jack. "You're really doing it."

The smile broke off his dad's face as he stumbled. The slow, sludgy fog of a bad dream enveloped him as his dad's legs buckled, sending him crashing knees first to the rough concrete. Jack launched himself but didn't get there in time. He collided into his dad, only making it worse.

"Dad?" Jack sprung up, pulling his dad back up and setting in back in the chair. He picked up the tartan blanket and set it over his father's unmoving, scuffed legs. "Don't feel too bad, alright? You did something ace just then. You'll get there. Show those doctors they dunno what they're talking about."

"I just want to be able to go get my newspapers on my own," his dad said, the fire gone from his voice. "Is that really so much to wish for?"

Jack rolled him the rest of the way to the shop in silence, paid for newspapers and shoved them in the bottom of the wheelchair. He wheeled his dad back home as fast as he could.

Tam waited for them at the bottom of his front steps. He looked up, eyes going wide as he saw the state of Jack's dad. "What happened? You alright?"

"Just had a wee tip, that's all. You look like you've pulled an all-nighter. What's eating you?"

Tam scrunched his eyes shut and shivered all over like someone just stomped over his grave. "You need to take it back."

"What?"

"The spider. Y-you need to take it."

"I thought—"

"It's all yours." Tam trotted over and pressed the ice-cold jar into Jack's stomach.

"But..."

Tam hopped up the steps and slammed his front door closed.

His dad cocked his head. "That's the biggest damned spider I've ever seen. You're not considering bringing that thing inside, are you?"

Jack's innards tightened. The spider had transformed overnight, growing to the size of a tarantula. Its limbs rubbed against edge side of the glass, with hardly enough space for it to turn itself around. Rows of calm, glassy eyes examined him. Vibrations tickled his palm as the spider tapped the jar with a hairy front leg laced with gold.

The other spiders were gone.

IN HIS BEDROOM, Jack set the jar on his desk below the motorbike helmet that hung from a peg on the wall. The angry red and black lines painted on the helmet called to him with its leathery sweat smell. It'd been so long since he'd ridden a dirt bike.

He leaned down to examine the spider, remembering how its tiny, glittering fangs tore chunks from the big black one. Despite that, he felt no fear for the thing – only a soft glow that warmed his insides. The lid was unscrewed halfway before he realised what he was doing. He screwed it tight and set it back on the desk.

The wind bounded through the open window, flitting magazines open, rifling through image after image of bikers doing stunts.

The single bed creaked as he leapt back on it and took out his phone. He searched *how to look after a spider* and thumbed through the lists of articles. When he did an image search, not one looked like the spider he had in the jar.

He took a shoebox from his cupboard and lined the bottom of it with an old t-shirt and poked some holes into the cardboard. Now all he had to do was figure out what pet spiders ate, except other spiders that was.

"Tam's a scared old lady," he said, walking to the desk. "We'll be alright. I made you a wee house. See?"

The box tumbled to the carpet.

The jar lay empty.

Jack spun about, searching in every corner, then the ceiling. An angry buzzing noise grew nearer and nearer. Panic clamped his heart. What if the spider was poisonous? What if it got to his dad?

Silky spiderwebs hung across the gap between the open window and the frame. It billowed in and out like a silver beach towel. It was so thick he could barely see through it. A flash of gold darted to the centre of the web. The spider gobbled down a struggling bee. The buzzing stopped.

It made short work of the bee. When it was done, it lowered itself to the windowsill by a single thread from its bulbous rear.

"Hey, wee guy." Jack put his hands on his knees, lowering his voice. "Hungry fella, ain't you? I'm sure I could find you something to munch."

It lifted one of its front legs and tapped the windowsill three times. It moved like silk down the wall. When its forelegs met the floor, it loped forward, blurring across the maroon carpet in a blur.

"Just don't bite me and we'll get along fine." Some primal part of his brain told him to scat, to grab his bike helmet and make spider-paste out of the ungodly thing – he'd had plenty of practise shutting that part of his brain off.

The creature jolted to a stop inches from his feet. It pawed the air, waving a cream and brown leg like a baby asking to be lifted up. Jack bent down, laid his hand palm up on the floor. The spider tiptoed onto it, tickling his hand so much he felt it in his elbow.

It lay on his hand weighing next to nothing. Jack straightened, slowly drawing the spider close to his face, seeing his reflection in its eight intelligent eyes. "What the hell are you?"

It spoke in a mighty, vibrating baritone. "What is it that you see?"

Jack dropped the spider. It made a small *oomf* as it hit the carpet, wiggled its legs, then flipped itself the right way up. "You are safe, my child. You may come out now."

He found himself in his cupboard among his forgotten riding leathers. Rows of hanging t-shirts with brash colours brushed him as he clambered out "Y-you can talk?"

The spider waved a front leg again. "Make me a seat of your hand again, if you would be so kind."

Jack cradled it in both palms and held it inches from his face. He caught the aroma of unknown spices and dust rising from it. As he exhaled, its coarse hairs parted.

"This is all a dream," said Jack. "I attempted something stupid on my bike and got wasted, didn't I? This just can't be real."

The memory of flying up a ramp soared within in. Gone was that magical weightless feeling as his beloved, gnarly two-stroke rumbled beneath him. Grief stung his heart all over again. He'd had to sell the bike to help his mum sate the burly men who chapped their door for money.

"I'm talking to you in your mind," said the spider. "I am Weaver, though I have gone by many names." The spider shifted, crawling closer to Jack's face. "You have been chosen."

"Chosen?"

"You are my saviour, Jacky-boy. And I can be your salvation."

"Is this why Tam freaked out so much?"

"I'm afraid I had to resort to scaring him. He was bathing, and—"

A shriek rang through the house. His mum struggled with someone, fighting, knocking things over. An almighty crash sounded, and Jack laid the spider on his pillow, then sprinted to the living room.

A tall man in black stood over his dad, his face half hidden by a bandana. He had a fistful of t-shirt held in one gloved hand as he cocked a fist back to strike. Blood trickled down his father's face. He held the Bible up like a shield as if it could stop the burglar's blows.

His mum sprawled in a heap in the corner, her hair streaked with bright, red blood. There were jagged pieces of purple ceramic all around her. She didn't move.

The sound the gloved fist made when it struck the side of his dad's head made the blood in Jack's veins boil. He threw himself at the man's back, putting an arm around his neck and yanking back with all his might. The man's spine popped. He grunted, twisting out of Jack's grip. The burglar stumbled, tripping over Jack's motionless mother.

"Old boot," the burglar said, getting to his feet.

The man ran to a window in the hall that was wide open. Jack sprinted after him. He wrapped his arms around the burglar and slammed him down to the floor. His foot ached as he kicked the downed man in the side as hard as he could.

The man gasped between blows. "Let me go. Won't see me again. Promise. Argh!"

Jack walked around the whimpering man, barring the way to the window and the front door. The burglar scuttled back on his hands and Jack followed him into his bedroom.

"My dad's in a wheelchair," said Jack. "You heartless prick."

As the burglar got to his feet, he did a double take of the window and the thick web covering it. "The world doesn't need more wheelchair fuck-wits. Best if someone just put him down like a dog." The man reached into the folds of his bomber jacket, bringing out a long knife with angry, serrated edges. "I think I'll just lay you all to rest. Starting with you."

Jack took a slow step back, and another, until he stood in his doorway, not knowing what the hell to do next, not daring to take his eyes from the man before him and the gleaming knife. "You'll have to go through me first."

"Brave wee prick, ain't you?"

Weaver swung from the ceiling, wrapping its thick legs around the man's face. He let out such a keening noise of agony it ached in Jack's eardrums. The spider clung to the burglar's face despite his attempts to pull it away. There was a sharp tang of ozone on the air as the man's struggle came to a pathetic end. His hand dropped to the carpet and all was silent.

Jack tiptoed closer. "Y-you're eating him."

Weaver tore meaty chunks from the man's face. The spider didn't stop eating flesh even as its powerful voice reverberated in Jack's skull. "I must rebuild my strength for the dark trials ahead of us."

"You killed him..."

"He would have slain you. That, I cannot allow."

Jack's mouth went cold and watery. Half of the burglar's face was already gone. The dark cave of an empty eye socket seemed to stare through him. "What are you?"

"As you protected me, I protect you. We're in this together now, Jack. Our fates are one."

"I—"

"Do not worry." Weaver sunk its teeth into skull. The cracking, crumbling noise it made echoed up Jack's spine. "Fear not. There will be no remains."

"Jack! Jack!" his dad shouted from the living room. "You alright?"

Weaver crunched into bone. "Our bond is made sacred. Go now and heal with your family."

The spider had devoured most of the man's head. The innards of his brain fluffed apart like candy floss in Weaver's huge fangs. Those sharp points glinted with oily blues and greens.

Jack ran.

"ARE YOUR LOVED ONES WELL?" asked Weaver later that night.

Jack stood slack-jawed, unable to take his gaze from the spider that clung to the wall by his bed. It padded backward, fixing him with rows of deep, concerned eyes. It had grown to the height of his old dirt bike and looked just as gnarly with its zigzag patterns of gold, brown and cream. His brain couldn't adjust to the size of it as it clung there unaffected by gravity's rules.

"T-They're fine," said Jack. "Dad's a bit cut up and Mum took a heck of a whack to the head. Still a bit in shock from someone just creeping in and trying to kill us all. I mean, who does that? Some serious scum about here, likes. I convinced them not to phone the cops."

"We must help each other."

"Help? How?"

"Tell me what you need, what your soul yearns for, and I will make it happen."

"What my soul yearns for..."

"I will make it reality. I am forever in your debt."

Jack paced the room, stepping over the line of dried blood where the burglar had perished. The spider was a thing pulled from the very worst of nightmares, yet it had saved him. It had saved them all. Jack felt no sorrow as he remembered the way its midnight fangs devoured the prick who'd attacked his parents.

"Can you fix my dad? Make him walk again?"

The spider lifted a front leg and ran its tip along the wall making a sound like a sweeping brush. "Faith can heal all wounds, child."

The room darkened as Weaver crept over the window. Moonlight shone atop its mass of prickly hairs.

"I must practise," said Weaver. "Bring me someone sick. Someone with a sickness that is somewhat more... curable. And I will prove to you that it can be done."

"Can you really fix him?"

"Once I find my old strength, he will walk again. Find a person laid low with any kind of sickness and bring them to me."

Jack shook his head. A small laugh sighed out of him. Had he wiped himself out on his bike? Had he died and this was his version of hell?

The giant spider scuttled slowly down the wall in two large steps, its long hairy, jointed legs whispering along the carpet as it trod toward Jack. "Place your faith in me and he will walk again, Jacky-boy."

"I-I do. I believe."

Weaver turned its muscular head. Silver moonlight glinted along its black eyes like slick pebbles. "Once, there were others like me. The world has grown so cruel. So cold. We will make it righteous once more."

"Righteous?" Bones crunching and popping replayed in Jack's mind. "We killed someone."

"Sometimes the road to a better world is paved with regrets."

A warmth spread up his face. Gently, he laid a hand on one of Weaver's bulky hind legs. A sense of purpose thrummed through him, a roaring just like he once felt at church when the Father painted vivid images with his words.

"I'll find someone."

THE NIGHT AIR clawed at Jack's chest as he snuck out of the house in search of someone who needed cured. He had no idea how he would convince them into his home and didn't think 'my giant talking spider can help you' would cut it.

He put his hands in the pockets of his leather biker jacket, watching his shadow lengthen on the path as he walked under the dull yellow glare of a streetlight.

Something caught the corner of his eye. An old man pulled at the handle of his living room window with shaky effort. Mr. Arnold shuffled back to a large brown chair. When he lowered himself into the seat, Jack could almost hear the old man's relief.

Could Weaver save Mr. Arnold?

He took a step toward the old man's gate. A grumbling noise stopped him. He turned. A tall man stood before him. Lit by the streetlight behind, the man seemed like a standing shadow.

"You look pure lost, sweet cheeks," said the shadow in a weaselly voice. "Your folks not warn you that a fine piece like you would get snatched up? You like parties? Bet you do, eh? Bet you're wild."

The man moved forward. His unbuttoned trench coat hung off his naked body. Jack caught the strong smell of whisky radiating from him. The man spread his long arms and lunged at him. Jack side-stepped and the man's head clattered against Mr. Arnold's wall.

Jack tapped the prone man's hairy leg with the toe of his hi-top. The scabby man didn't move. He just lay there, his mouth hung open, his brown coat riding up beyond his scarred arse-cheeks.

He grabbed the unconscious man by the arms and dragged the sicko home.

THE WEB that Weaver had spun cut across Jack's bedroom, spanning from one wall to the other. The drunk was wrapped tight in a silky cocoon in the centre of the massive web, suspended in mid-air. The web was so thick he could barely see through it. Weaver leaned over the unmoving drunk, studying him intently.

Inside the stained trench coat, Jack found a beaten wallet. The man's name was Peter Drysdale. No money, no address, no clues to what he did or who would miss him.

Weaver plucked at the web like it strummed a guitar string, making the whole web quiver. "This is one sick man, Jacky-boy. A poison eats him from the inside of his very being. A poison of his own making."

"He was trying to get me to go to his house. The sicko," said Jack, lost in Weaver's large eyes.

"This man, this Peter, must repent these sins if he is to be truly saved. He must learn—"

Peter groaned and his eyes shot open. The web shook as he struggled against the wrappings that held him tight. "Let me out, you wee fanny."

The naked man squirmed, trying to break free of the bandage-like webs, becoming still when Weaver moved closer him, slowly tiptoeing toward Peter's face. The man's pock-marked face drained of colour, and Jack thought he was going to let out a blood-curdling roar and wake his parents, but all that escaped the man's dry lips was a thin, pathetic whine.

Weaver moved in nightmare-slow motion in an agonising, taunting gait. Something green dripped off its bared fangs, pattering onto the carpet.

"I can smell the sickness within," said Weaver. "Peter, you are in great need. My messenger has brought you to the right place. A place of salvation."

"Don't be scared, Peter," said Jack. "Weaver, that's the, ehm, big spider there, he says he's gonna fix you."

"Get away," shouted Peter. "Get away. Mammy? Mammy, where are you?"

A glinting, green-tipped fang buried itself in Peter's neck. The man let out a short squeal before his head slumped to one side. Bright green liquid glowed in the dark of the room and dripped down the dead man's neck.

Jack stared beneath the suspended body as drips of blood pattered on the carpet. "What you playing at? You've killed him."

Weaver looked down upon Jack, then it tore into Peter's head, yanking its muscular head to the side. There was a squishing, cracking sound, then Weaver tossed the man's head up into the air by its hair. Little specks of hot blood spattered Jack's cheeks. Weaver caught the head like a dog playing with a chew toy. It crunched through bone, gulping it down.

"I thought you were saving him?"

"This is the only cure for those like him, Jack. He was drowning himself in his own sickness." The spider continued to crunch as the voice boomed in Jack's head. "There is no room for such scum in our future."

"You can't keep doing this." Jack took two careful steps back towards his bedroom door. "I'll get the police. You can't just go around killing folk."

Weaver stopped mid-chew, its rows of cold eyes turning toward him. "Stop me? You think you can abandon our cause after two souls perished in your very bedroom? Remember, it takes great sacrifice to cast the impossible aside."

There was a faint smell of musty cinnamon in the room. Something tickled his nostrils. He rubbed at his irritated eyes. "Cast the impossible? That's what my dad said."

"Come closer, my angel."

He thought his legs would crumple under him as he stepped closer to the feasting creature tearing its prey to shreds. "You said you could make my dad walk again."

Weaver shook its bloody maw of a mouth and made its way down to the bottom of the web. The eight eyes were no longer filled with anger and beheld him with such a look of pain. The spider shuffled closer, halting its slow exaggerated steps inches from Jack's face. Its fetid, hot breath radiated from the thing's entire body.

"I can give you everything, Jack. But first you must *believe*."

JACK LAY in a cold sweat dreaming of the last time he rode his beloved dirt bike. He jerked the throttle, demanding the most from the screaming engine as he whooshed up ramps and flew through the air, his stomach floating as he reached the zenith of each jump. His dad leapt up and down, the only person watching on the side-lines, yelling his support until his booming voice began to crack.

The front wheel wobbled, the handlebars whipped to the side, and the dirt and pebbles came rushing to meet him.

He jolted awake, throwing his arms in front of his face as if he were about to smack into hard dirt and gravel. He rolled over and smothered his face with his pillow, laughing and crying hysterically into it.

The dream had made him forget all about the spider. It lay in a great hulking mass, clinging upside down above his bed. Its bulbous shape had grown, almost taking up half of the ceiling.

Weaver's legs were hunched under itself, and it hung upside down, eyes open but unfocused. Was this how it slept? It was the darnedest thing he'd ever seen.

Jack blinked as his balance wavered. His grip on reality was slipping away from him. He slid off his bed and tiptoed to the door. Spots of copper smelling crimson dotted his white t-shirt. The spider left no trace of the murder that had happened here.

How much bigger would it get? How many more people would it devour?

His doorbell trilled a long *ding-dooooong* through the house. The spider scratched and shuffled above him. He felt its eyes laser into his back. It tapped an uneven rhythm with its thick legs as he turned to face it.

"Jacky-boy," said Weaver in its deep voice. "I had the most marvellous vision. I will make your father walk again." It crawled along the ceiling until it was directly above him. "You're not thinking of betraying me, are you? Do not abandon on our cause. We will cure this cruel, cruel world."

Jack saw twisted reflections of himself in the spider's black eyes.

The doorbell chimed again. A familiar voice yelled outside. He rushed out of the room and down the hall to open the front door.

"Hey, Mr. McKenzie. What is it?" Jack leaned against the door.

"Tam here?"

"Tam? No. Not seen him for a few days."

"That can't be right," said Tam's dad in a clipped, panicked voice. "You think your folks have—"

"They've been stuck inside. Coming down with the cold, or something." Jack started to close the door. "If I see him, I'll tell him to get straight home, alright? See you later."

"Hang on." Mr. McKenzie shot a hand out, stopping the door from closing. "It's just not like him to be out all night. You sure you've not seen him? I don't care if you've been getting drunk in there or whatever. I just need him home."

"He's been out all night?"

"Is that a web in your hair?"

"I should be getting back to my old man, you know."

"What's that smell?" The surly man pushed on the door, putting one foot inside.

"Don't—"

A series of bassy thumps came from Jack's room. He imagined Weaver beating at the ceiling, making it sound like someone upstairs was galloping around.

"Oh." Mr. McKenzie walked over to the steps leading up to his own front door. "Wee bugger's just sneaked in. Sorry to bother you, Jack."

He closed the door. The cool of the dark hall chilled over him. The thumping grew. Weaver scuttled out of his bedroom and toward the living room. As it moved, it tucked its legs in as its huge bulk barely fit in the narrow corridor.

He sprinted after it. The curtains in the living room were closed. The TV cast silver, flickering light around the room. The spider had climbed its way up on the couch between his mum and dad like some other-worldly pet. They both lay with their heads back, staring at the ceiling, mumbling incoherently as if clawing their way from the same nightmare.

"What have you done? You said you'd save us!" said Jack, looking about for something to whack the great spider with.

Weaver stood, stretching as if it were a cat about to curl up and take a nap. It laid a bristly foreleg on his mum's lap. "Do you not feel their great agony, Jacky-boy? I couldn't stand by and let it go on. I simply gave them a little *something* to help. Help them with the pain that shakes their world. Until we can find a more permanent solution."

"Gave them what?"

"Just some medicine, is all."

Jack collapsed to his knees and tugged at his hair. He fell forward, curling into a ball, knocking his forehead off the warm, dirty floor. "Did I die that day in the church? This must be my own personal hell."

"I pray that you never perish, my chosen. We will shape this world into whatever we wish. Rise up and be the change this broken world needs."

Jack sobbed into the carpet. "I'm losing it."

Something stuck to his back. It tugged at him, hoisting him up to his feet. He kicked at the ground, pulling against the web as Weaver pulled him close.

"Don't fight it." The spider hauled him closer, its shining eyes inches from his. It laid a bristly foreleg on his shoulder. "I have only given them *medicine* to help with their pain. I will give you some so you can know peace. Would you like that?"

Jack stared at the dripping tips of the spider's huge fangs. He saw eight versions of himself in Weaver's eyes. "Peace?"

"Yes, Jack. This I give to you. Come. Take your medicine."

Weaver leaned in, yawning open its huge mouth. Its glinting fangs dripped green liquid on his shoulder. A hot slice of pain stung his neck where the tips of its fangs pierced his skin. A painful note registered from somewhere distant in his mind, drowned by the hot river of pulsing pleasure that roared in his bloodstream.

He closed his eyes and let it sweep him away.

JACK'S MIND WAS A DENSE, fluffy cloud. His mellow happiness slowly melted away as he breached the murky surface of wakefulness. He couldn't open his eyes, so he watched the flittering, purple shapes that flew behind his heavy eyelids.

His tongue felt too thick in his mouth. "Mum? Dad?"

An image of his parents lying prone in the spider's clutches made his eyes fly open. Webs touched every dusty surface in the dark living room. The TV fizzed its static snow, its harsh white noise echoing through the room.

Weaver gazed down upon him from its web that hung from one end of the room to the other like some giant hammock. It straightened its long limbs, examining him intently. A low purring, popping noise vibrated from the spider's bulky abdomen like someone revving a tiny engine.

His parents were trapped like flies awaiting their grim fate. He saw the whites of his dad's eyes as he groaned, as if he was having a nightmare he couldn't wake up from. The sound took Jack back to his dad's hospital bed when it was all touch and go, when it seemed his dad might not pull through.

"My soldier of light returns to us," said Weaver.

Jack picked himself off the floor where he'd collapsed. The grey room seemed to tremble beneath him as he straightened. "I don't know where you've come from, but you need to leave us." His eyes stung like the smoke of a fire burned nearby. "It was all lies. I really believed you could save us."

Weaver put a long leg carefully over Jack's mum, then crawled until it hovered menacingly over both his parents. They both stared up, looking but not seeing the beast's bulbous body just inches from their noses.

"Lies?" said Weaver, bellowing in Jack's mind. "You've got it all wrong, my special one. These acts I commit for you, Jacky-boy. I will cure your parents both. They only rest, see?"

Jack turned, drew back his fist and punched the wall. Instead of a great roar of anguish, all that escaped him was a keening moan. Gripping his hand, he spun back to face those bottomless black eyes. "You say I'm this special one? Well, if you can't fix my dad, I'm not helping you."

Weaver settled back in its web like a chastened dog, lowering itself even closer to his mum and dad's faces. "It hurts that you doubt me so. I *will* make him walk again. Then we will make this world a better place."

Jack stepped closer to the huge web, certain that if he touched it, he'd be sucked up forever, never able to escape the spider's clutches. "And how will we make the world a better place? Why do you need me?"

"You are my voice. Just place your faith in me, and you'll see."

"Faith? Faith? I'm all out of fai—"

What if this spider, which had appeared to him as a glowing, godly apparition, could really make his dad walk again? Such a miracle would mean they really could make the world a better place.

A man lives by his own limitations. Cast the impossible aside, and you can achieve anything your heart desires, his dad had said, right before he nearly walked again for the first time since the crackling church roof tore their old, happy life into kindling.

"W-Where's Tam?" said Jack. "What did you do with him?"

The spider crept closer, lowering itself so its fangs were inches from Jack's face. "Tam was a regrettable sacrifice, but he stood between us and our mission."

Jack shook his head, seeing Tam's warm smile as they scooped up spiders in a jar. "You're just going to keep on taking and taking until there's nothing left. No matter how much you weave your tales, no matter how many lies you pump us full of. No, I can't help you do this. And my dad wouldn't want me to, either."

Eight crestfallen eyes beheld him, and again he heard a clicking, purring noise coming from the centre of the spider. "Have I lost you, dear one?"

Jack took a step back. He ran his tongue along the numbed roof of his mouth. The TV flickered, making the room strobe in a deathly white. The rumbling sound coming from Weaver grew harsher like a swarm of maddened wasps.

He bolted for the door, slamming it shut behind him. The spider thudded off the other side. As he slumped to the floor on his side of the door, green bile crept up his gullet. What kind of son abandoned his parents like he just did?

"I'll find a way to stop you," said Jack.

"Oh, I doubt that. But I will not fight you. Maybe what you need is a test to prove your faith. Go and summon whatever help you can muster. I won't hurt your parents. This is my promise to you."

TEARS STREAKED down Jack's weary face on the way home from the police station. A moustached officer had turned him away, calling him a 'drugged up wee bastard.' The moon glared its yellow light, shining so bright he thought his eyeballs might burst. When he looked at his hands, it was like they were a million miles away.

"God, what's wrong with me?" He hugged himself, shivering all over. A laugh bubbled out his mouth at the thought of God. He doubled over, screaming unstoppable *hee-haws* at the path.

He drew in ragged breaths, knowing he'd chuck up the remains of his empty stomach if he couldn't get a hold of himself. Mr. Arnold's squat house stood like a mushroom before him. From the other side of his living room window, the old man shook his head, looking at Jack with such disgust. In all his days, Jack couldn't remember anyone visiting the old man.

Jack drew his leather jacket tighter around him and stumbled home.

Shame rose up his gullet as he opened his front door. "Mum? Dad?"

He went into the silent house, stepping over and under webs. He walked right into one that covered the length of the hall like a wall of silk. It wrapped around him, the warm, stickiness of it made his bones shiver. It clung to his hands as he slapped it off.

A corridor of webs covered the dark corners of the hall. He caught movement in them and stopped. What he saw almost sent his soul crashing out of his body. Hundreds of little spiders looked down on him, fixing him with penetrating glares. He could see flashes of cream, brown and specks of gold.

"You better not have hurt them," he shouted.

The living room door swung slowly open, spilling light from the overturned TV that continued to spill out its static snow. In that dead light, a river of spiders parted before his feet as he walked into the living room. Hundreds upon thousands of small creatures swam to each corner. They made a scuttling, swarming sound as they moved away.

He tiptoed dreamily into the centre of the room, feeling a million eyes on him. Weaver was hunched in its huge web as if sitting upon a great silken throne. Jack's mum and dad lay on the web, drawing in shallow, uneven breaths.

"You came back," said Weaver, now grown to the size of a car. "I knew you would."

"How?" Jack shook his head. The sea of hairy spiders that blanketed the floor and walls moved as if it were one. Fear gripped him from the soles of his feet to the back of his neck.

"Let me introduce you to our little army."

"How did you—" Jack gasped, covering his mouth.

A tattered corpse lay in one dark corner. He recognised the grey spiky hair at once. Tam's dad's long face had been bitten away and his torso was burst open, a hollowed-out cavity where something had exploded from its chest, splattering spots of blood all over the wall. A stream of spiders flowed from the body and covered every corner of the room.

Jack bent over and threw up a stream of thick, globby puke that splattered on the carpet.

"A cause as great as ours needs followers. It needs acolytes. This," Weaver raised a foreleg as if addressing a huge audience, "is our army of peace."

"Peace?" Jack wiped his mouth. The thick air of the room seemed to cling to his lungs.

"An army to help spread the word. An army to conquer fear and instil morals. An army to bring in a new era. An army to shout our voice to every corner of this heaven-forgotten place. Your voice, Jack. Your voice."

His dad spluttered. "Jacky-boy? Is that you, my son?"

"Dad?" Jack raced over, spiders skittering out his way, revealing the sickly grey carpet beneath.

His old man stared glassy eyed at the ceiling. "You did it, Jacky-boy. I can feel my legs once more."

Relief made Jack's knees buckle. He knelt beside the web in which his father was tangled and held his clammy, cold hand. "It wasn't me. It was Weaver."

Weaver made its slow way down to the ground and padded over to stand beside Jack. The gigantic spider's back shimmered and crawled with countless miniature versions of itself, mesmerising him like slow shifting sand.

"You should've seen it, Jacky-boy," said Weaver. "It was a most wonderful thing. But it took its toll on him. He rests now."

Cables of sinews strained in his dad's neck as he raised his head to look at him with misty eyes. "Faith need not have a beautiful face. Be the cure this abandoned world needs."

"Dad?" Jack laid a hand on his father's face, the unshaven bristles tickling his palm. His dad drifted off to sleep again.

Weaver bared its nightmarish green fangs. "Believe, Jacky-boy. Believe in me. In us."

Jack scrunched his eyes tight shut. Images of fights in the streets. Infants crying with no parent in sight. Dogs barking through the night. The sounds of break-ins. The agonised screams of girls. It all crossed his spinning, clouded mind. He opened his eyes. "No-one ever gave us a chance or believed in us. We've been abandoned. We make our own fate."

"'We make our own fate.' I like that. You were born for this. Do you see?"

"And you were sent to me for the greater good."

"We must cure more sick people."

"Aye, we must help them."

"Find me another worthy of our help."

THE FIRST STREAKS of dawn lined the distant horizon in a flare of purple as Jack stepped out into the chill autumn morning. As he loped down his steps, a blanket of spiders followed in his wake, eating up the path behind him.

Sickly, billowing webs coated every hedge, tree and fence. The town had been wrapped under eerie grey sheets. No one except him made a sound in the predawn light, and the small stones under his trainers echoed down the street.

The only person awake was Mr. Arnold. The TV light bounced over his hairy knuckles as he clutched a bottle of golden whiskey. He poured more of the alcohol onto the table than into the tumbler as Jack watched from the path. The man shook violently. They could save this man. End his suffering.

He crept to the door, the eyes of a million followers at his back scuttling about the hedges that lined the winding, cobbled path to the front door. Would the old man go to a better place? A place where he could live without pills?

Kirkness lay in silence as he reached the door.

Jack raised a hand to knock.

The world felt like it was squeezing down on him. A streak of golden light shone on the door, and on Jack's fist. He lowered it. "I-I can't. I just can't."

He ran a hand through the lightning bolt shaved into the side of his head. This wasn't right, was it?

His dad's calm voice rang in his mind.

Be the cure this abandoned world needs.

Jack groaned, turned and kicked a shrub, sending little spiders flying in all directions. They quickly consumed the plant again.

With a shaking hand, he raised his fist.

He knocked on the door.

WE THE DARK DENIERS

Jim Vates could hardly see a damn thing through his sunglasses. He stumbled after Kev and Stevie, unable to see ten feet in front of him. They walked towards the wall of tall trees that surrounded the town of Kirkness.

"Right lads," said Kev, throwing his rucksack on the grass. "Here's a good spot. Let's get the tents pitched before we crush the beer. Don't wanna be poking about in this darkness half-tanked."

Jim set his rucksack down, his shoulders breathing a sigh of relief. "Did you even read that last post I shared? Darkness does not exist. It's all a game to keep us cooked up inside – nice and compliant."

"Would you shut your pie trap?" said Stevie, his rat-like teeth nibbling his lower lip. "Had enough of your bollocks, likes. Nearly midnight and you're cutting about with sunspecs on, and—"

"Ehm, could you rephrase that please? Us dark deniers don't like the term midnight. It implies that there is a night, which is the lies *you* choose to feast on. Enlightened people use the term post-evening. Inclusive society and all that. The sky is only as sunny as you choose it to be."

Stevie flicked his tongue like he tasted something foul on the air. "Whatever."

Jim sat on the dewy grass. Every rung up his spine protested. He really should keep to his diet. That wasn't going to happen tonight with the beer and crisps he'd packed.

He could just make out his two friends at the edge of his dampened vision as they bustled in their packs. Metal clanged on metal as tent poles hit the ground.

Outside of TheDarkIsLies.com, it was hard to get anyone to see the truth – that darkness was a lie that humankind taught itself over the years. According to the latest articles, humankind had imagined the darkness when predators stalked every inch of the earth. Those times were long gone. The day of the permanent sun was here. If only he could make them see.

Don't leave me here, Mummy. It's creeping in—

He popped the tab on a beer a took a large drink, chasing the shivers away. He savoured the cold harshness of the beer as it scratched the back of his throat.

Stevie made a noise of exasperation and kicked his bag, its contents spewing out. "Let's just get trolleyed. If we're drunk enough, we won't feel the cold anyways."

"Now, that's something I can agree with," said Jim.

Grasshoppers chirped nearby as they faced the tall trees. Branches swished in the breeze, making a noise like static on an old telly. Those trees surrounded the town of Kirkness on Scotland's east coast. People vanished in those trees.

"Kev," said Jim, scratching his sizeable gut. "You joining us for a beverage?"

Kev wrestled with a tent pole, the tip of his Viking beard touching the grass. Of the three of them, Kev looked the only one who'd put up a decent fight. Jim's bulk would be his undoing and Stevie looked like a nervous, skittery bug.

"In a sec," said Kev.

"Well," Stevie belched and threw an empty can on the ground, "I'm gonna take myself a post-evening piss."

"Charmer, that one." Kev's tongue poked out his mouth as he jabbed a pole through a piece of cloth.

"Your wee bro," said Jim. "Was it near here where... Forget it. Worst subject ever."

"Who, Melv? I left him back at the house. Bet the tike will try to follow us up here." Kev stared at the ground, shaking his head. "You'd never believe the crap he pulled earlier. Coco Pops all over the floor. Rascal. Made me clean it up, too. I'll crush up his transformers for that one."

"Kev?"

Kev smashed a tent peg with a small mallet. "Aye?"

Melvin had been six when a sicko lured him into the woods. Thinking about the things they'd shown in the papers made Jim's gums curl. No shame. Never mind that they'd printed out the word 'night' on numerous occasions, they'd also shared the most gruesome of details, sparing no thought for Kev and his folks. They never caught the person who did those things. The news had never quite sunk into Kev's brain that Melv was gone.

Why does the dark have to come, Mum? Make it bright forever. Please? I can't take it...

Jim stood, his balance wavering. "I'm gonna go check on Stevie."

He left Kev staring at the ground, his eyes stuck somewhere in the past.

It felt like someone breathed on his face as he stepped into the forest. The air turned moist like a rotten swamp burbled nearby. He could barely make out his own hands in front of his face. The plastic tips of sunglasses scratched the side of his head as he rested them atop his scraggy hair.

He found Stevie hanging upside-down, his legs folded over a thick branch. He gave Jim a salute and crossed his arms over his scrawny chest. The large tree creaked as he swayed gently back and forth.

"I could totally be a bat," said Stevie.

"I can see it in your face."

"You're winding me up."

"Call you Bruce Wayne from now on."

"I don't take the piss out of you with all your post-evening crap. I want to be a real, actual bat. I feel it inside me. Like it's always been there."

"You do you, man. Free the bat inside."

"I bloody well will."

"Good."

"Good."

Jim itched the chafed skin above the waistband of his jeans. "You planning on sleeping like that, or you coming back to the—"

A branch cracked.

Jim peered into the depths of the forest. The light sure did play tricks in post-evening. A wet, snuffling noise echoed like a pig nosing for truffles. He stepped forward, squinting his eyes.

"What's out there?" said Stevie.

From behind a large tree, a shadowed figure crept into the open, its movements oily and powerful.

Night light, night light!

Jim fell over a root, air thudding out his lungs as he landed on his rear. The creature stalked forward on four muscled legs, its clawed hands digging into the earth. Jim scuttled until his back hit a tree. His legs went on motoring beneath him as he tried to kick himself away from the beast. Clicking sounds vibrated from it, growling out a mouth packed with razor teeth.

"Wha-What is it, Jim?" Stevie asked, vocal cords straining as he tried to twist round to see.

"Darkness is the absence of light," said Jim. "That which is absent, isn't real. It's not real. It can't be real."

The closing scent of wet animal crowded him.

Mummy's here with cookies my wee man. It's bright and light and magical. Nothing to be afraid of.

"Jim! You better not be winding me up." Stevie almost fell off his branch.

The creature was close to Stevie now. A couple of sinuous steps forward and it'd be underneath him. Spit foamed from its rumbling jaw. Drool pattered the leaves below. Jim's head pulsed, his mind on an elevator, crashing to the bottom floor.

It rose to its full, awful height, taller than any living creature had any right to be. The corners of its wide mouth flickered in what Jim thought was a smile.

It lifted a huge hand and raked at Stevie's back.

His head made a dull *thud* as he hit the ground, neck popping at an awkward angle. He sucked in a breath to let out a scream, but the creature pierced its glassy claws through his chest.

Jim put his weak, rubbery hand on the rough bark of a tree and hauled himself up. Stevie's coppery blood dotted his face.

Blood and foam dripped from the beast's elongated mouth. The thing's eyes flashed yellow as it turned its slithery attention upon him. His stomach turned to black lead. It snorted, then loped into the forest, kicking up a spume of leaves in its wake.

"Well," said Jim, putting his sunglasses back on. "That didn't happen."

KEV FINALLY GOT the tent to stand on its own. It trembled in the breeze like a struggling sail. He tapped his phone, using its torch to find his bag of snacks.

Melvin's giggly voice echoed in his mind. He missed the wee guy. He didn't like being away from him for this long, but he'd play with the rascal all day tomorrow. Maybe even bring him out here. He'd be old enough to camp out soon, and—

Where is he, Dad? What do you mean you don't know? Don't you care? Something's happened!

He unscrewed the lid on his hipflask and gulped fire. He sucked in a breath through gritted teeth, welcoming the syrupy feeling that oozed up his calves.

There'd be ice cream and football with Melv tomorrow. He could almost see him skipping and dancing around him in a circle, longing for adventure in the forest.

Not in the woods. No, no, no!

He ripped open a bag of onion rings, spilling them all over the grass.

Where the hell were Jim and Stevie? And wasn't Melv just here? Where'd he get to? Turn your back on that boy and poof, off he goes like a wee rocket.

Jim waddled back to the camp. His ridiculous sunglasses hugged his face, too tight for his large head.

"Where's Stevie at?" said Kev.

"Ehm, hanging out, I guess," said Jim, licking a thumb and pawing desperately at his chin.

"You alright? Shaking like a scared Chihuahua."

"Fine, aye. Just enjoying catching some rays with my buds. Been too long since we last done this."

"True that, man."

"Can I ask you something personal?"

"Shoot."

"Your wee brother."

Kev ripped out a clump of grass, squeezing its juices into his palm. The green scent drifted up to him. "What about him?"

"What if someone was to challenge you on that? Test your belief. Like, with actual proof, too. What would you do?"

"I'd rip their hair clean off their skull, tell them they were being idiots of the highest calibre while introducing their face to the ground on several occasions."

"Even if the evidence is... compelling?"

"What you trying to say, man? That my brother isn't real, or something? What kinda crap is this? I won't hear it, man. I refuse. You can kiss my—"

Clicking echoed from the trees. It was a sound that took him back to pedalling a bike downhill, screaming at the devil with Melv's arms clutched around his stomach. The playing card taped to the spokes on the wheel clicked like machine-gun fire.

Don't let go, Melv. Stay close!

Something darted about, snapping twigs. It sounded bigger than a rabbit.

"It's back!" Jim shot up, faster than the big guy had any right to.

"What?"

"What? Nothing. Something. Nothing. I mean — argh!"

Jim doubled over, pulling at his hair with two gnarled hands.

Kev went to him and put an arm around him. "What's got you so bent out of shape? Just a deer or something. Jeez."

The rising, plastic smile on Jim's face made cold fish dance about in his belly. He wanted to slap it off of him.

"What happened to Stevie?" said Kev.

"He's gone bats."

The wind picked up, sighing through the trees. Kev stared at the ring of darkness at the edge of the cold torchlight.

"Melv?" called Kev. "You in there? Wee rascal."

"Aye," said Jim, his back teeth showing in the corners of his awful smile. "Aye, that's it. That's totally it. Get the wee man. Off you go. If he's here, then that can't possibly mean—"

Jim cracked himself in the jaw with his own meaty fist, making the sunglasses tumble onto the grass. He grabbed Kev's arms, fingers digging in. "Go get Melv. Into the trees and scoop him out. We need him. His wee voice. His piggy laugh. Go."

"Alright, calm down."

Kev shook free of Jim's desperate grip and took out his phone. A white cone of light showed moths fluttering about as he walked to the trees. His skin cooled as he crossed the threshold, into the forest.

"Melv?" he called.

Nearby, someone sucked in a long, shaky breath.

"Are you two setting me up? Stevie that you? Gonna pummel your face in for this one, likes. Had me going." He moved forward, brushing a small branch out of his face. "And Melv? Get your wee butt out here or I'm telling da—"

Why was he thinking about his dad? He hadn't been around for the best part of a decade. The news vans, the hounding questions, the non-stop visitors with sad-eyes and flowers—

He shook his head, the piney scent of the forest stinging his nostrils. "Melv? Come get me, bro."

Something crashed through the trees.

"Bro?"

JIM FOUND his coat in his rucksack and buttoned it up with jittery fingers. All this sunshine and not a friend to share it with. Stevie flapped around as a bat somewhere, and Kev had just up and left him to play hide and seek with his definitely alive little brother. They didn't even invite him. Some friends they were.

"All is well," said Jim, thumbing his sunglasses back up his nose. The shivery sun's rays were strong. The first prickles of heat sweat dotted his forehead. "All's fine in sunshine town."

They'd better hurry back before he got his greedy mitts on the munchies. He'd promised he'd try and cut back, watch his weight. Two things weren't to be argued about in life – the false construct of darkness and heart disease.

Crack, pop, crack, snap. A slow series of twigs broke in the forest.

"Nothing. Calm it. Nothing out there. See? Squint the right way. Voila. Dazzling Sunshine and — stupid specs shop! Can't see anything properly."

The frames of his glasses creaked as he took them off, squeezing, almost snapping them. The dark lenses blocked out the silvery sun, but he couldn't see an inch of anything else with them on. He placed a chubby hand on his pounding chest.

It slobbers inside the cupboard. Make it go away, Mummy. Don't leave me in the dark!

He took in a slow breath and placed his sunglasses back on.

"Stop being a baby. Stevie's fine. Still in his tree. Kev and Melv are darting about like funsters. Join them. Not every night you get a post-evening as clear and glorious as this."

It can't hurt you if you don't believe in it, my wee baby boy. Hush now.

He stepped into the trees, tiptoeing forward, holding his arms out in front of him.

"Guys? You here? Stop taking the piss."

Something blurred past him, leaving a trail of hot, fetid breath.

Jim gasped, stumbling back. He pawed at his face, knocking his glasses off. Their frames cracked under his boot as he moved slowly forward.

The beast with the midnight black fur slunk low to the ground, its tongue brushing the grass. Glistening blood shone on its chin.

"It can't be."

Mum promised him the beast from the cupboard was gone. She'd chased it off with the light. He still remembered the hurting in her eyes as she promised the darkness wasn't real. It was a lie. All you had to do was *see*.

He could still feel her clammy, skeletal hand in his as he closed his eyes.

He stepped forward.

"You don't exist."

Hot breath blew his hair, carrying with it the smell of slick mushrooms.

A sharp tug at his stomach made him gasp. A burning sensation ripped up his torso.

"See..."

All he had to do was *see*. See that the creature simply wasn't there. Shine a light on it and it vanished.

He stepped forward, through the burning.

He opened his eyes. Frazzled dots buzzed in the corners of his vision.

The sun was so beautiful. Its rays blazed the top of his head.

Stevie flapped about the blue sky, doing loop-de-loops, a huge grin plastered up his gremlin-like face.

The scent of dandelions and vital things bursting with life hit him in the chest as he walked on through the forest. His steps were surer and lighter than they had been in years.

A six-year-old boy zipped in front of him. After the boy bounded Kev, his beard bobbing about as he gave chase.

"See? This is it. They can't get us here."

BLOCKS

"What's the issue, you skinny piece of pish?" the ogre of a man in a yellowed vest bellowed from his doorway.

Maybe your prick of a son shouldn't have smashed my two-year-old with a spade, Ewan O'Connor thought. He took in a deep breath, almost able to taste the beer seeping out of the large man's pores. "Calm down. I just came to have a word—"

"Don't you tell me to be calm, you splotchy looking bastard. Let's settle this like men." The man spread his chubby, sausage arms out wide. "C'mon then, what's it gonna be?"

Ewan looked down at his shoes and shook his head. Slashes of violent pink and muddy orange paint covered his white overalls. A rumbling pressure was building inside his head as he thought of his little Blake and the ragged, nasty scar that curled above his left eye.

"You're nothing but a cissy-boy, with a cissy-boy son."

The brute stepped back and pushed the front door closed. Ewan shot out a palm, his wedding ring clinking off the white PVC, halting its progress.

"We're not done," said Ewan.

The big man's eyes lit up, a slimy smile slanting up his face. Out on the street a crowd of boys gathered, hollering for some action. "Last chance. Beat it, or I'll stomp a hole in—"

"Dad," a small shout came from behind the mound of seething flesh.

"Beat it, James. Daddy's talking."

A rake of a boy slid under an arm, fixing Ewan with the same petulant glare as his father. He clutched an orange can of Irn Bru that was nearly the same colour as his fiery mop of hair. "Who's this muppet, likes?"

"You smacked my boy with a spade," said Ewan. "You should say sorry—"

The large man moved fast, shoving Ewan with a clammy hand. Ewan tumbled back, laying a hand on a pile of sodden cardboard to stop from falling over.

"Try telling my boy to be sorry again," the ogre said. "I dare you. You'll be picking bits of my shoe out your arse for weeks."

Ewan stood up and wiped his dirty, wet palms on his overalls. He ground his teeth. A cold static buzzed around his brain. The feeling grew, pushing behind his eyes, begging to be let loose. "You're not even wearing shoes, you prick."

The kids who'd gathered on the street tittered then fell silent. The dead-leaf October smell mingled with rotten oranges as the wind whipped at the overflowing bins just metres from where they stood.

Ewan didn't move as the flubber-train rumbled toward him, a pressured storm gathering inside his head. He let it well up, thinking about the endless tears his little boy shed because this arsehole didn't teach his son it wasn't okay to open people up with shovels.

The man cocked a doughy fist ready to smash him to pieces. Ewan squinted and *pushed,* shooting the swirling thunderstorm at the man's head. He collapsed and kicked at the ground, his knuckles turning white as he clawed at his oily temples.

His gran had called it 'the Crush'. She could crumple empty tins of beer with the blink of an eye. He'd watched her crush uncountable cans after she'd emptied them down her throat. He was ten when she first got him involved, handing him a cold beer to finish off.

The man rolled around on the path, tearing at his hair like rats gnawed at his skull. "Argh, fuck. Make it stop."

A sweat broke out on Ewan's forehead, cooled by the howling wind. He focused on his head, forcing the built-up pressure toward him. "Only if you tell your boy to say sorry."

"James, say it."

James scowled at Ewan. "But Blake struts around like he's a wee prince."

"Say it or I'll make you wish you had."

"Sorry," James muttered, and slammed the door.

The letter box clanged, and the thunder inside Ewan dissipated. The world drained of all its colour, and his bones turned winter cold. It felt like a hot needle had been pushed through each eyeball. He knew he'd be useless for days, unable to think straight.

The brute hauled himself off the pavement, and fixed Ewan with a bewildered stare. "You've got some kind of devil in you."

"Hardly," said Ewan, lowering his voice. "If I find out your son has so much as breathed near my boy, then I'll be back. You got that?"

"I-I'll sort the wee shite oot, don't you worry about that."

Ewan marched down the path and through the crowd of shocked teens who parted to let him through, and began the short walk home, his head pounding with each step.

His gran had forgotten she had the ability at the end, though every now and then when he entered the dusty room where she'd die, he'd notice a crushed-up pill box or crumpled pack of cigarettes.

He licked his dry, cracked lips and muttered to himself. "I could murder a pint."

HE DROVE from work the next day in his dented pick-up truck with its furious green dragons he'd detailed up its sides. The low sun squealed rays of agony into his eyes as he raced to collect Blake from nursery on time, praying that a certain shovel-wielder had behaved himself.

When he got there, Irene glared at him, clutching Blake's hand at the nursery's gates. Blake had an arm wrapped around a large black block, struggling to hold it against his small frame. The sunlight beamed off the block, and Ewan saw magnificent orange swirl around its surface like shifting, glittery sand. It burned little dots into his vision. When Ewan insisted Blake hand it back, Irene was adamant it didn't belong to the nursery, then turned her nose up and stomped off to lock up.

Stones crunched under the truck's large wheels as he pulled into their driveway in front of Connie's spotless ice-blue Mercedes. He thought, not for the first time, that he stood out like neon green in this part of Balekerin, where everyone went to work clad in drab greys and blacks.

Blake's shoes squeaked on the wooden laminate floor, sending a wave of pain into Ewan's ears. The wee guy bolted for his toy chest in the corner of the living room, setting his block to the side with a slow, gentle care.

His wife's phone-voice drifted down from their spare room, and he snatched a beer from the fridge, gulping half of it down in one go. The cold, harsh fizz scratched the ever-present itch at the back of his throat. He closed his eyes, sighed, and took another long pull.

Blake sprinted around with a dragon in each hand, making them do loop-de-loops, breathing pretend streams of fire everywhere. "Oh, he's a bad dragon, he's going to the jail."

Ewan poured the rest of the beer down the sink, and joined his son, picking up a fluffy green dragon, making it nibble Blake's nose, smiling from ear to ear at the sound of his son's soft giggle.

The day's fading light poured in through their patio doors, and Ewan stared at Blake's block, mesmerised by the way the sparkling oranges mingled with twinges of fiery red. The colour made languid swirls that contrasted against the deep black background that seemed to inhale any light that touched it. He crawled over to it, running a thumb along its warm, smooth edges, lost in its exploding, colliding colours. What was it that kept the colours moving around like that?

The stairs creaked as Connie bounded down, her earbuds still in. She made a *yap-yap-yap* sign with her hand as she walked over to them, kissing the top of Ewan's head, then gave him the dreaded sniff.

She said bye and hung up the phone, then looked to Blake. "Hey dragon-scales, Mummy's done with stinky work. You hungry?"

"But I no need to eat." Blake bashed two dragons together.

Ewan continued to stare into the blocks, knowing his wife's narrowed eyes were on him.

"You promised me you were off the beer," said Connie. "We'll talk about that later, shall we?"

He nodded and tried a smile, but it felt more like a grimace, and he slid along the floor to sit beside his golden-haired boy, who turned and jumped into him, almost knocking them both over. "Woah, careful, wee guy. You've got a sore noggin', remember?"

That took the playful steam out of Blake, and he traced small fingers along the white paper-stitches that still shone red underneath, staring blankly at the block in the corner. Now that Connie had put the big light on, Ewan could see the orange shifting about like oil in the world's darkest puddle.

"Where did you find that block?" said Ewan.

Blake stared, not blinking. "James bad."

White rage gripped Ewan's stomach. "What he do now?"

"He went stomp on Blake, he a baddie. He gone now, he no make Blake cry no more."

THE NEXT DAY Mr. Dennison called to say his only booking had cancelled, so he didn't need to come in today. Work at the garage was drying up. At this rate his wage would barely cover the cost of Blake's nursery.

It had been days since he used the Crush on James's dad, yet it still felt like the front of his brain was being clamped by white-hot tweezers.

Since he didn't have to work, he stayed at home with Blake, stomping around the house being daddy-dragon, pretending the floor was lava.

If it didn't have teeth and wings, that boy simply didn't care, so it was strange to see Blake run over to his block every other minute, swivelling it around, whispering to it that it had 'been a baddie.'

By eleven o'clock, Ewan was knackered, and he'd gulped down an ice-cold beer before he noticed what he was doing. Connie hadn't cornered him like he'd expected. She only asked him if he was okay, and gave him that concerned, disappointed look. He'd have preferred a punch in the nuts, it would've hurt less.

He recalled the first meeting with their marriage counsellor when the drink had nearly stripped all he loved away from him. Now he seemed to be slipping back down that ever-slippy slope.

"Dad, Dad, you play with me." Blake bolted through the kitchen and grabbed his hand, and he joined his son in the land of dragons.

The doorbell rang. Blake grabbed his police-dragon, scrambling to answer the door. "I'll get it, I'll get it, I'll get it."

They raced to the door, and Ewan opened it to see a soaking policeman, droplets of rain trickling off the brim of his black hat.

"What's happened?" asked Ewan. "Is it Connie?"

"Your wife's fine, far's I believe. Can I come in? I'm as wet as a..." he trailed off looking down at Blake. "Oh, look here. A member of the force has already arrived."

"The force is another word for police," said Ewan, seeing his son's confusion. "Come on in, officer, before you get waterlogged."

"Oh, call me Deek for old time's sake."

Derek 'Deek' Anderson was a gentle giant, and his presence usually did enough on its own to keep the peace in most situations. His large boots squelched on the floor as he entered.

"Blake?" said Ewan. "You go play while Daddy speaks to the policeman."

Blake galloped to a shadowy corner, gently setting the blue and yellow dragon on the dark block.

"Bad guys go jail," whispered Blake.

"Can I get you a drink, Deek?" said Ewan.

"Nah, I best get going soon as I can." Deek expelled a chest full of air. "There's a kid gone missing from Bayview nursery. The poor mum's clawing her heart out."

"Aye? Geez."

"We're asking around to see if anyone knows anything."

"Who went missing?"

"Wee lad called James McDonald. I hear you had a tussle with his dad. Scared him real good from what they say." Deek leaned in. "And the fucker deserved it. He's a real piece of work, let me tell you." He reached into a pocket on his protective vest, pulling out a tiny notepad.

"James?" Ewan looked to his son, who was rolling around because a bad dragon set him on fire. "I was only up there to have words with the dad, but it kinda got out of hand."

"Can you confirm your whereabouts between twelve and five yesterday?"

"Wait, you think I stole that kid?"

"Sure you didn't. Still need to ask, though."

Ewan felt a familiar pressure building up behind his eyes and forced them closed. "My boss at the garage will tell you. I was working, busy finishing yet another horrible paint-job for a boy racer. I was on that job most of the day, until maybe half five. I had to rush to grab the wee guy from nursery." He shot both palms up. "My wee guy, that is. Irene gave me the stink eye for showing up late if you want to check in with her."

"Sure, sure." Deek folded the notepad and shoved it back in his pocket. "We've got the dad in for questioning, but all he does is moan about his heed."

"I'm pretty sure you're not supposed to share stuff like that."

"Nothing stays quiet for long here. Well, I best get on my way, continue my rounds."

Blake appeared between them. "James was bad."

"Oh ya!" Deek clutched at his chest. "I didn't know dragons could be so sneaky, gave me a fright there."

Blake shot them both a frowny look, an angry crease appearing above his brow. The boy tottered back over to his block, wrapping his arms around it, muttering to it. "You be good boy now, alright?"

Ewan turned to Deek. "Well, eh, I suppose..."

"Let me know if you hear anything," said Deek.

Ewan closed the front door, and before he knew it, he was stood by the kitchen sink, another cold can of beer in his hand, glugging it down as Blake stacked up a pyramid of dragons.

He took another large swig, thinking about the look of petulant defiance on James's face when he watched Ewan use his mental strength to squeeze his dad's head.

"You drinking the stinky booze, Dad?" said Blake.

Ewan dropped the can in the sink. "You're getting awfully good at that sneaking up thing."

Blake scowled at him, and he felt like his eyeballs were about to pop loose from their sockets. He tasted something acrid on the air like someone burning plastic as an electric buzz jolted its way down his neck.

He clutched at the counter to stop from toppling over. The walls of the kitchen pressed in on him. "Daddy's just chucking the booze out, see?" His hand shook as he held the empty can upside-down. "A-All gone. See?"

"Booze bad. You drink booze, you go jail."

THE NEXT DAY, Ewan got home from work, frantically tidying up dragons of all sizes before Connie and Blake walked in. They arrived five minutes later. His heart turned into a heavy grey lump seeing Blake juggling another block in his small arms. His eyes went dry as Blake placed it atop the other, and the shadows gathered thicker in that corner.

The new block had streaks of vivid pink and purple flowing out from the darkness that sparkled like pearlescent paint.

He trod over to Blake, pulling him out of his little yellow jacket. Blake picked up a fluffy pink dragon, rubbing his eye with a balled-up fist.

When Ewan sat cross-legged next to Blake, he caught a whiff of the stale-milk smell of stiffened paint on his overalls.

The blocks were hypnotising him, drawing him in deeper as he stared into their fathomless depths.

"Babe," he shouted to Connie who rummaged around in the kitchen. "Where'd he get this other block?"

Connie slammed cupboards, opened and closed the fridge, then opened another cupboard. "I've got to head out to the Welliger place in ten minutes. He wants to host a viewing. Last minute thing, but the commish on this will be well worth it." She came through, munching a cereal bar. "I was going to ask Irene, but there was an awful palaver. Police vans and everything."

"They find who took that James?"

"Worse, a wee lassie went missing. Blake's not going back until they catch the sicko who's doing this." She looked at her sparkly watch. "I got to bolt, soz."

She knelt and kissed his cheek, then did the same to Blake, who leaned against the wall, hugging into his pink dragon, stroking a fluffy wing.

Ewan scooched over to his tired little boy and set him in the seat made by his crossed legs. Blake hugged into his chest, and Ewan rested his chin on top of his head. Fine blond hair tickled his neck.

They sat in silence, and he thought about how Connie was so driven. She rushed here or there with a purpose he both loved and grew jealous of. It felt like he wasn't pulling his weight.

Blake muttered a nursery rhyme under his breath. "That's the way the story goes, pop goes the weasel."

Ewan took out his phone and texted his mate Charlie.

You about for a chat tomorrow? I've had it with the garage. Time to try our wee venture, if you're still game?

He rocked Blake gently back and forth. "What you do at nursery today?"

"Masha make Blake sad. My was crying."

Ewan's insides screwed up when Blake's bottom lip trembled, trying his best to fight back the tears. "Hey, hey, it's okay. Did you tell a grown up when it happened?"

Blake sniffled and snuggled in closer. The setting sun poked through the clouds, pouring the last of the day's light through the big window, lighting up the blocks in the corner.

The magnificent pink of the new block made his insides quake. Little Masha was a girly-girl, always decked in candy-floss pink from head to toe.

"B-Blake?" Ewan felt a stone in his throat. "Tell me where you got those blocks."

"I made them, they mine's. I go," Blake clapped his hands, "*squash*, and no more being bad at Blake."

Ewan stared at both blocks. The fierce pinks and oranges stung his eyes in the sunlight. The room spun around him as he struggled to draw in enough breath. "Listen, did you—"

There was an urgent knocking at the door and whoever it was rang the doorbell three quick times. Ewan set Blake on the couch and opened the door. A shattered Deek stared back at him.

"Is it about the nursery?" said Ewan.

"Afraid it is. How'd you know?"

"Connie said there was something happening when she picked up Blake."

Deek clomped into the living room, twisting and wringing his black hat. "Two kids missing in the same week. Something just feels," Deek turned and looked down at Blake, "off."

"So, Connie was right? A lassie has gone missing?"

"Aye, wee Masha, she — you awright there, Ewan?"

He forced his eyes closed and leaned against the frame of the living room door. "Aye, aye. I'm just... aye," he finished lamely.

"Is that beer I smell?"

"Ehm..."

Blake pushed himself off the couch, and toddled over, fixing Ewan with a stare under a furrowed brow that would've been comical if it wasn't for the freezing blood that crept from the top of Ewan's skull. It was as if his head was stuck in a frozen vice.

"Policeman silly," said Blake. "You no drink stinky booze, Dad."

"No," croaked Ewan, tasting copper at the back of his throat. The pulsing blood inside his head returned to normal as Blake turned his focus on the concerned policeman.

"It's awfully unsettling," Deek leaned toward Blake, turning his hat round and round. "Did you see anything, wee guy?"

Blake let out an almighty shriek. "My Dad good, he no bad. He no go to jail. You go away!"

"Well, I... I..." Deek dropped his hat. "Argh!"

The big man balled up on the floor, screaming and clawing at his temples. His body contorted, and the sickening pop of bone made

Ewan retch. When Deek eventually stopped yelling in agony, silence engulfed the house. As bone snapped and sinew ripped, Deek's mass crumpled in on itself, getting smaller and smaller.

There was a flash of dark light that consumed the whole room. The light prickled Ewan's face like a burst of flame. When the heat died down and he opened his aching eyes, he tasted melted rubber like someone had set a tyre alight.

All that remained of Deek was the zigzagging swirls of yellow and blue that twisted inside the new block's midnight black.

EWAN PACED THE LIVING ROOM, peeking out the closed blinds every five minutes to check on his neighbours. He held his breath each time a car whispered by the house, but the street remained quiet. How sure could he be that no one saw Deek enter the house before Blake crushed him into a block? There was no police car parked on the street, so Deek must've done his rounds on foot.

He picked up his phone and text Connie again. *Home, asap, please xx.*

He'd sunk three beers, trying to deny the memory of Deek's muscles twisting off bone, and the popping noises as he was crunched into a block. He opened another tin. The ring-pull made its welcoming *pssst* sound, and flecks of foamy beer showered the back of his hand.

"What you doing, Dad?" said Blake.

"N-Nothing, son. How about we skip bath night and just get ready for bed?"

Blake's softly spoken words rammed him in the chest. "I don't like Daddy drink stinking booze."

Ewan inhaled one last mouthful of beer, rounded up all the cans he had in the cupboards, and emptied them down the sink, one by one, watching the dark foam making its glug-glug noise as it covered the plughole. The deep, malty smell of beer filled the kitchen.

When he was done, he peeked out the blinds again. He saw nothing, hearing only the wind barrel down the silent street. "Right wee dude, come get your jammies on."

Blake's head popped up from behind the three blocks, a spiral of brilliant orange, blue, yellow and pink wavered over his features like he was stood in front of some magical pool of water. He came bounding over, launching himself on the couch head-first, sat up then pointed at the telly. "Can you watch the dragon film with me?"

"Jammies first." Ewan held a green pyjama top, ready for little arms to wriggle through. When Blake was dressed for bed, he threw his arms out, wrapping them around Ewan's neck, snuggling into his shoulder. A small, warm hand traced circles on Ewan's back. He kissed the back of his son's head, warm tears swarming in his eyes. "Daddy's scaly monster."

He savoured the vital smell of Blake's hair, squeezed him close, then placed Blake on his knee.

"When I was a kid," said Ewan, "I used to watch your great-granny crush tins of fizzy juice with nothing but her mind. She called it the Crush. D-Did your eyes hurt when you... squashed the policeman?" He pointed to the blocks hunkering in the dark corner.

"My eyes go all hurty, and bad guys go *pop*. Then they boxes. No bad, no more."

"I can do it, too, but I can't make people into boxes. Listen. You can't just go boxing people up because they're bad. Understand?"

"James said you a bad word. He said you make his dad hurty."

"That's no reason to turn him into a block."

"But he was bad, and I do crush, just like Daddy, and he gone now. No more punching Blake."

"You need to tell a grown-up when that happens, okay? No boxing, no squashing, no crushing, got it? We're in deep trouble now."

He hugged his son close, watching *How to Train your Dragon* for the millionth time, waiting on the police coming to haul his dragon-boy away.

THEY DIDN'T COME for Blake that night, and Connie refused to believe him. He threw himself at her in a confused, garbled mess trying to explain what their son had done – that he was responsible for three missing people.

"Listen to what you're saying. Wouldn't there be blood or some other evidence lying about everywhere? Even you've got to see how daft it all sounds," she'd said, then stalked up the stairs. She stopped mid-step and called back down to him in a loud whisper to not wake Blake. "Crushing people into blocks? Really? Maybe the drink has finally gone to your head."

He paced the living room until the early hours, going over it in his mind, how Deek's eyes went dead right before the unholy black light transformed flesh and bone into block. The icy chill that had run through him when Blake glared at him was like nothing he'd ever felt before. Was that what the Crush was like when you were its victim?

The next morning, he gasped awake, punching at the air all around him like the world pressed him in from all sides. Downstairs, Blake spread his arms, flying through the living room like a dragon. Connie stood gazing out at the rising sun through the closed patio doors.

When she turned, half her face was lit by the sun's early rays, and his heart forgot how to work when he saw the light catch her hazel eyes. She had a tiny circle of deepest brown beside one dark pupil. When he'd met her in the pub all those years ago, the sight of those smiling eyes made his pint tumble out his hand and smash all over his shoes.

Connie came over and wrapped her arms around him, nuzzling into his shoulder. They stayed, not speaking, for a long minute as their son ran lengths of the home they'd made together, the peach scent of her hair bringing back a million little memories.

"Sorry for being so harsh with you when I got in last night," she said.

"You're right. I've been on the sauce. But I poured it all out last night. I'm done."

"Promise?"

"Promise."

"You still think our boy's a people compactor?" she chuckled as she moved away from him.

"You didn't hear it – the sound he made. You've got to believe me."

She waltzed through the kitchen, grabbed a cup from a cupboard and thumped it down on the counter. "That's enough. Do you not hear how that sounds? You need to get out the house. Me and the flying monster need some quality time."

It felt wrong grabbing his coat and heading to the pub to meet Charlie, but what else was there to do? Wait until someone came knocking?

His shoulders tensed as he leaned into the biting October wind on the way to the pub. The inside of the Bane's Arms was a dark and dreary place that smelled like wet dog. A crowd of greyed faces swivelled to sneer at him before turning back to their drinks. A glistening pint sat on the bar beside his friend Charlie, calling out to him.

Charlie turned on his barstool, a haggard look on his long, unshaven face. "So, the man with the skills, struggles to pay his bills. You finally serious about giving our business a chance then, aye?"

Ewan balanced himself on an unsteady stool, tracing a finger down the cool condensation covering the golden pint. "I can paint circles round the boss's son, but he still gets all the work. I'd be amazed if that arse could stay in the lines in a kid's colouring book." He could almost taste the beer. "Aye. Let's do it. What we got to lose, eh?"

His hand shook and it started its unstoppable journey toward the pint when his phone vibrated in his pocket. It was Connie. He held a hand up to Charlie and walked over to the pool table. "Everything alright? Babe? Connie?"

He heard Connie juggle the phone. Sharp puffs of breath crackled down the speaker as if she was running.

"Talk to me, babe."

"It's Blake. He... He..."

"What's all that noise?"

"You were right, Ewan. You were right. They're trying to take him. Oh, God. A policewoman came, and Blake just, he squished her. Her bones folded in on themselves like a god-damned accordion." Her voice cracked. "Our Blake wouldn't do that, would he?"

"What's happening? Is he okay?" He waved to Charlie, and started sprinting, the wind billowing through the mouthpiece. "I'm on my way."

"No. Blake? Stop it. Don't. Argh—" The phone cut out.

He ran as fast as he could, the blowing wind pushing at his back. When he got there, the flashing lights of three police cars painted his house in urgent streaks of red and blue. Two of the cars had skidded to a stop on their front lawn, tyre tracks stopping just before the front window.

He leaned over, hands on his knees, taking in great gasps of air, hearing nothing but the crackling of radios sounding from the police cars begging for updates.

"Oh-oh, what you doing? Get back on there," his son's angel voice sounded from the back garden. "Dad? Dad, that you? Look what I building."

His hand trembled as he swung open the large brown gate. He crunched over stone chips to the uneven slabs that covered half the garden. Mingled with the scent of dewy grass was the cough-inducing reek of burnt rubber. "Oh, Blake, what have you done?"

Blake toddled in his dragon onesie, a fabric tail swishing back and forth in the wind. He wrapped both arms around a new block with flashes of molten, hypnotising silver. He juggled it, then reached up on tiptoes to place it atop the others. When Blake spun round, Ewan flinched.

"My making a castle," said Blake. "Like in the dragon film."

Out here in the daylight, the blocks sang with life, a kaleidoscope of colour that lit up the whole garden. Ewan counted, his heart growing heavier with each one. There were eleven blocks in all, each with its own harrowing set of colours.

His eyes stopped on a block that shone with enchanting hazel with flecks of deepest brown. The wind nearly bowled him over. "What have you done?"

"They try take Blake to jail. Blake no go to jail. They silly."

"Is that one Mummy?"

Blake stared at his fort of clashing colour, thumbing the stitches on his forehead, his lower lip sticking out. "I no mean it. It was a accident."

He heard the blaring urgency of a police radio. The torn quality in the dispatcher's voice made a ball of ice lodge in his stomach. He strode over to Blake, who turned and leapt into him, wrapping his arms around his neck, letting out whopping little boy sobs that wet Ewan's chest.

"I don't want to go to jail," said Blake. "I need Mummy back."

Sirens shrilled in the distance, calling to take his boy away. "How about we go for a big drive in Daddy's dragon truck?"

He felt Blake nod.

"You need to do everything Daddy says, okay?"

Ewan raced to his truck and buckled Blake into his seat, then bolted into the house, grabbing as much of Blake's toys, wipes and spare clothes he could stuff into a holdall. He scooped up the keys to the Welliger house Connie had been trying to sell. When he slammed the pick-up's door shut, he saw neighbours pointing their phones at him, swarming outside his house.

He put his foot to the floor and his tyres spun, making stones fly everywhere. They pinged off the empty police cars as his truck launched itself forward and out of the street. If he could just make it to the big roundabout, then he would be heading in the opposite direction of the police cars barrelling their way to his house.

In his rear-view mirror, he saw Blake reach over to the bag, and grab his pink dragon, hugging into it as he wiped at his wet, red cheeks.

Why hadn't he talked to Blake about the Crush earlier? He could've stopped this from happening.

His throat was as dry as dust, and his heart nearly fell out his mouth as he approached the big roundabout. He took his chance, not daring to stop, hearing the sirens gaining on them. A car skidded to a halt mere inches from them as he spun around the roundabout.

Tyres squealed as he gunned it down the straight road, whizzing by rows of dying trees. They'd need to ditch the truck at some point – its angry green dragons would be a dead giveaway. They could hide out at the empty Welliger house and devise a plan.

Once his heart slowed, he glanced in the rear-view seeing nothing following them. "Blake, listen to Dad. You can't go making people into blocks anymore. What you did back there was very bad."

His son sniffled, shielding himself behind his dragon.

"You need to promise me you won't do it again, okay? If you do, they'll find you, and take you away to jail with all the other bad people."

"My no go to jail!"

"If they find us, you'll go to jail, and I'll go to jail, too."

The pained sob that Blake howled clawed at Ewan's soul.

"Listen. Calm down. It'll be alright. If you do what Daddy says, we'll make sure we both don't go to jail, okay?"

He glanced once more in the rear-view mirror. His son's puffy face had morphed into a vicious scowl. A wave of heat slapped his face, and his blood hit boiling point. He could hear the hammering of his heart in his tense, hot ears. The fire spread its tendrils, roiling through each section of his brain, and torched its way down his neck. He tasted burning plastic though nothing was on fire.

"Blake. Stop." His voice came out thick and he couldn't tear his gaze away from the reflected stare.

Muscles tightened as he gripped the steering wheel. His ribs ached, pushing into his lungs.

The truck sped along the road.

NIGHTMARE SOUP

"Billy, you up? Come get your soup, you lazy toad," my gran screeched from the kitchen. "Don't let it get cold. You won't like it when it's cold."

Her pinched voice bounced around the small bungalow shattering a tense knot between my ears like a smashed bottle, glass shards slitting the back of my eyeballs. She was like this whenever I had a late night, shouting me awake, forcing me to eat what I thought of as her 'nightmare soup'.

Opening my eyes was an experience. As the thin light spilling over my cramped bed hit my pupils, flowers of molten pain shot up my eyes, a feeling like barbed wire twisting inside my brain.

Clothes from last night lay scattered on the floor as if I'd peeled them off before collapsing in a heap. I scrunched my eyes shut and squeezed the bridge of my nose, winching as my clumsy fingers found a swollen mess. Taking in a sharp breath, I tasted whiffs of coppery blood, the green of muddy grass, and, surprise, the apple and cinnamon of a girl's perfume.

A smug smile played on my lips as I tried to remember what the hell happened last night. A caveman grunt escaped my lips and I chuckled – big mistake. I held my breath, the pain ricocheting around my skull reaching supernova levels like my brain would splatter out my ears and across my bedroom walls at the slightest sound.

"Billy, get your arse out here. Grammy's special recipe, brewed just for you."

She cackled like an honest-to-God witch and I buried my head in my arms until the whirlwind of white pain abated. I braced myself and sat up, the world sloshing around me, hot, yellow bile almost shooting out of my nose. I shuffled to the edge of the bed and pushed myself up, the single bed bowing under me.

Flashes of being chased down a narrow street outside the Drumnagoil Arms sizzled like a short, grainy film in my mind. There was beer, mud, trees, blood, and escalating threats of violence against my person. Good times.

I stumbled to the open door, my skin aching all over like I'd caught the flu. I rolled my jaw, running a tingling hand across my face. I must've had some amount of laughs last night, my cheeks were on fire. It felt like I'd grown a week's worth of beard in one night.

The soup was always the same, crammed full of floating veggies of unknown origin that bobbed around in the steaming black liquid like musty croutons of hell. Its unique scent drifted through to my room, somewhere between diesel and soggy mushrooms. It was enough to make my bowels shrink. It made me think of green things stewed in a cauldron, but I knew I'd gobble it up – it always helped me feel like myself again after a rough night.

My feet were encased in mental concrete. Each time I stepped on the scratchy carpet, fresh pain cancelled all my thoughts. I closed my eyes and shambled forward, bashing the crown of my head off the doorway. A cough of pain rumbled out my dry throat and I slapped at my thick skull as I walked down the narrow hall.

In the living room, I coughed into a balled fist, the rot of turgid soup billowing its cloud around me. My belly rumbled like a mini earthquake as Grammy glared at me like I'd just pointed a gun at her. She kept her wide, sorrowful eyes on me as she set a huge wooden spoon next to the bowl.

My throat constricted as a bubble plumed in the centre of the soup, morphing from black to deepest green. It popped, letting out a strangled burst of steam. My heavy eyes turned away from the soup, focusing on black pots stacked in the kitchen, green sludge dribbling down their sides like drying phlegm.

"Sooner you start, sooner it's over. Go on."

Her thin wrists poked out of a baggy, black top that covered her like a poncho, motioning me to sit. She looked every part the witch with her long, tussled hair that was more silver than black these days, and the ever-growing wart that lived on the very tip of her nose. She'd been the one who took me in when life tried to spit me out. A warm tingle swam around my chest seeing her fuss so much about making me feel better.

I sat on a wooden chair, thighs brushing the underside of the table as I squeezed myself in. The chair below me shifted, and my hand slapped the table inches from the soup, a droplet of black liquid sloshing over the bowl hitting the table, turning shades of midnight blue then green as it dribbled off the side and onto the carpet.

"Och, watch it, you," said Grammy, mopping it up with her sleeve.

I must've looked a right state. Hunched over, staring down into the soup, I caught how I smelled – like sweaty football boots stuffed inside a cupboard for two weeks.

I drummed my fingers on the wood, a pressure pulsing under my fingernails as I hunted for memories inside my sludgy cave of a brain. I must've gotten into another fight, no doubt over she who smelled of apple and cinnamon. Stuck in this dead town on the arse-crack of Scotland, there wasn't much else to do for fun except getting in a scrap or two.

Grammy hovered over to the window, peeking out of their bungalow and into the wall of trees lining the other side of the country road. She turned her hazel eyes on me, then flicked them away again, pretending to stare at something outside.

"Come on." My deep, scratchy voice caught me by surprise. "I won't bite."

"Just you eat your soup, dearie. You'll feel all the better."

I took in a deep breath and regretted it, a tang of tar and soggy strawberries sailed up my nose, grabbing my tonsils. The huge spoon shook in my hand like a baby trying to hold cutlery for the first time.

I blinked down at my hand. Slashes stained the back of it, the wounds red and seeping. I traced a finger along the sensitive skin and a thicket of rough hair sighed under my fingertip.

Grammy gasped and I stood, nearly knocking the table over. I steadied the bowl before the nightmare soup was lost to the floor. Flashes of blue and red painted the cramped room as a car screamed to a halt in our gravel driveway.

"Crap, crap, crap." Grammy strode over, her pointy Adam's apple bobbing as she grabbed my spoon, scooped up a ladle's worth of inky soup and shoved it in my mouth. "Time to eat up, Billy. Quick."

The liquid trickled down my throat, hitting the base of my empty stomach, a numbness spreading up my spine.

There was a pounding at the door that reverberated in the small space. "You alright in there? Is he there? Is... *it* in there with you?"

I smacked my lips. "Grammy?"

She set the spoon in my hand and squeezed my shoulder with a gentle hand. "Soup will make everything better. Eat up."

I looked into the soup, a funhouse reflection staring back at me. The mirror surface of the black liquid showed protruding teeth sticking out the corners of a huge jaw.

The police hammered the door again, threatening to knock it down.

"Eat your soup, dearie," said Grammy. "There you go. You're starting to look more human already."

THE DUMPS

A heatwave of diesel fumes hit Mark McWilliams as he hopped off the bus and into the school yard, his hands clutched high around the straps of his backpack. He kept his eyes firmly on the gum-pocked ground.

"You'll be fine," he said to himself. "Don't let them see you. Blend in. Be a ghost."

Before he ran to the bus-stop earlier that chilly autumn morning, he managed just one spoonful of sorry cornflakes. The milk sat heavy atop his stomach, ready to whoosh its way up his gullet. A stone of ice touched his throat – his mum should've been here to see him off to school. Especially today.

"You have a splen-tacular day, my wee dude. Learn something cool or you're not getting back in here," she would've said, patting his shoulder. He was lost without her here to guide him through these awkward teenage years.

"Awfully quiet this morning," said Tommy, their shoulders touching in the press of sweaty kids. "You alright? Eye's ain't so smiley today."

Mark glanced to his side, not meeting his friend's gaze. He caught the fiery impression of Tommy's ginger hair under his army-green baseball cap.

"Bad sleep, I guess," said Mark.

"Wonder what this assembly's gonna be on, then. Pure boredom, guaranteed. Am I right, Dragon?"

His dad's collection of bearded dragons had grown over the last year. They lived behind darkened glass in every corner of their clammy living room. The first had appeared two months after the cancer sucked the life from his mother. His dad often held a chunky lizard on his shoulder, petting it, muttering soft as if it were a babe. The house filled up with their desert smell that lived in all Mark's clothes. The weirdness of it was enough to put his friends off coming to see him, earning him the nickname 'Dragon'. Those damn lizards were the reason he'd drifted from his friends. He didn't feel close to anyone anymore.

Tommy whistled. "New sneaks? Sweet."

The crispness of the three white stripes against the black felt stood out among the sea of black, scuffed shoes as they shuffled toward the main entrance like herded sheep.

"Aye," said Mark, clutching his bag straps until his knuckles popped.

He felt Tommy's unsure gaze. Normally, he'd be the one clinging to Tommy, not wanting to face the harsh reality of Kirkness High School alone. He held tight to his secret, praying he could make it through the day without anyone noticing him – a ghost in the halls.

His moist palms clung to the lining of his trouser pocket as he brought out his phone. Seven minutes left until the bell rung. Typical – the one day he wanted to arrive on time and straight into it.

They searched for a quietish spot to hang around until the bell called them to their weekly assembly. He walked towards one of the 'huts' that stood opposite the main entrance. During a Physics class inside that hut, he'd tried to use a Bunsen burner, his hands numb as the Scottish winter that seeped through the thin walls.

As he sat on the stone steps, he threw his bag off his shoulders. The material made a harsh sound like a scraped knee on concrete. Two boys snapped their heads up.

"Where'd you get the coin for the kicks?" said Jonno, his hair spiked like a character from a manga comic. "You and your old man been selling lizard babies?"

"Ha," snorted Eddie, wiping his nose and leaving a silver trail on his black sleeve. "Bet they tag team them. Nothing like a bit of father, son, lizard action, eh?"

Tommy stepped away from him, moving slow and silent as a frightened cat. Mark turned his attention back to the two pricks as they shuffled about at the bottom of the steps, ready to go.

Always with the lizards. He had fantasies of smashing their tanks, setting them loose, breaking their mystical hold on his dad. Losing his mum took away his dad's spark, leaving him dull-eyed.

Mark got to his feet. "That you having wet dreams about me, Eddie? Shucks."

"Hey, now," said Eddie. "I didn't. I—"

"I'll burst your nose for saying that," said Jonno.

"Come on, then." Mark stepped back, nearly bumping against the large doors of the hut. He put one foot in front of the other, ready for the rush.

A silence grew as the crowd sensed the coming violence.

Mark glared down at Jonno and Eddie, swearing inwardly at himself – this was not the way to go about being a silent shadow the whole day long.

Tommy's back hit the door, his eyes darting all over the place before he snuck under the metal railing and into the waiting crowd.

"Two on one's fine with me," said Eddie, licking his lips.

"Your mum said something similar," said Mark, instant regret cackling through him.

Maybe the kicking he was about to take would be a good thing. If he became gossip for getting knocked around, he'd draw them away from—

The classroom door banged behind him, making his breakfast almost take the southern path out his body.

"Break it up, lads," said a rotund, red-faced Mr. Halloday. "Before I batter you myself."

The bell trilled, rumbling in Mark's eardrums. It shattered everyone's attention, making them look up at the dull sky. The crowd shuffled toward the large doors of the main entrance, their promise of violence snatched away.

Jonno and Eddie levelled a promising stare at him, then turned and joined the crowd.

THE ASSEMBLY HALL filled with shrieks of metal chairs scraped on wood. The scent of cedar and cheap plastic mingled as he let out a long breath, searching for a seat away from the rising chatter. He shuffled along an empty row, setting himself down on a plastic seat, almost sliding off it. He wiped his tremoring hands on his trousers as a wave of green sickness threatened, its heat clawing up his neck.

"Nearly got your face caved in back there, eh?" said Tommy, sliding into the chair next to him.

"Good to know you've got my back."

Tommy took his hat off, releasing a wet dog smell as he scratched at his tangle of ginger locks. "Look, man. I'm—"

"Pupils of Kirkness, good morning," the headmistress crowed, standing erect behind a lectern on the stage, somehow managing to look down her nose at the crowd.

"This should be a long one," sighed Tommy, leaning back in his seat.

Mrs. 'Beaver-face' Paterson took to the stage after the headteacher's shrill introduction. She mumbled into the mic, shuffling her presentation cards, not daring to look up. The pupils who'd brought the drink and 'devil-fags' to the last school dance were all going to hell, and fast. A joint being called a 'devil-fag' caused a surge of laughter to pulse through the crowd. She waited it out before shakily moving on to boring preparations for the autumn dance.

"And I'd like to thank Mark McWilliams especially," said Mrs. Paterson, staring down at her trembling hands like she was about to faint. "For agreeing to man the welcome desk on the evening."

"Fanny!" shouted a boy, gaining a champion level of laughter.

"Settle down, settle down. Be nice to Mark. It's his birthday."

The intake of air prickled the back of his neck. Chairs creaked, everyone turned to face him. He leaned back, wishing he could crawl inside his polo shirt and die. Rows of predatory eyes gleamed – his secret was out, and it wasn't even first period.

"That's it for today," said the headmistress. "Away to class you go. Dismissed."

"Aw, shit," said Tommy, leaning against his shoulder. "You're for it now."

THE FIRST TWO periods of the day were a misery of threats. Happy birthdays were given with feverish grins. He couldn't recall a word of what was said in Maths and as soon as the bell sounded at the end of Chemistry, he bolted, leaving a gaggle of boys and girls in his wake.

His thighs screamed as he crossed the road. A car squealed to a stop inches from him, its tyres spewing grey smoke. The car honked its pathetic horn as he kept running. The driver hurled abuse at him, telling the chasing mob to 'mash that prick' for giving her such a fright.

He sprinted past the ice cream trucks, toward the park, hoping to hide in the bushes among the discarded beer cans and vodka bottles. Footsteps thudded behind him, closing in.

Someone grabbed his collar and yanked him down. His eyes nearly pressed out of their sockets as they slammed him to the concrete path, air whooshing out his lungs. They danced around him as he stared at the bleak, grey sky.

"Happy birthday, ya wee bastard," said Jonno. "Chucks, hold him still."

"Thanks for the effort lads," said Mark, "but there's really no need, honest. I—"

Beefy hands hauled him up. He stared into the cold eyes of Chucks, given the name because no one had ever seen him laugh. Chucks shoved his head between his damp thighs, pinning his arms up toward the sky. He was bent over and could do nothing about it.

A knee struck him where his arse met his leg, sending a shiver down his calves.

"One," yelled a jubilant Jonno, the crowd counting along with him.

"Two."

Bone thudded against muscle.

"Three."

The impact shuddered down his back.

"Four."

He clamped his mouth shut as his leg screamed.

The crowd went silent as Jonno kneed him the thirteenth time.

"Fooooouuurrrrrteen!"

The impact of the blow was felt all through his body.

"Enough, lads," said Mark, his ears burning as he tried to haul himself free of the vice-like grip. "Had my dumps now. If you don't mind letting me go—"

"My turn," said Eddie. "This'll teach you to have a birthday."

"Stop," roared Mark after Eddie's fourteenth knee to the back of his leg.

"Alright," said Eddie. "Let him go, Chucks. Hate to see a pussy crying on his birthday. Maybe he'd like his real present now."

"Present?" said Mark as Chucks pushed him away. He took three limping steps away from the semi-circle of kids who'd all counted and cheered so loudly, mortified at the thought of the girls watching him squirm while his arse was on full show.

"Go on then," said Eddie. "Turn around. Eyes shut."

"You for real? No chance."

Jonno's arm was a blur as he threw a small object at Mark like a baseball pitcher lugging a fastball. Pain melted up his bare arm. He slapped a palm on the area as he sucked in a breath through his teeth. Next to his new trainers lay an egg. It hadn't cracked.

He turned and ran as the crowd threw more eggs at him, some cracking and splatting their goo all over his back, some almost piercing his skin and dropping to the ground. Others lobbed warm milk over him. One girl sprinted by his side and dusted him with a cloud of flour, stinging his eyes.

An egg burst against his cheek bone, making him yelp. His lungs were on fire as he ran blindly back to the school, praying for the bell.

. . .

In Home Economics, he stared down at the ruin of his new trainers. Where they'd been black, they were sooted in yellowed flour. The crisp white stripes were splatted with yoke yellow. He smelled like mouldy cheese spread. He ran a hand through his hair, picking out pieces of eggshell.

He'd made it through lunch by hiding in the toilets, praying the mob wouldn't come hunting. The reek of his ruined polo shirt stayed his hunger as he crouched on the toilet seat. He could've gone home, but they'd have called him a pussy. More than that, he couldn't face his dad not noticing he was home early.

Mr. 'Daft' Daphne hardly noticed the chalky paste as he continued with their lesson on how to make a salad 'traffic light' sandwich. Mark quickly shoved the tomato, lettuce and carrot on the bread and wolfed it down. His stomach thanked him even though it tasted like the inside of a plastic bag.

"H-Happy birthday, Mark," said Veronica, not looking him in the eye, her large glasses perched on the end of her nose.

His cheeks burned red, though he doubted she'd see that under all the flour. "Thanks. Could kill Beaver-face for telling everyone like that."

"Least they see you. I really do hope you have a marvellous day. Ehm, bye."

She marched back to her desk, head down.

The home time bell thundered. The school kids knocked over chairs and stormed out into the halls. Mark held back, speaking to the English teacher about some poetry competition and his thoughts on how to write a poem – no chance he was getting the bus home today. Pupils wrinkled their noses whenever they got near him. He'd walk home, air the embarrassment out.

From the window, he watched the kids swarm onto the buses while Mr. Lamont prattled on about the joys of Keats and Wallace, and how he might want to start with Heaney and move on to Dickinson, and he had a book somewhere for Mark to borrow, and did he ever consider the richness of a rose in spring, and—

"I'll catch you later, sir," said Mark. "Gonna miss my bus, so."

The promise of autumn rain lay in the air as he stepped through the empty corridor and out into the light. He'd survived a day at school on his birthday. An infinity of bruises would scream at him as he scrubbed off the gritty flour on his skin and in his hair.

He stared down at his new trainers. It was like he wanted them to notice, wanted them to ask how he'd gotten them. They were finished. Maybe that would be enough to draw his dad into a shouting match – it would be something at least.

"Think you're done, aye?" said Tommy, hands folded behind his back.

Mark's stomach almost crashed out of him. Tommy stood at the gate with three other boys who Mark once called close friends – Otto, Chucks and Kane.

"Leave me alone," said Mark. "I just want—"

"Happy birthday to you," they sang in unison, their harmony as grating as chirping lizards. "Happy birthday to you."

Tommy stepped toward him, taking his hands from behind his back. He held a cake with the word 'Dragon' in slimy green icing.

Mark felt the low wind drive at his eyes. He smiled as Tommy stepped, careful not to drop it on the gum-laced concrete.

"You didn't have to..." said Mark.

"You smell like a monkey," their voices rung with confidence now. "And you look like one, too."

He caught the sweet taste of icing as Tommy stood before him, his eyes wide under the shade of his baseball cap.

"Tommy, man," said Mark. "You didn't have to."

"Just a wee thing to say sorry for earlier, you know? We cool?"

"Course, man. Course."

"Wish," grunted Chucks from behind Tommy.

Mark closed his eyes, taking in a deep breath, feeling his chest rise then fall as he let it all out. What to wish for? His mum back? His dad back?

Tommy punched the cake into his face. He stood still, raspberry jam inside his nostrils, the velvety sponge drooping off his cheeks.

They roared with laughter, picking up pieces of fallen cake and shoving it down his back as he stood frozen to the spot, his hands still held out to receive it.

"Ha, ha," said Kane, prancing around him. "Ya birthday fanny."

Mark clawed cake and icing away from his eyes, watching the lads skip away. He licked at a piece of it, tasting its sugariness, a smile hidden under the mashed sponge.

ONCE UPON A FLAME

Everyone knew the story of old lady McCrory. She bundled up her man then set him alight, and chased her son into the night. And that's why the good folk of Pitlair made her life unbearable. Hurling abuse and rocks at the old lady was something of a community sport in this forgotten town on the east coast of Scotland.

I'd have been out of here faster than you could say chemical equilibrium if that was me. The story goes that she sacrificed children. She and her husband would lure them inside their bungalow that hunched at the end of the street like a dark, poisonous mushroom, burning the bairns as an offering to their sick gods.

It's impossible to tell how old McCrory was. She'd been an old hag when Grandaddy first told me of her, sitting me on his bony knee, the leathery scent of his cigar clinging to my long, dark hair as he breathed fire into the tale. Six-year-old me was spellbound as he told me in rich detail how they roasted the kids on a spit like a pig. How, if you listened carefully, on full moon nights, their screams could still be heard on the wind. How's that for my earliest memory?

Grandaddy's gone, rest his rotten soul, and McCrory chugs on, unchanged these last two decades since I started keeping tabs on her. It was hard not to, especially after moving into a flat right across the street from her. Talk rippled through the town for days after each appearance, but had anyone ever seen she was really a witch?

I'd asked Grandaddy that same question. I rubbed at my cheek. The red sting of his slap still echoed through the years.

The full, crisp moon called to me as I sat in my rocking chair by the window. A flutter of shadow caught my eye as I stared at McCrory's small home. From the depths of an unkempt hedge that lined her small patch of garden, two eyes stared back at me, reflected by the light of passing cars.

I should've used the autumn break to turn around my chemistry grades. Professor Brown's stern talk rung in my mind, saying he'd never seen a girl who enjoyed making cool clouds of exploding colour instead of focusing on the ins and outs of chemical reactions.

"Come on, ya old hag," I said, leaning forward. "Show me who you really are."

Grandaddy always said never to make a wish on a full moon night. I lived to learn the truth of that.

"HEY, McCrory! Roasting any bairns in there?"

The slurred voice of the man shouting in the street shocked me awake, almost tipping me out of my rocking chair. Blurred by the light spattering of rain on the window, two men stood outside McCrory's house, passing a large bottle between them. I slowly slid the window open, the scent of leaves and cold, wet concrete revitalising me.

"Bitch deserves a lesson," said Billy, his gruff voice forming a cloud of mist inside my stomach like dry ice.

"No need to get all huffy, man," said Gogs who was half man, half boulder, no neck. "She'll get what's coming to her one of these days."

"No," said Billy. "It's past time she boiled in her own skin for what she did to those poor wains."

I closed my eyes, remembering the last time I'd heard that cold hiss in Billy's voice. One night in Pitlair Tavern, he cornered me, his face growing redder, the vein tracking down his forehead popping as my rejections got shorter and nastier. He grabbed my forearm, fingers biting into my skin. I did the only thing I could – booted him in the nuts and ran out the door.

The autumn night swarmed around my neck as I leaned on the windowsill, glaring at the pair who taunted McCrory.

"Yo, Billy," said Gogs. "W-What you doing there? Aw, don't, man. It's just a cat. Leave the thing alone."

Billy knelt, holding his hands out to the side, cornering the black cat who stood its ground. Even from up here, I could see its white teeth and the ridge of frenzied hair running along its spine as it snapped and hissed at him. Billy shot forward, not grabbing it, but punching the cat in its side. The hollow thump its wee body made caused the blood to drain from my face.

The cat ran around in sick circles, something inside it broken. It leapt at the fence, digging its claws in, and hauled itself up. Billy booted one of its back legs, its tortured yelp breaking the silence of the night.

My guts danced around inside me. I couldn't watch, but I couldn't turn away, either. I bit my thumb, keeping the rising scream within me. Last thing I needed was these two idiots playing with me the way they did with that poor cat.

Billy's giggle floated up to me as if from a dream. "Hold the bastard still. Aye, just like that. This should get that old witch's attention."

I leaned out the window, almost tipping out. "Hey! Leave that cat alone or I'll phone the cops, ya pair of arseholes."

The cat danced in Gogs's arms, clawing his doughy face. He dropped it and it dragged itself down the path to McCrory's front door, disappearing from view.

Billy swivelled toward me, the moonlight hitting his shaved head, his menacing eyes smiling.

"Rowan, Rowan, Rowan," he said. "Where for art thou tits, my love?"

"Same place your manliness went – somewhere you'll never be able to find," I shouted before my mind could tell me it was a bad idea. "That how you get your kicks, by cornering a helpless wee animal?"

"You should know."

I glared down at him, my lower lip tensing. If I had the arm-strength, I'd have lobbed my chemistry books at his stupid, cruel face.

"C'mon, Romeo," said Gogs, tugging at Billy's elbow. "I can't get done by the fuzz again, you know that."

Although I was higher, Billy seemed to sneer down his nose at me. "You and that old witch chums now, that it? Always knew you were made of evil stuff."

"Well," I squawked, coughed, then tried a more threatening tone. "M-Maybe you should stay away from us. We'll, ehm, hex you right up, rot your teeth, and turn your blood into oil, and all that..."

"Don't like the sound of that," said Gogs. "She ain't serious, is she?"

Billy turned and skelped the side of Gogs's head then barged past him, walking down the sorry street. He turned, walked backwards, giving me the middle finger, his face full of burning promise. Great.

I thought about closing the window, shutting out the pained yowling. Before I knew it, the cold of the night scarfed its way around my neck as the shared door banged shut behind me with an air of finality about it.

I paused on my side of the street, my black boot tapping a small puddle as I gnawed at the plastic end of my hoodie's drawstring. Worse than the sound of pain-crazed shrieks was the thick, stony silence.

I marched across the road, shoving my hood over my head, flicking my hair behind my ears as I walked McCrory's cobbled path to her storied front door. I raised my hand to knock when the sound of cloth scraping on concrete stopped me.

McCrory lay on the path, huddled in a ball. She tugged at her fuzz of white hair with one bony hand while the other clutched at her leg. Her attempts to keep her suffering quiet were worse than if she'd screamed the whole street awake. She shifted her injured leg in a cycling motion as if both the pain of moving it and the pain of keeping still was too great.

The bitter scent of overgrown weeds and dying dandelions mingled with McCrory's dusty, flowery perfume as I hovered over her. I eyed the street at the end of her cobbled path, my lips pressed tight together.

"Let's get you inside," I said, leaning down to help her up.

"No need to trouble yourself, dearie," she said. "I—"

An agonised wheeze escaped her as I lifted her under the arms and dragged her towards her door. She held her pained leg aloft as I hauled her backwards, over the threshold and into warm darkness like we'd entered a cave.

I shuffled blindly backward, my arms beginning to quiver as my eyes adjusted. The huge living room was furnished like a dark cellar. Dusty books and bottles were stacked on every shelf and worktable. I blinked away a fit of dizziness and looked around the room that was somehow too large for the small house.

I plonked McCrory down on a worn chair opposite a huge fireplace. The house tasted of cat, rotten timber, and the unmistakable odour of spilled beer.

"You alright, Mrs. McCrory?" I said, hand on her shoulder. "I'll get you an ambulance."

McCrory straightened her injured leg, her lined face rippling with pain. "No need to fuss over an old bag like me. I've survived worse. And please, call me Janet."

"You sure? I think I'd better call someone, I..."

The soupiness of a weighty dream settled on my shoulders. I was here, in the witch's home where she'd apparently dragged all those kids to their smoky deaths.

"Wait, your name's Janet?" I said. "Janet?"

"Aye, what's wrong with that, like?" she asked. "Cheeky sod."

"Not exactly a witchy type name."

"There's a lot in a name, Rowan O'Conner."

"How?" I gulped, suddenly too hot, skin prickling up my sides. "You know my name?"

"I'm not daft, lass. Know exactly who's watching me. Only way an old bat like me can survive in this dump."

"They hobbled that cat. It dragged itself back to your door after Billy kicked it, injuring its leg – the same leg you're holding right now."

"Aye, lass."

"You were the cat, weren't you? You are a witch." A gleeful giggle escaped me, a sound I hadn't made since I was about eight.

"Do me a favour, will you? Grab me a beer. Through there. Watch your head. In the fridge is generally where it's kept. Pft, it's like you've never experienced beer before, good lord."

She held out a pale, shaking hand as I set a tankard of frothy beer in it, the red in my cheeks simmering down as I looked around. I could've fit a whole lab in there with space enough to swing a cat. Her chair was the only seat in the large room. I sat cross-legged by the fireplace and its dead charcoal smell.

McCrory took three long gulps of beer. "Ahh, that's the stuff. Bit slow on the uptake, aren't you? People round here been calling me a witch for decades now."

"I never thought it was actually possible, though."

"If enough people say a thing, usually means there's a nugget of truth to it." She took another long sip, the tension around her eyes easing. "Now, my dear. If you don't mind, I have a wee bit of recovering to do, it seems. Those boys really did a number on me."

Billy's fierce eyes roared into my mind. "Can't you, I don't know, cast a spell on them? Teach them a lesson?"

"They'll grow out of it. They usually do. I may be getting on a bit, but I can handle a kicking."

I stared up at the frail old lady who struggled to keep a pleasant smile plastered across her lined face. There was nothing threatening in her hearty, grey eyes. The rug I sat on cushioned me, bidding me to relax and stay a spell.

What stories she must have. And how long since she'd had the chance to share them? I couldn't just leave her here, surely? I needed to make sure she'd be alright, that she'd—

"Beat it," said Janet. "Aw, no need to look like I just stole your last biscuit. You're welcome to come back tomorrow, if you'd like."

THE NEXT DAY, I sat on the plush rug by a crackling hearth drinking the smoothest hot chocolate I'd ever tasted. I closed my eyes, the heat from the fire flushing my cheeks as I tried to ward away the shame of sneaking over here like a shady character buying drugs.

Janet lay back in her chair, her leg up on the footrest of the recliner. I wondered what Grandaddy would say about me being here.

He'd probably have yanked me up by the hair and given me a few teeth-shuddering slaps.

Janet's eyes opened, her slanty smile melting away the memories. She wouldn't hurt me, those grey eyes said. I liked to think myself a good judge of character, but wasn't I the one who'd once thought Billy a nice-looking chap worth talking to?

"So," I said, "do you chant at the moon? Cook up spells in a cauldron? Fly a broom?"

She took a drink of her beer, licking the white froth from her top lip. "There once was a time when I thought myself unstoppable. I could fly with the crows, water dance with the seals. The truth of it is, if you're gifted enough, you could do anything you imagined. Me? I chose to use my gift for nothing but evil."

My fingertips squealed against the mug, the skin beneath my nails turning white. "The stories are true then?"

"Ah, now to the real question."

The life seemed to seep out of Janet's eyes like the moon vanishing behind misty cloud. She swirled her battered tankard, the beer sloshing around before taking a long swig. The room felt like it turned to absolute zero as she squinted down, examining me.

"If you don't want to," I blurted, "it's—"

"Aw wheest, don't cause yourself an aneurysm."

The fire popped, sending a wave of warmth up one side of my face. I shifted my legs from under me, hugging my knees to my chest, feeling every bit the child waiting for a scolding.

"It's all true," said Janet, eyes staring into a dark, empty corner of the room beyond me. "I told myself it was all Robert's fault, but I can't go on giving my husband the blame for what we did. For what *I* did. I was so taken by him at the start, that I didn't see the darkness that ruined us. He made me believe we did it for the good of the town, that Scotland her very self was at stake."

She hacked up a cough, splotches of red growing up her neck. "Sorry lass, go top me up. I'm thirstier than a nun in a strip joint."

"Janet!" I said, taking the proffered mug, my face going scarlet.

I poured another cold beer into her tankard, its wooden edge rough on my skin. I wondered how many beers it had held in its lifetime as I set it back into Janet's waiting, shaky hands.

She downed half of it in one go. "Ah, that's the stuff. Get yourself one, lass."

"I'd rather keep myself grounded, thank you." I sat cross-legged by the fire again.

"Suit yourself. What was I saying? Oh, aye. Was about to divulge my darkest secrets to a stranger."

"Are we still strangers?"

"No. No, I guess not." She sighed, staring into the fire. "Not a night goes by when I don't hear those wee bairn's screaming. It was all for nothing. That's what stings me hardest. He always made me feel like it was my fault, saying the next sacrifice had to be bigger. I believed him. Stupid old hag. Please make no mistake about it – I was a monster led by a bigger monster, but that's no excuse for what I did."

She leaned back, the chair creaking under her as she stared out the window at the setting sun. "I deserve every curse, every stone thrown my way. I deserve that and more. And I'm sure I'll get it one of these days."

It was official – I sat in the company of a child killer. She must've carried them kicking and screaming into this room where I'd enjoyed hot cocoa. My phone felt like a stone in my pocket. Should I call the cops and tell them she fessed up? Something inside me told me to slink away, pack my things so I never had to be reminded of what she'd done.

I'd had my share of twisty men in my life who always knew how to make everything my fault, no matter how big or small, no matter where the logic lay. My mug scraped along the stone fireplace as I set it down, the orange of the fire dancing over it.

Janet ran a thumb below one eye, and then the other, then seemed to crumple into herself like a broken dam.

I shot up to my feet, throwing my arms around her, holding her head against my shoulder until her sobs eased. I held her face in the palm of my hand, wiping her wet cheek. When the tears stopped, she gave me a pained smile, and I sat back down.

"What did you do to him?" I said.

"You're a bright one, so you are. We had a son. His soul was as dark as his father's. Robert suggested we use him as a sacrifice." She traced a finger along the rim of her drink. "I roasted my husband just like those bairns. My rage scared my Evan so bad I never saw him again. Word spread, but no copper ever came to the door. I would've confessed everything back then. When they eventually showed up weeks later, I guess it was too late. I doubted they would believe Robert brainwashed me into it. So, I kept my gob shut. Denied everything."

"Men about here don't seem to have changed much," I said, absently stroking my throat.

"You mustn't let the rough times taint who you are destined to be."

A torrent of bad memories rose to the surface. Pinned shoulders. Meaty hands around my throat until blood pounded in my temples. Countless slaps, backhands, and razor-sharp words – all delivered by the men I'd been closest to.

Janet cleared her throat. "Call me an old fool, but it was more than curiosity that dragged you here."

I stared into the dancing fire, strange shapes appearing and dying into shadow as my eyes went dry.

"Is it weird that I never want to leave?"

AMBER HEADLIGHTS SWISHED along my bedroom ceiling as cars drove through puddles in the street outside. I tried to lift an arm. It was dead as if it'd been punched over and over until numb. I couldn't move anything else except my eyes. My breath came out in short, ragged gasps as I tried to lift my head from my damp pillow.

A shadow pounced onto my windowsill, its claws clacking on the wood as it ducked under the open window. Its green eyes drank me in as I lay unmoving, my eyes starting to ache from looking down the length of my body.

The mattress shifted as the cat pounced on my bed in a liquid movement. I tried to scream, but all that escaped me was a pathetic, toothless wail. The harsh pads of the cat's feet tracked up my stomach, over my chest, peering down into me, its green eyes laced with yellow swirls like distant galaxies.

The reek of fish mingled with a smell like a hundred rotting books as its jaws opened, showing me rows of sharp, capable teeth. The vibration of its rage rumbled down its paws, irritating my skin. I gazed up, helpless, wondering what it would feel like to get your face flayed off by a cat and if anyone had ever died that way.

The pressure on my windpipe increased as it leaned closer, almost cutting off my air. Its frenzied eyes widened, showing me a reflection of my own fright.

My muscles kicked in and I shot up, dragging in lungfuls of cold, luscious air. I tried to shake off the nightmare, but the angry cat noise roared inside my mind, piercing the centre of my skull. I couldn't shake it away.

I kicked off the covers and raced to the window. The cat's wailing burst from McCrory's place.

Through the twinkling of moonlight on broken glass, I saw the rise of flames from inside Janet's house. White smoke began to drift out the living room as Billy and Gogs laughed away, snapping photos with their phones like they'd just lit a bonfire.

"Janet..."

I jumped into my jeans and top from yesterday and raced down the stairs, across the street, blood pumping around my chest like the mixing of explosive chemicals.

"Hey!" I shouted as I stood outside the house, the growing flames licking my face with crackling heat. "Leave her alone."

Billy turned slowly, the orange light making shadows bounce about his face, flames dancing in his delighted eyes as he opened his mouth and ran his tongue over one of his incisors.

"She's got you wrapped in her web, hasn't she?" he said. "Bet she's teaching you how to snag wee kids as well. Can't have that in my town."

I stood my ground even though my stomach skittered around. He stopped in front of me, close enough for me to taste the sour Jack Daniels on his breath. He held out his hand, a single flame flickering at the end of his thumb – a lighter.

"This'll sort you out," he said.

A cold stone touched the base of my spine. "Wha—"

Billy whipped a can of deodorant from his pocket, closing one eye as he aimed. The deodorant hissed. I threw my hands up, a tongue of fire burning through the fabric of my top. Pain erupted up my forearms and I tumbled to the ground.

"What you playing at?" said Gogs.

He wrestled Billy away as I rolled on the path, the pain ascending until white lights strobed in my vision. I looked at McCrory's house, now engulfed in fire. I pictured her, relaxing in her chair. They must've lobbed a Molotov cocktail or something through the window, trapping her.

Billy struggled out of Gogs's grip, dropping the can, the burnt fragrance of tangy fruit and pine making me gag.

"I'll kill her," said Billy, stepping toward me again. "I'll—"

Gogs stepped behind Billy, swinging a fist, cracking the back of Billy's head. Billy dropped to the pavement, spittle flying, eyes vacant. His head thudded off the concrete, a sound that made me throw my hands over my mouth.

Gogs stood open-mouthed like a lost fish, staring back and forth between me, the fire, and the unmoving, splayed form of Billy.

I got to my feet, ignoring the swelling of burnt skin along my forearms. I ran to McCrory's front door, the metal handle nearly roasting my palm as I opened it. The heat that billowed out blazed on my hair like the hottest summer day.

"Janet!" I screamed, the heat and smoke attacking my throat.

I coughed, shielded my face, and entered. Smoke swam across the low ceiling as if alive, darting above me and through the now open door. Sweat poured down my face. I held a breath, said a quick prayer, and made my slow way to the living room, crouching low.

Janet was a human torch, flailing about, slapping at her legs. I blinked, the afterimages of her morphing into a cat and back into a human again, making me dizzy. Transforming made no difference – the flames raged upon her.

I ran past, avoiding her screaming eyes as I darted into the small kitchen. The tap almost scalded my skin off my fingers as I filled up a pot. I doused her with it twice before the thin air went to my head. I stumbled to the floor, wheezing, my lungs scraping in every particle of oxygen they could find.

Janet crawled over to me, reaching a blackened hand out. Her eyes blazed white panic, her skin bursting red all over.

I gathered every last piece of energy and rose to my feet. I grabbed Janet under the arms and shuffled backward toward the front door, molten sparks blazing into my skin. Each made me grit my teeth so hard they nearly snapped.

Close to door, Janet roared at me to stop. I set her down. She fumbled with something on the floor as I regained my strength, picking her up again, hauling her the last few steps, over the threshold and into the autumn air. Raindrops hit my skin, singing pleasure and agony.

I set Janet on the path, my fingers hovering over her, scared to touch her ruined skin. My own skin was charred in places. Clear juices seeped through my cardigan that was now attached to my skin. That was nothing compared to Janet. Her lips trembled of their own accord as if I'd pulled her from under a lake of ice. She was red and puffy all over, one eye melted closed, white ooze trickling out of it.

I looked around for Billy, swearing the next time I saw him I'd kill him.

"Janet," I said, my voice croaky. "Stay with me. You're not allowed to leave me, you hear? Why didn't you run away?"

"C-Called you. Too late. Seen," she coughed, little splutters of spit hitting her lip. Her breath came in uneven, laboured hitches. "Seen it burst. Burst in my window. Like a star. Deserved to burn. I deserved this."

I held her limp hand in mine, the rain soaking me through, chilling me to the bone. "Take it easy, alright. I-I'll get help."

With a trembling hand, I reached for my phone, cursing myself a fool for not calling for help the instant I saw the fire start from my bedroom window. Gawkers lined the street, some concerned, others with playful, hungry eyes. One old gentleman held a phone to his ear. I heard him tell the fire department to get here now 'before that old witch's house lights up the whole damned street'. I put my phone away.

"Burned up," said Janet staring up at the sky, rain glistening on her face. "Never thought I'd go out like my sisters."

I squeezed her hand, planting a kiss on her forehead. A tear trickled off my nose landing on her forehead. Her dying breaths were an agony of effort.

"You can't leave me, you understand?" My voice burst with an urgency and a love I didn't know I was capable of. "You can't."

A small, knowing smile curled her lip. "All that I am is in here." She placed a small volume in my hands, her wrists shaking with the effort. "It's your time now. Don't let it. Let it consume you."

She sighed, her eyes rolling in the back of her head. She looked relieved as she let escape her last breath in this world. I hugged her close, sobbing into her shoulder.

Lights from a rushing fire engine played over us as she went slack in my arms, growing as light as a bag of twigs. Out her mouth flowed a burst of colourful dust that circled me in gold and silver light.

"My time," I said, looking at the thin book, its edges curled and blackened.

A hexagon symbol in its centre glowed with warm light.

I RAPPED on the door until my knuckles hurt, the November chill settling around me like a mist, the hood of my jacket keeping my throbbing ears warm. I batted away a tear as I waited, a river of heat pulsing in the pit of my stomach as I recalled sitting alone at Janet's funeral. Father Brown had refused to say a word as it would taint the 'good book'. Well, I had my own book now.

Three crows screamed murder into the still day as Billy opened his door, his bloodshot eyes protesting against the light. He squinted, his eyes turning fiery, raising his voice to be heard over the caws and roars in the tree behind us.

"You?" he said, surprise turning to bright malice. "Should've known you'd show up. You here to grass me up to the police? I heard McCrory crisped up real good – like she deserved."

I removed my hood, trying my best to keep the ghost of a smile from my lips and failing. "What goes around, comes around, Billy-boy."

"What you—"

"You killed her. Wrote her right out of the game. Well, sort of."

"Sort of? Get away before I smack you in the mouth, bitch."

He shoved the door. I concentrated hard, stopping it from closing, my hands in my pockets.

Billy's eyes went from menacing to little boy frightened. "You're like her."

The air warped behind me as a crow landed on my shoulder. I stepped into the house.

"Oh, no, Billy," I said. "I'm much worse."

THE NIGHTMARE TREE

Haider squeezed his girlfriend's pale hand as he glared at the row of trees that lined Cuttie Hill park. Among the guardian-like oaks and sturdy birches, a misshapen tree clawed at the sky, its blackened bark glistening in the summer sun. His eyes went dry as he squinted at it from his spot atop a small hill. The tree's ashen skin seemed to pulse with life.

"Jeez." Caitlyn whipped her hand out of his grip. "Don't have to hold on so tight. Not gonna fly away."

Vitality thrummed out her blue eyes. His fingertips brushed little figures of eight on the back of her smooth, unblemished hand. She was forever ready for summer. Even in winter, she'd wear shorts and flowery clothes, refusing to let the cold ruin her sunny outlook. The scent of her orange-laced perfume lit him up inside. She was the only thing he had left. As the summer breeze danced through her sandy blonde hair, he knew he couldn't live without her.

"Sorry, gorgeous," said Haider. "I—"

Caitlyn grasped the top of his t-shirt and pulled him close, kissing him in that soft, yet urgent way she had that set his mind racing.

"Bairns down there," she said, pulling away. "Better not corrupt their wee minds."

"Aye, right. It's Pitlair. Wee minds are probably full of God knows what already."

The sun beamed on her porcelain skin as she gave him a half-lidded glance that made his heart jitter like an excited schoolkid.

"I'll corrupt you nice and good later, alright?" she said.

"Or now's good. Now works for me."

"Calm down, ya rocket. Plenty time for that." She shielded her eyes from the glare. "Don't see days like this often. Bairns actually being nice, no-one starting their shit. Makes you believe it can be a nice place if it tried."

Haider wasn't so sure about that. Pitlair, stuck in the forgotten crack of Fife on the east coast of Scotland, was an attraction for stowaways and a dumping ground for rehabilitating ex-prisoners. The people here were always on edge. Murder was the word on everyone's lips after a spike in the usual rate, which wasn't exactly low to begin with.

"What you staring at, babe?" said Caitlyn. "Something got you all bug-eyed."

"That tree always been there?" said Haider.

He couldn't take his eyes from it. It called to him to come trace his fingers along its unnatural skin. A high-pitched ring pierced his head. The tree's brittle branches leaned towards the sky.

"Must've been," said Caitlyn. "Looks like it's been burnt half to death though. Relax, chum. Not gonna get up and eat you."

Haider clutched at the grass, digging his fingers into it until they were green and moist.

Caitlyn flicked his hand with her index finger. "Come back to me, buck-o."

The spell broke. He pulled his attention away from the tree. Its secret song still rung in his ears, dissipating slowly like he'd just conked his head off something hard.

A pang of sadness flashed through him as he glanced at his girlfriend of three years. She'd been there when he needed it most. He bit down on his lip, burying the stupid question that always wanted to burst forth. The perfect ring waited in the store, but it would cost a few more months' pay.

Whenever he'd joke about marriage, her eyes got as skittish as a red-eyed sheep. In his dreams, she was mother to their three kids – two boys, one girl. He'd continue with his dad's painting and decorating business, earning enough so she could spend her days looking after their children. A big foolish grin would near enough break his face every time they came rushing up to him after work, and—

"What you thinking there, camper?" Caitlyn walked her fingers up his thigh. "About what I'd do to you if we had this hill to ourselves?"

"Move in with—"

She squealed a note of excitement and thumped her feet on the grass. "Can't keep it in any longer. Glasgow uni accepted me, babe. Ain't that pure aceness? Me. Going to uni. Dad will eat his shit hearing that. I might make him, the prick. I need to get out that house before something bad happens. Oh my God, the parties will be banging. First stop, Glasgow."

"Next stop, the world..." he finished.

This was it – his worst nightmare set into motion. He'd said all the right things as she worked on her photos for her portfolio, even posing in a few of them. Inside, he'd prayed she wouldn't make it.

At a job repainting the toilets at Fife college in Kirkcaldy last week, he read the lurid promises and interesting threats. They'd brought him in to cover up the graffiti – not the most exciting job, but he was in no position to turn away work. One line had stolen his breath:

All that you love will be taken away.

That scribbled message in black biro stewed in his mind. Ever since that day, he felt something cold and sure building inside – he knew she'd leave him.

"I'm so happy for you, gorgeous," he said, hugging his knees close to his chest.

"I'll get my own room at the digs through there. Hopefully meet some stellar new peeps. Full on uni experience here I come." She sighed, plucked a daisy and twirled it between her perfect fingers. "Can't wait to see the look on my dad's stupid face. Said I'd end up on jakey row. That I'd be begging him for money the rest of my days. Not me. I'm off to uni, ha. Eat that."

A little boy toddled up the hill, chuffing with effort as if he climbed

Ben Lomond. He turned, waved his arms at his dad who stood at the bottom like a goalie waiting on the world's most important penalty kick. The boy ran and leapt into his father's arms. The dad picked him up and spun him round, his little legs dangling loose and free. Sweet laughter chimed in the air.

"Proud of you, babe," said Haider.

"Positively brimming over with excitement."

"I am. It's just..."

"Come with me. I know it's mostly a pig's sty, but I'm sure they still get their houses decorated in Glasgow."

"You know I can't."

She exhaled a rough breath through her nose then chewed at the inside of her cheek. "Won't, you mean. You need out that house, Haider. If I can't drag you away from what happened, nothing can."

He pushed his knuckles against the centre of his forehead, trying to get the world to slow down. The dryness of his throat sang for a cold drink of cider to drown in. "You think I can just move away from them and magically forget?"

"Just try. For me? The things that happened in that house... I don't know how you can stand it."

"I'm not leaving them. I don't expect you to understand."

Caitlyn got to her feet, slapping loose grass off her knees. "What if I need you with me? You ever think about that? You know I want to be with you, ya big oaf, but I can't stand it here. I can't be held down to the same place as the rest of the world spins on. Don't you know how much I need this?" She started walking down the slope, past the gleeful family enjoying their infant summer. A scowl creased her eyebrows as she spoke over her shoulder. "I'd rather die than stay here."

He watched her stomp on down the hill, kicking at the grass. She cast a furtive glance at the strange tree before keeping her eyes on the ground.

He shook his head, staring down at the green grass. "All that you love will be taken away."

2.

. . .

LATE THAT NIGHT, Haider drowned his gut with ice-cold White Lightning, relishing the scratch of harsh cider bubbles at the back of his throat. As a family, they used to squash together on the couch and get sloshed, or chill and watch a film. The room swivelled about at the edges as he sprawled on the couch, staring up at the ceiling. He clutched the cold can of cider and tapped his fingernail against it. The hollow *ding* it made echoed through the empty house.

On the big chair across from him, a vision of his dad appeared, looking like he had at the end. Red veins burned purple on his nose. When he spoke, he did it with a pained wheeze like someone had belted him in the stomach.

"It's official, then? She's leaving us," said Ramsay McFarlane, as he clutched a phantom can of Guinness.

"Aye, Dad," said Haider. "Guess so."

"Well, you gonna do something about it, or just melt into that couch?"

Ramsay's jowls flubbered under his chin. His skin glistened with sweat just as it had when he'd clutched his chest and tipped out of his big chair. That was five months ago. The doctor said Ramsay was dead by the time he hit the floor – a broken heart will do that to you.

"You not got anything better to do than rib me?" Haider asked. "Afterlife not the rave you'd thought it'd be?"

"Everything I love is right here."

Haider took a long pull on the cider, glugging the rest of the can. He squeezed its centre, the metal crinkle hurting his ears.

Ramsay drank loudly of his Guinness, smacking his lips when he was done. The scent of the foamy, beefy beer stained the air between them.

"Get that tidy bird of yours in here," said his father. "Show that lassie what a McFarlane is made of."

"But she'll never..."

He was alone again.

Haider sighed and plonked his feet onto the coffee table in the middle of the room. The drunken feeling like he'd just stepped off a fast roundabout was no longer pleasurable.

Caitlyn hardly set foot in his house. His mother, father, and brother all dying in the space of six short months was too much for her. Freaked her out. So, he kept his imaginings to himself.

"Am I just making you up? Or are you really here, watching over me?" he said.

Seven months ago, they'd huddled on this couch, having a proper drink to celebrate how the family business was going. McFarlane & Sons were the only painters and decorators in Pitlair, and enough jobs came in to remove debt's boot from over their heads.

Now, the house, the company, the van, were all his. Some called him lucky to have his own company and no mortgage at the ripe age of twenty-three. Such idiots ended up with a sore face.

He struggled to his feet, walked down the dark hall, and into his parent's bedroom. That's where he found his mother.

She lay in the crisp centre of the double bed, covers tucked around her small frame like a mummy in a sarcophagus. Mist rose from the sheets like winter frost touching the morning sun. Cold seeped up to him as he looked upon his quivering mother. He'd earned her cobalt blue eyes but had more of his father's sturdy frame.

She'd been the first to go.

Routine operation, the doctor said. In and out in no time. Hardly even worth checking in on her. She'd be out as quick as a jiffy, ready to do, do, do the conga.

"Lying prick," he said.

A routine operation to remove a benign cyst from her arm left her with an infection that raged through her small frame. Her duvet shushed across the floor as she shivered under it, complaining about how cold it was.

If only he'd pushed instead of listening to the doctor's lazy advice. They'd waited. Waited to see what happened since 'these things normally sorted themselves out'. If he'd heeded his churning gut, he might still have a family.

"N-Not your f-fault," said Greta McFarlane, white pluming out her shaking jaw. "W-Win C-Caitlyn over. F-For me."

His dad had gone next. One month later. His heart caved under the stress of burying his wife of twenty-eight years. He'd been a mess without her, finding whatever solace there was to find at the bottom of a can of Guinness.

A week after they'd buried their dad, his brother Jace decided to hang himself. Quit. Just like that. Right when Haider needed him the most.

He glared at Jace's bedroom door. A boil of packed heat shifted in his stomach. "Why'd you have to quit on me like that, man?"

Caitlyn had helped carry Jace's casket, shouldered the weight. She'd jerked about, grimacing, but refused to drop it or ask for help. All through the misty misery that followed, she didn't push him with words. She held on to his hand, letting him know she'd always be there.

All that you love will be taken away.

Haider groaned and kicked the wall. His big toe screamed at him. He wished he could go with her – to see her living out her dream. But he couldn't leave his family here. He had a hard enough time leaving to go to work every morning. What if he left one day and they vanished?

He marched back to the living room and into the adjoining kitchen. The golden light of the fridge spewed over empty shelves. All that lay inside were stacked cans of cider.

Liquid sprayed over the back of his hand as he popped a can open. The metal sound it made following by the whoosh of gases made him lick his lips. He brought the can up to take a drink.

A black something fluttered past the living room window. Haider set the can on the counter and walked through, peering out into the night. Backlit by the orange fuzz of shaky streetlights, it blurred past again.

"What the," he said, his nose inches from the glass.

Bats sometimes flew overhead at night, but never this close to the street. And never on their own.

Something *slapped* the window.

A black leaf clung to the glass, its frayed ends trembling in the wind. It was the deepest shade of indigo, a colour that reminded him of slimy liquorice.

A dull ringing built inside his head as he set his moist palm against the glass. The leaf was just about the same size as his hand. A shock zapped up his wrist. He jerked away from the window, massaging his palm. A knot of red fire numbed the centre of his hand.

He squinted at the it. Dotted along the lower half of it were rows of black bumps like tiny, wet pebbles.

"Alien leaf..."

When they'd been wee boys, he and Jace spent their days crashing through the trees, getting into all kinds of bother. Jace loved nothing more than to freak him out by finding leaves dotted with red spots. Those diseased spots were a sure-fire sign that aliens had taken the tree over. If you touched them, the red dots would zap into your brain and turn you into a raging zombie. Haider would try to laugh this off, tell Jace he was being an arse, but he'd bolt as soon as Jace brought a leaf with those red dots anywhere near him.

A hollow spike churned in his gut at the memory of Jace's laughter and the scent of forest in those summers that he wished would last forever. They'd been tag team champions, and now he flew solo.

The leaf unpeeled itself from the window. It didn't fly off. It flipped and turned about, hovering like a mocking magpie, zooming off and coming back into view.

Before he knew it, his coat was around his shoulders. The leaf whisked into the night ahead of him, leading the way. He followed its path, keeping his gaze fixed on the pavement to avoid eye-contact with angry dog-walkers and gangs of kids who wouldn't think twice about pasting him and stealing his wallet.

He zipped up his coat, nibbling on the metal zip, tasting its coldness. The world strobed around him in a drunken haze. Caitlyn's deflated eyes came back to him. He could be her rock if she let him. If only he could make her stay.

The leaf spun ahead, leading him to Cuttie Hill park and the tree.

3.

. . .

The brittle branches of the strange tree kissed the stars. That's what it looked like to Haider who craned his neck, tracing his eyes over its broken, zig-zag limbs as it clawed at the night sky. The stars had never seemed so far away.

The leaf had spiralled to a stop and lay limp at the foot of the tree beside one of its thick roots. Those roots tumbled and slithered over each other like eels packed in a shallow river.

Cuttie Hill park lay in silence. Blood throbbed hot in his ears as he craned his neck too far. He fell onto the packed dirt.

"Why did I follow you here?" he heard himself say.

The smell of dry dirt hit his nose as he stood, beating his palms against his jeans.

Wisps of steam ghosted from groves in the tree's trunk. Slashed into its bark were the words:

All that you love will be taken away.

A chill swept down from the top of his head, making the skin at his temples prickle. His mouth bobbed uselessly up and down. The tree's skin creaked as its branches twisted of their own accord. He clutched at his hair as sand-like blackness swallowed the words. Flashes of pain exploded behind his eyelids as he pressed his knuckles against his eyes.

"You can't be here," said Haider as his vision strobed back to normal.

Black syrup oozed down the tree like molten metal. The smell of battery acid and ozone made him hold his hand over his nose.

He stepped towards its pulsating surface. His hand hovered inches from the bark. Heat radiated out from it as if it were some slumbering beast and not a deadened tree. Something coiled inside his stomach, clawing its way up his throat.

Dotted along the black surface of the bark, hundreds, thousands of dark bumps swarmed as one.

The words came from someplace deep inside, some automatic, dormant place.

"She can't leave."

He closed his eyes and reached for the tree. When he placed his palm on the moist, tepid bark, dots swallowed his hand, turning it charcoal black.

In his mind, he shot through vast space, trailing past comets and burning purple suns. Peace trembled within him as he burst through to empty space, nothing but dancing stars in the distance. The power breathed within him, waiting to be freed.

"She can't leave."

4.

HE SLATHERED paint over a kid's wall. The duck egg blue colour made his empty stomach flip. It had to be the world's crappiest colour. The sun beat through the curtainless window, bouncing off the fresh paint, making his eyes stream.

The hangover had plagued him all morning. He woke with a crashing sore head and couldn't eat a drop for breakfast. The hazy image of him walking out into the night and talking to that damned tree played over and over in his mind as he sank into the meditative rhythm of brush strokes.

The creamy fumes of the paint were the only thing keeping him going. People complained about the stink it left, scared it would make them high or something, but he loved sniffing it, inhaling it in great lungfuls. He was mid-sniff when his phone rattled about in his overalls.

"You alright, babe?" he asked.

"No, I am not fucking alright," said Caitlyn.

"Woah, what happened?"

Her long breath burst down the phone's speaker. "Least you'll be happy about it. The bastards. Can't believe they'd just whip it all away from me like that. Was about to start packing up my shit. They..."

The sound of her fighting back tears tore at him. "What did they do to you? I'll—"

"They took it all away, Haider. Rescinded. That's a fancy college word I didn't even know until today. Guess I'll be trapped here in this bastarding place forever. I can't do it, Haider. I can't—"

"You're staying?" He covered his mouth, hiding the tug of a smile that tickled his face.

"I was a clerical error, apparently. Gonna write the biggest complaint those booky bastards ever seen." She streamed out a cold, empty giggle. "That's not the worst of it. They said..."

"What?"

"They said my standard wasn't nearly good enough. Had the cheek to call my work pedestrian. That anyone could churn out those standard images. I don't have an artful soul. That fucking hurt."

"That means you're not going, then?"

"You prick. Breaking my heart here and you're all chipper cause I'm trapped in this house, listening to my folks half murder each other every night. I need gone."

He said he'd finish up his job and meet her at her house later. She'd be spiralling, clawing at the walls.

His skin shone pink as he scrubbed at the dots of duck egg blue. He fussed with the collar of his nicest polo shirt, ignoring his dad's jibes about him getting awfully 'poofed up'.

A photo that he'd framed on the dusty mantelpiece held his attention. The way Caitlyn had been able to capture him as he looked down on an empty beach sang to him. He knew positively zero about art, but the picture pulsed with some sort of life. He took a long drink of his cider, not taking his eye from the black and white image.

Caitlyn's straining voice echoed in his mind as he ran a thumb over the photo frame she'd bought him for his Christmas. She'd given everything to her photography.

She can't leave.

The can slid from his grip. Cold cider splashed over his toes and sizzled into the carpet.

"It was me."

He marched through to the kitchen, cracked open another cider and inhaled half of it.

It couldn't be true. He prayed his night visit to the tree was nothing but a dream. The wish. It had come true. But how was it possible? There was no way Caitlyn got refused based on her work. She was talented enough to snap her pictures all over the world.

"What the fuck is going on?" said Haider.

"Language," said Ramsay, appearing in his big chair.

Haider floated over to the couch and threw himself down on it. "It was me. I went to the tree. I made the wish. Now she's stuck here."

"That's my boy. Cheers." Ramsay lifted his black can of Guinness then took a long swig.

"You think this is what I wanted?"

"Course it was."

"But, I..."

Ramsay's image vanished, leaving him alone. He groaned a long, frustrated note into his hands. He'd find a way. Get her back into uni. Help her get away, even if it meant losing her.

The driving wind whistled at the window frame. He got up and leaned against the windowsill. The grey afternoon blurred past in a gale of crisp packets and crinkled cans of juice that tumbled on down the street. The glass was cool on his forehead as he rested his head against it.

A black shape slapped the window, making him jump back.

A cold stone pulsed in his bowels. The leaf had returned. It spun in front of his house, refusing to follow the detritus swept by the gale-force wind.

All that you love will be taken away.

The words echoed in his mind as if whispered by some Godly being.

"Nope," he said, stepping back. "Not happening. Nopey, nope."

"Don't beat yourself up, son," his dad said, reappearing in his big chair. "You did what you had to."

"S-She's family," his mum stuttered from the doorway. An aura of white mist dusted off her shoulders as she clutched her duvet around her. Her eyes widened as she trembled. He followed her stare.

The leaf see-sawed toward the window. He recalled the alien dots and its indigo veins as it had plastered itself against the glass before he followed it out into the night.

It floated closer, reaching out to him.

"What the — argh!"

The leaf phased through the window, darting at Haider like a malicious wasp. He danced to the side, out of its path, then shot his hand out to catch it between his thumb and forefinger.

"Smooth moves, son," said his dad.

The leaf buzzed, sending a jolt up his forearm. He traced his finger along its blackened edge. Sucking in a pained breath, he dropped it. It lay on the floor, lifeless.

A line of hot blood trickled down his finger.

5.

HAIDER PUSHED Jace's bedroom door open. The stale air seemed to rush at him like some air-tight chamber had just been opened. A bar of sunlight streaked up the wall, illuminating a glossy Mötley Crüe poster.

The door to a walk-in closet lay open. Inside, Jace hung from his rope, his body rotating slowly. His bloodshot eyes mocked Haider as he stepped further into the room.

Jace had left him with no goodbye, no clue, nothing. The shock of finding him, of clawing at the rope always came roaring back to him whenever he entered his brother's empty room.

Jace's voice strangled its way out of his snapped windpipe. "Bro..."

Of all the death that had touched the house, this is the place Haider avoided the most. He ignored his brother and marched to the ruffled bed, getting down on his hands and knees and sticking his arm under it.

The room still held the stain of Jace's cheap, woody aftershave that he'd sprayed so much that it made Haider gag in his presence.

The cold of the metal frame sent a fright up his arm as he reached under the bed. He found the felt covered box and brought it out, the poker chips clinking inside.

"All in," said Jace.

The leaf crackled in his hand as he carefully took it out of his pocket, avoiding its razor-sharp edges. He winced as his finger touched the black bumps at the base of the leaf.

"Zombie."

"You shut your face, you quitter bastard." Haider shot up, pointing a shaky finger up at Jace. "Makes you think you can talk to me, eh? You've no right."

His fingertips were slick with moisture. It looked like he'd spent the morning thumbing through a newspaper. Charcoal black covered his fingertips. He'd crushed the leaf in his grip as he'd raged up at Jace. The leaf unfurled in his palm, returning to its previous shape.

"Caitlyn," said Jace.

"You don't talk about her."

"Tree."

Haider glared up at Jace, at the angry purple colour that mapped from his crooked neck. Jace's feet dangled less than an inch from the carpet. Had he not been such a short arse, he'd still be here, still helping Haider to deal with the loss of their parents.

Blazing sunshine spat its way through the window. Haider closed his eyes, remembering the way the leaves tickled his calves as he and Jace blasted through the forest, getting up to all sorts of boyish mayhem.

When he opened his eyes, the swaying corpse was gone.

Poker chips clattered on the bed as he emptied it and placed the leaf inside.

He'd tried to get rid of it. When he threw it out the window, it curled back round, and phased through the glass. When he tried to set it on fire, the flame wouldn't take. He buried it, ripped it up, flushed it down the toilet, but it always returned. It was the same leaf each time. He'd come to know its contours, its black veins that shot from its spine.

He slammed the box closed and threw it under Jace's bed and skittered out of the room, feeling as if a hundred eyes crawled over his back.

He picked up his coat and left for Caitlyn's house. She lived at the bottom of a graffitied street where dogs roamed like stray cats with no owners in sight. As he turned into the path that led to Caitlyn's door, he caught the stench of weed and piss that made his nose crinkle.

Caitlyn's parents could be heard through the walls, screaming and roaring at each other, pushing one another's buttons until it came to blows. His lip curled as he approached the dented door. She didn't like to talk about it, but he knew she'd been on the other end of both her mum and dad's angry fists more than once.

He didn't knock. The door swung open on a dark hallway. The noise of an argument bounced off the close walls. Something about money – always about money.

Caitlyn's room was the first on the left. He tapped at the door and entered. The walls were covered with photographs – a lifetime of pointing her camera.

She lay on the bed, furiously rubbing at her eyes before turning to face him. "Took your time."

"Sorry, gorgeous. Look, you wanna get out of here? Folks blaring and all."

"Just cause your parents were happy. Think you can judge everyone else."

"That's not what I'm saying." Haider sat on the end of the single bed, the smell of lavender creeping out at him.

"I'm just waiting on one of them offing the other, so I can be rid of them both. Fuckers."

"You don't mean that."

Caitlyn folded her head between her arms, breathing into the duvet. Her voice was muffled. "Take me away."

"Come live with me."

She whipped herself up, glaring at him. "You'd love that, wouldn't you? Cook me up inside that dead house of yours, get me all preggers and turn into golden oldies before you can say holy-fuck-what-happened-to-my-life."

Haider leaned back, holding his palms up. "Take it easy, babe. I'm on your side here, alright?"

"Sure about that?"

He opened his mouth and slammed it shut, biting back the retort that wanted to escape.

Mr. and Mrs. Doran continued to knock verbal lumps out of each other. Haider felt the pressing urge to go have words with Caitlyn's dad, but that usually meant more heat for Caitlyn once he was away, so he learned to ignore it, banish his urge to step in.

"Did you get any further with the uni?" he said.

Caitlyn flopped back onto the bed. Haider eyed her flat stomach, remembering all the times he'd kissed her there, the taste of her soft skin.

"Nope," said Caitlyn. "Vultures meant what they said. They even threatened to have me blackballed so I'll never get accepted anywhere. Pricks."

"Maybe it's a good thing. What's for you, will not go by you, and—"

"What are you, eighty-four? If you think I'm staying here, you're three syringes short of a shooting gallery."

"Caitlyn, I only—"

"Don't dare try to talk me down." Her blue eyes caught fire as she sat up again, pointing a finger at him. "I can't stay here. I won't."

"It doesn't have to mean that. Just come live with me, alright? Get away from these muppets before something serious happens. I worry about you, you know? Think about it this way. You could save money, figure out your plan and take the next step." He gulped away the spike in his throat. "And I won't stop you. No matter what you want to do."

She stared down at her covers, tracing a finger along the lines of an orange flower. "Haider, I worry about you, too. Living in that house where all that stuff happened. I don't know how you handle it. Would it be so bad if we both moved away? Away from that death house? Leave with me, Haider." She fixed him with those piercing blues. "Please?"

"I won't leave them."

"See? You'll not be budged, and I need the fuck out. Where's that leave us, eh? Didn't you ever wanna be an astronaut? A race car driver? Singer in a rock 'n' roll band touring the world? You ever have a dream?"

"No."

"That's the saddest thing I ever heard."

Jace had done enough dreaming for the pair of them, bragging about all the escapades he'd get up to once his band kicked the big time. Haider never had any wishes to move away, to see the world. He was happy here, with his family.

"Why do we have to decide everything about our lives right this very minute?" said Haider. "Move in with me. You can sort yourself out, and—"

"Sort myself out?" She blew out a cold laugh. "Nice. Because your life's all planned out, eh? Paint houses, find a wifey, get her pregnant, have some sprogs, grow old and live ever so yucky happy."

"What's wrong with that? Isn't that what everyone wants?"

"Not me, I... Just leave, alright? I need time to think. About everything."

He laid his hand over hers, shocked by how cold it felt. "I love you, gorgeous. You know that, right? Take all the time you need. I'll always be here."

"Sure," she said. "Not like I'm going anywhere."

6.

"It was supposed to be me that kicked the bucket first." The big chair protested as his father massaged his chest. His face was the colour of beetroot and he slurred his speech. "Said I'd save her a space up there when I finally keeled over. Wasn't supposed to happen this early. Supposed to be carting about in wheelchairs with a bunch of grandkiddies to embarrass. God, I loved that woman. I don't know how to be without her."

The room wobbled in Haider's drink-infused haze. He rubbed his hands together to ward off the February cold. Without his mother, the family were rudderless, stranded on some distant, unknown shore. Jace hardly left his room, while he and his dad drank their pain away into the wee hours.

"I keep thinking she'll just swan in here and join us," said Haider, the sting of tears hot in his eyes. "Dad? You ain't looking so hot."

The night howled outside. Haider blinked, the feeling of a soupy dream settling around his shoulders. Flocks of black leaves flew past the window. Suddenly, he knew where and when he was, and what was about to happen next.

"Dad? Listen to me. You need to lay off the sauce. Got me? We need to stop this before it's too late. Before you—"

"Can't stand it anymore," said Ramsay. "The world is just so... nothing without her, you know?"

"Dad?"

"Nothing without her."

"Let's call it a night. I know it's shitty, but we need to get back to normal. We can't lose you, too."

"Jace needs you. You should go see him."

Haider glared at the open door. "Well, he decided not to join us."

"Aye, it's—" Ramsay pounded his chest, the thud reverberating through the room.

The wind died. The stillness rung in Haider's ears. Yellow streetlight shone off the rows of suspended black leaves that hung in the air, watching.

"Dad?"

His dad clawed at his face as his eyes rolled in the back of his head. The can of Guinness dropped out of his hand, spilling a black puddle into the carpet.

"No," said Haider, fighting to get to his feet. The couch had turned soft as molten toffee, refusing to let him go. "Not again."

Ramsay spluttered, pounded his chest one final time, then fell sideways. He landed in a heap next to the glugging can that continued to empty itself onto the floor.

Haider clawed his way off the couch. He knelt beside his father, holding his head, trying to sit him up. Black tar erupted from his father's mouth. The substance smothered Haider's chest, almost burning his skin through his sodden t-shirt.

Haider looked down at the tar that stank like raw beef. Within the dense, shiny liquid, black leaves unfurled like small, opening hands.

"Not again."

His father's blood-tense body had vanished. The back of his hand came away black as he wiped his running nose trying to breathe through the tears.

He stood as if drawn by string, pulled toward the dark hall by the instruction of his nightmare. Outside his parent's bedroom he heard a familiar, weak sobbing.

"C-Cold," his mum said. "So c-cold."

White smoke billowed from the gap at the bottom of the door. It stung his eyes, tasting like the summery coconut perfume she'd worn every day.

In the wake of her death, when Haider needed her the most, he would sneak into the bedroom and spray that perfume, inhaling the memories the smell brought.

The mist was gone.

The dream led him on. On towards Jace's room. His stomach turned yellow and clammy as he approached.

Tree roots burst through floorboards, buckling the doorframe in deafening splinters. The gnarled limbs looked like pythons coiling, waiting.

The taste of brown forest hit his tongue as he stepped through the ruined doorway, stepping into the dark room.

"Jace?" said Haider.

Jace hung once more, his eyes sparked wide with hurt. He didn't swing inside the closet. The noose was tied around the thick branch of a blackened tree – the tree from the park.

He knew it from its writhing body, its buzzing lifeforce that seemed to roll up his calves as he neared it.

"Jace?"

Jace's mouth bobbed up and down, a line of black blood spilling out as he tried to speak through his warped windpipe. "All that you love..."

Haider strode forward, grabbing his brother's dangling legs. He hugged them tight, then pushed up with all he had, trying to take the weight of Jace's purpled neck.

"Taken away," said Jace.

Branches snapped and popped above him, falling to the floor. The tree shifted about, collapsing in on itself. A hole appeared in its dead centre. Haider gazed into it, feeling the weight of an empty universe calling back at him.

White pain burned along his brain, causing his limbs to give in. He crumpled to the floor, staring up at the creaking tree as it folded, being taken in by the black hole.

Thin twigs like spider's legs walked over his brother's face. Soon all Haider could see was the whites of Jace's wide eyes as the tree swallowed him, wrapping him up in its web.

Haider tried to get to his feet, but his body refused to listen. "No!"

The tree shrivelled in on itself, taking his brother.

Haider moaned and twisted in his bed. He fell, cracking his nose off the floor. Blood swam down his throat and trickled down his lip as he sat up, gasping. His t-shirt was soaked with sweat.

He punched his bed and roared his anguish at the ceiling. His scream echoed through his dark, empty home.

7.

NO MATTER how many coats of emulsion he used, the house still reeked, causing harsh apple bile to rise up the back of his throat. Underneath the cat-piss stench crawled an odour like green, oily sewage.

The day dragged as he sweated out the remains of cider and last night's dream. His family hadn't appeared since he screamed himself awake.

He took out his phone, knowing he was hounding Caitlyn. Spirally panic gripped his thumbs as he typed out a hasty message that he instantly regretted as soon as he hit send.

I need you with me. Don't you get that? If you don't then you can just go ahead and leave. I won't stop you. x

His lips curled over his gums as he read the message over.

"Dummy," he hissed.

He typed out a message crawling back on himself, saying he didn't mean it, then deleted the text.

The dead ammonia smell buzzed around the bedroom, clawing at his nose like ravenous midges. The reek seemed to puff out of the carpet wherever he stepped. He hoped it wouldn't seep into his cover sheets.

He grabbed his roller, dipped it in the tray of white emulsion, then smushed it up the wall.

Should he tell Caitlyn? Admit that her dream got cancelled because he'd stood before a tree and made a wish? He knew that would be the end of their relationship. And she'd probably stave his skull in.

"Probably deserve it," he said as he rolled, little flecks of white raining on his forearms.

As he stepped to the side, he tripped, nearly crashing headfirst into a mirrored wardrobe. The roller made a moist *splat* on the grey carpet, inches from the cover he'd laid down to protect the floor.

He got down on his knees, scooped up the roller, then scrubbed at the carpet.

"Shit."

That white stain would probably cost him his entire fee and more.

He felt around for whatever had tripped him. A mound stuck out like a hockey puck. Against the wall, the carpet lay uneven, frayed at the ends.

The owner, Liddy, had left him to it, barely glancing at him as she escaped into the muggy sunshine.

On other jobs, he'd had some right good laughs when snooping around. One time, Jace uncovered a box hidden under an elderly gentleman's bed. DVDs with titles such as *The Fat and the Furious 3* and *Uncle Boner's Back Door Trip 9* had them in hysterics.

"Why'd you have to quit on me, bro?" said Haider.

He reached over and tugged at the frayed carpet. It came away in a neatly cut section, uncovering a small hatch. The thing that had stuck out was a handle that looked like a doorknocker, covered in faux gold.

During his years painting in other people's homes, he'd seen his share of dodgy things. Drug stashes, sex swings, he'd even spotted a dead rabbit decaying behind a telly.

He flexed his hand, hesitating over the handle, listening just in case the owner came home.

As he opened the small hatch, a waft of sick air exploded up his nose, making him wretch and gag. The cool of the dark space chilled over his face as he leaned down again, peering in.

The girl had been dead for some time.

Ribbons of her skin had come away from her face as if chewed. The bone of her teeth shone through her cheek. She sat against the wall, arms clutched around her small legs as if he'd rocked herself to sleep. It was her hair that made the tears bite his eyes. Ginger and full of fire like it yearned for the summer sun.

Fifteen minutes later, his head spun as PC Johnson stormed into the house. The detective riddled him with questions, making him feel as if he'd been the one to stuff the little girl down in the dark.

He'd helped himself to the blackest of coffees. The cop continued to pummel his ears with questions under a broom of a moustache that covered his top lip.

The owner swanned into the house, chucked her keys on the table next to Haider's coffee mug with the words *World's Best Mum* writ in red letters. She sighed and sat next to him before she noticed the detective.

When PC Johnson told her of Haider's discovery, breaking the news in the slowest and gentlest way, Liddy only shrugged, admitting that's where she kept the 'wee shite.'

That was the worst of it – seeing a little girl's life reduced to a shrug.

Haider almost threw up again when he had to step back into the bedroom to collect his painting gear.

A police photographer snapped photos, the flash of the camera making strobes of purple appear whenever he blinked.

The man crouched at the edge of the 'murder hole', his chin creasing as if he was about to break down in tears. Haider guessed the man had a daughter of his own.

He nodded at the man as he set about folding his cover sheet. How could someone be driven to such a vile act? There was a special place in hell for those who harmed bairns he decided as he clipped the lid on the large tub of emulsion.

A bar of sun lanced through the window, beaming its radiance over the unmade bed. The sunlight ended just before the pillow. He walked over. Something poked out from under it.

A black leaf.

It was silky to the touch, just like the one he kept under Jace's bed. He spun it by its stalk. This one was thinner, its veins and cracks somehow angrier than his.

He placed it back under the pillow, then marched out of the house.

8.

THE NEWS of the girl left to wither in the dark blew through the town like a gale. His phone had *dinged* non-stop since he'd made it home after giving his full statement at the police station. In Jace's silent room, he stared at his bright screen, praying one of the thirty-odd messages was Caitlyn. It was just more gossipmongers looking to feed, looking to find out the gruesome details of how wee Katrina had perished all alone as her mother slept above her. The phone made an unsatisfying *thud* as he threw it against the wall.

He dropped flat on his stomach, then reached under the bed. Dust motes played around his face as he drew out the small box. He placed it on the bed and opened it. Weak daylight shone on the leaf's midnight surface as he gripped the stem between his thumb and forefinger. A chemical cold seeped down his arm, tracking its icy fingers to his elbow as he spun the leaf slowly.

What did it all mean?

Liddy Morse was heading to Broadshade at her majesty's leisure. A shiver tapped its fingers up his spine at the thought of the imposing prison and its red walls. Liddy's shoulders slumped like a weight had evaporated off her shoulders when they snapped the cuffs on her. She'd started spilling the heart-splitting details before Haider got the chance to leave the room.

What did she wish for? To not be a parent anymore?

The crawling of eyes made his skin edgy. He set the leaf back in the case and clapped it shut.

"What did I do, bro?" said Haider.

"Happy," said Jace. His voice struggled out his mangled windpipe.

Jace leaned against the doorway, arms folded as if posing for an album cover. Daylight glimmered off his black leather jacket. With his long hair and their mother's scrawny build, he looked like the frantic drummer of a hair metal band. The red and purple bruises that shone on his neck only added to that image.

"You think this makes me happy?" said Haider.

"Aye."

"Screw you."

"Champs."

Haider gnawed his lower lip, his temples packed with fierce heat. They'd made a good team, looking out for each other at high school. Jace loved to brag how they were the tag team champions of the world. Haider had felt invincible then.

"We're not champs anymore."

Jace kicked back from the wall and stood in his way as he stomped toward the door. His skin crackled as he phased through the image of his brother.

Panic flitted around his chest as he thought of how he'd stood before that blackened tree, making his wish. He imagined Liddy standing there, staring up at its alien bark, touching its writhing, humming surface.

He opened the fridge, his hand hovering over a tin of cider when his phone chirped against his thigh. Caitlyn.

Hotshot. Stop with all the naggin, he he. Im comin over. We'll talk and whatever ;-) xxx

She chapped the door hours later. The last of the day's sun lit up freckles that fluttered across the bridge of her nose. Red roses burned on her cheeks.

"Gonna let me in or..."

"You pissed?" he asked, moving to let her past.

"Allowed a drink in the circumstances, I think."

He couldn't help but laugh as she slalomed to the living room, the denim of her jeans scraping off the wall a few times in the process. The heaven of her orange perfume mingled with the sour tang of vodka.

She shook her head as he set down two ciders on the table. "Bound to have something stronger than that cissy juice. I know your dad must've kept some voddy about here somewhere."

Haider gazed at the big chair, exchanging a look with his father who shrugged. A pleased smile sparked up his ruddy face.

He fished out a bottle of vodka from the depths of a kitchen cupboard. The gargle of fizz filled the room as he poured them both a vodka and coke.

"You gonna tell me about that wee lassie, then?" said Caitlyn. "Sounds fucking awful. What a piece of work the mum must've been. You alright?"

Haider took a long drink, then ran his tongue along his teeth. In the big chair, his dad took a large chug of his Guinness, a sly look on his face, before tipping him a wink.

Caitlyn smacked her lips together after taking a drink. She lay back on the couch, shuffling herself comfortable. "If you don't wanna tell me, I'll understand. I—"

"It's fine, honest. It was terrible, you know? Poor wee lassie. Trapped like an unwanted guinea pig down there." Ice clanked against his teeth as he finished his drink. He set the glass on the table. "I can't stop thinking about how the mum wanted rid of her bairn, and how there are less... costly ways of doing that. Could've gave her up, you know? Shopped her to an orphanage. Would've sucked ass, but least she'd still be alive. She was just a wee ginger angel, laying there all huddled up. Sun will never touch her again. Babe?"

Caitlyn snorted a gentle snore as her head fell to the side.

"Babe?"

He moved a strand of hair from her face, tucking it behind an elf-like ear.

"N-Needs you." Greta stood by the window in her duvet shroud.

"Aye, son," said Ramsay, big chair creaking under him. "And you need her. What's the problem with making her stay?"

"She doesn't want to," said Haider. "She doesn't want me."

"Come off it now, eh. She's here, ain't she? I mean, you put her to sleep with all your yapping, but—"

"A wee lassie died, Dad."

"N-Not your f-fault," said his mother.

"The tree, though. It's all connected, somehow. What if I end up doing something just as awful?"

They both vanished. He clenched his fists and slumped back onto the couch, glaring at the ceiling. "Why you always gotta do that?"

"There are other skies than these," Caitlyn mumbled. Drool shone in the corner of her mouth.

The clink of the vodka bottle as he poured himself another drink woke her. She sprung awake, cocking her fist, ready to deck him one before she came back to herself.

"Woah, Cujo. Calm down," said Haider, holding his palms up in mocking placation.

"You like sneaking into girl's houses, aye?" she said, flopping back down. She lay a hand on her forehead.

"What? We're in my house, donut."

"Bet you get up to all sorts when you're visiting those bored housewives, eh? You've been in half the houses in Pitlair."

"Only to paint their walls."

She spumed out a raspy laugh.

"What's so funny?"

He poured her another drink as she slapped her thighs, eeking out every last note of musical laughter. He downed half his drink. The vodka clawed its warm way up the back of his neck.

"You said you wanted to talk," said Haider.

"Just kiss me, ya clueless arsehole."

She yanked the top of his t-shirt, pulling him close. They butted teeth, giggling, kissing again. She was all rough talk and games, but when it came to this, she was as soft and as gentle as anyone he'd ever been with. They kissed slow. Soon, he tasted the perfume on her neck as she pulled him on top of her. Everything was forgotten as they moved with each other for a dizzying, heart-pounding spell.

When he landed back on earth, he poured a drink and downed it in one, then poured himself another. He put his t-shirt back on as his heart hummed happily in his chest.

"I guess we should talk now," she said, fixing her bra.

"We'll figure it out, gorgeous."

"I need out. I don't have many options. But that won't stop me."

He pointed at the mantelpiece – at the framed photo she'd taken of him at the beach. "Why does it matter where you are when you can take awesome photos like that? I heard wedding photographers make a—"

"Weddings? Weddings?" She pressed her fingers on her cheeks. Glistening red shone when the taut skin tugged at her lower eyelids. "You want me to round up wedding guests for group shots and all that pish? Don't talk to me about weddings. Have me doing graduation photos next."

"You don't have to do it forever. Just build it up and save like crazy. Maybe your dream needs some elbow grease, you know? Nothing worth having comes easy, and all that."

"You sound like an old hag." She groaned as she sat up, taking a long pull directly from the bottle of vodka. "Had it all planned out."

"So did I."

"Doesn't sound like our plans match up."

He looked away, chewing on the inside of his cheek. The sticky taste of cola syrup fuzzed over his teeth. "Why don't you move in with me?"

"You daft as well as deaf?"

"Think about it. Spend the next year or two here. Work on your portfolio, or whatever. Get away from your dick parents. You could live with me scot-free."

"And be your lawful little house-bunny? The world's waiting on me, Haider. You don't know what it's like to hear it calling your name."

"It's a long game, babe," he said, setting a hand on her shoulder. Her skin was cool to the touch. "Stay with me. Please? I'll cook you breakfast in bed, like, all the time. I'll make all your wishes come true."

"God, that's pure cheese."

She flicked her blue eyes up, piercing through him. A cold note beat within his chest. How to show her she meant everything to him? How to make her see she could be happy here?

She slumped into his chest, forcing him to lay on the couch. The alcohol pulsed within his ears as he dozed, feeling the rhythm of her breath on his skin. His heart beat against her ear as he ran a finger through her silky hair. A tear warmed its slow way down his cheek.

9.

"MR. MCFARLANE?" said the scratchy voice on the phone. "PC Johnson. I was with you for that whole, ehm, Liddy Morse situation yesterday."

Haider itched the side of his nose. The milky scent of emulsion warmed his nostrils. "I was just there to paint, alright? Told you all this already, and—"

"Hold your horses, son. We were both there when Liddy confessed in rather sordid detail."

"Then how can I help you, officer? Got a job to get back to."

"I've got a Caitlyn Gardner here at the station."

"What happened?"

"Had herself a little episode. Caused quite the scene."

The springs on Haider's van jiggled him around in his seat as he rumbled into the bumpy car park. The sun tried to burn its way through a dense blanket of cloud. He saw its attempt at sunshine prickle off the large windows as he skidded to a halt outside the police station.

He shoved the heavy doors open, stepping into the cool of the brown panelled office. The glum day shone through rows of stained-glass windows. His boots clomped on the floor, echoing in the large space as he made his way to the reception desk. The receptionist diddled at a crossword, not looking up. Her permed hair bounced with life as she shook her head.

Haider opened his mouth to speak when the front doors burst open. He flinched as the doors swung and crashed off the wall. A hulking figure was sandwiched between two struggling policemen. They tried to march him forward as if dragging him to death row.

A smell like engine oil mingled with the panelled wood as the large man was led around him. The wide-eyed officers held an arm each, guiding the shackled man as if afraid he'd burst out of his restraints and murder everything in sight – looked capable of it, too.

"It made me do it," the man roared as he fought against the tide. "The leaf. Have to believe me. It cut me, officers. Wouldn't hurt a fly, me. Chop the bastard down. I love that woman, I didn't mean to—"

They slammed the man into a set of doors that flew open. His protests became muffled as the doors closed.

"Lot of aggro about this place of late," said PC Johnson, appearing at his side as if by magic. "More than usual, that is."

"What he do?" said Haider.

The detective scribbled on a clipboard and chucked it over the desk to the receptionist who had yet to look up from her crossword. "You don't wanna know what mess that big fella left behind. Let's go get your woman friend."

The detective led him through the large doors where the hulking giant had just been taken. They walked through a maze of corridors that all looked the same.

"Old dear called it in," said PC Johnson, talking over his shoulder as he marched on. "Found Caitlyn screaming her wee head off at the edge of town. She was kicking at the pavement. Weirdest thing she ever did see, is what she told the desk. Anyways, we showed up and tried to calm her down, but she was having none of that. Scratched us up pretty good. We had to restrain her, you know? Before she did anything to hurt anybody."

PC Johnson stopped before a large, iron door. "She's been in this cell for the last few hours, cooling off. I gotta ask." The officer leaned close. The salty sweat stench was enough to make Haider's nostrils twitch. "She on drugs? You know? Spice? Acid? Anything that makes your mind go all twisty?"

"What? Course not."

"You sure? Said a lot of strange things. Awful lot of stuff can go on behind a partner's back, you know."

"No drugs."

"History of mental illness in the family?"

Haider thought about her parents. There was always some fight to be had it seemed. It was like their world wasn't right without one. And they gunned for Caitlyn. She'd never opened up about what happened behind closed doors, but the scars were clear enough to see. The thought of her parents' glassy-eyes and harsh voices made him yearn for his own mum and dad. His mum would sit on his dad's knee as they watched a film, snuggling up like school kids in love.

"Come off it. She's not that bad, surely?" said Haider. "She's had a couple of rough days is all."

The copper raised his bushy eyebrows and Haider wanted to smack them clean off his face. The key clanked in the lock, echoing down the row of cells that stank of piss and stale puke.

They let her off with a warning. She stayed silent, not looking Haider in the eye as PC Johnson man-handled her out of the cell as if she were some feral beast.

"Ice cream," she said once they stepped outside. "Now."

He stole side glances at her as they walked down the busy road, avoiding the stumbling men who openly wore their drug habits in front of the establishment charged with stopping them. She bit her lip, her blue eyes filling as she fought back the tears. He stayed silent, knowing that she needed time to come back to herself, then she'd let it all out in one big stream of frantic hand motions and jerky, anger-stilted sentences.

Her eyes were cast somewhere far-off as she took a seat on a wooden bench outside the shop. He squeezed her hand then ran in. A ghost-twitch smile tugged her lips as she took the proffered tub and its two hefty scoops of mint choc chip ice cream. She folded her legs under her as she tucked in.

"What in a rat's arse is happening to me?" said Caitlyn.

"Take me through it, gorgeous," said Haider. "And take your time."

"This rate, you'll be forced to cart me off to Stratheden in a white jacket."

"Stop with that nonsense. You're fine."

"Fine? Ha. Like something in my head's gonna pop at any second. You ever feel that way? Like you can't take one more thing?" She gazed at him, fierceness melting away from her eyes. "Course you have. If it'd been me found them like you did, I'd have floated off to the looney bin ages ago."

"I didn't, though. Cause I have you."

She scooped the violent green ice cream, biting down on the plastic spoon. A shiver seemed to wriggle through her.

"What happened, babe?" said Haider. "Tell me."

"It won't let me leave."

"What you mean?"

"The town. This place. This forsaken shite-hole."

"Home, you mean?"

She flinched like he'd nipped her. "Home? Yours maybe. Not mine."

"You'd probably not feel at home anywhere."

"What's that supposed to mean?"

"I mean, maybe you're... Sorry. This isn't helping. Just, go through what happened. Please?"

She shoved the last of the ice cream in, closing her eyes as she savoured it. When she opened her eyes again, she seemed to have come back to herself.

"I gets on the bus," she said, "to head down Leven. Got a wee photo shop there. Was gonna pick up some prints. The bus just died. It was weird, though. Normally you can tell when you get on a right chugger that it's gonna give up the ghost. This was different. It just sputtered as it approached the end of town."

"So, the bus breaking down got you upset? Could've just walked it."

"Oh, really? Smart arse. I'm not that much of a fragile flower." She pressed her lips together, making them look like two white worms.

"Go on."

"You'll think I'm nuts. I started walking. I remember thinking how I could get a shot of the trees as they twinkled with sunlight. Catch it just right, at the orange part of day and the contrast would be beautiful, you know? That's when I smacked my head right into it."

"Into what?"

"Promise you won't think I'm crazy?"

"I'm not the one to judge people in such matters."

"Ha, true that." She let out a long, mint-laced breath. "It was like plexiglass. I thumped off of it, landing right on my arse. I must've looked a right fanny running into exactly nothing and bouncing off it again. Tried walking round it, but nope. I even stumbled out into the field, and nope. It's all around. Right where the town ends. Something's keeping me here, Haider. I need out. Let me out. Let me—"

He wrapped an arm around her and held her tight as she sobbed. The plastic-like scent of the cell's mattress danced in his nostrils as he rested his head on her.

The tree had its hold on the town. Haider, Liddy, and that brute who was dragged past him. Who knew how many others had leaves of their own?

He should've felt like the biggest prick in the world, being the reason Caitlyn was confined here. With the summer breeze humming over his skin, the love of his life in his arms, he felt like a million quid. Everything he needed, right here. He tried to shake it off, but a smile tugged the corner of his lip.

10.

"I DON'T KNOW if I can trust myself to go home right now," said Caitlyn as she stepped through Haider's front door.

"It'll be fine, babe. Promise." He stepped out of the muggy air into the cool of the dim hallway, closing the door behind him. As she neared the living room, he turned and locked the door.

As he opened his mouth to ask her what she wanted to drink, a familiar cold seeped into his skin. The door to his parent's bedroom creaked open. White steam billowed out like a fire raged from within.

Greta's icy gaze pierced him. "G-Give her what she n-needs."

His mouth hung open as he took her in. The thick duvet wrapped around her skeletal frame made her look like a shaking druid.

"Hey, paintbrush," called Caitlyn from the living room. "You coming or what?"

He looked back at the open door. His mum was gone, but he still felt the mist on his face like he'd just stepped out of a freezer.

"Has to be a way out of this mess. We'll find it," said Haider, lowering himself on the couch next to Caitlyn.

Beer spat on his palm as he twisted caps off two bottles of beer. He absently raised a toast to his dad, who nodded back at him from the big chair.

Caitlyn followed his gaze, sighed, then shook her head. She grabbed her bottle, knuckles going white as she took a deep drink like the beer couldn't get into her system fast enough. When she was done, she wiped white foam from her top lip with the back of her hand.

"Heart's been ripped the fuck out," she said. "You get that? All my dreams since I was yay high, gone because some old bastard thinks he knows what art is. I'd be happy to exist on beans on toast the rest of my days if I could get out of here. Just me, my camera and the world. It's all gone now."

"It's not gone. You can still do all of that."

"Not if you have your way."

"You think I did this? Told the uni to bin your application, then made a dome, or whatever, form around the town?"

"You've got me right where you want me." She shot her beautiful blues at him. "I can see it in your eyes."

"What's so wrong about wanting you to stay? Last time I checked, that was what normal couples did. Stayed together. Became a family. Lived a life. Grew old and useless together."

"You could come with me, you know? Nothing holding you back here." She stared at the big chair. "Anymore."

"But—"

"But you won't. You won't leave this dire place because it's got its talons in you. So, don't go acting all put out because I won't do what you want, when you won't do the same for me."

Heat billowed up the sides of his neck. He drowned a torrent of strained feelings under a wash of beer.

"Why do you need to rush so much?" said Haider. "Move in here, then we'll see what your options are. Take it a step at a time. Figure it out. Surely, you can get experience up and down Scotland. Plenty beautiful here, you know."

"You don't get it."

He shoved his bottle down on the table. A rush of foam fizzed out the top and ran down the brown glass. Its malty scent filled the air. "You just want away from me. That's what this boils down to, eh? Just want to party it up and 'find yourself' by travelling the world. Got news for you, hen – you're already here. And I love you too much to just watch you go."

"What did you just say?" Caitlyn's nose crinkled as she glared into him, leaning forward as if gearing for a fight.

He stood and walked to the window. The sun had won its war with the thick cloud. Its warm light spewed over him as the image of the black leaf returned in his mind.

She can't leave, he'd wished with some primal part of his gut. And he'd meant it, too.

When he turned around, his dad smiled up at him, holding his can of Guinness close to his lips. The sun streaked off the sweat on his reddened forehead.

"Sorry," said Haider. "I just want to see you happy, is all. I thought I could be that for you. Feels like—"

"We weren't meant to be. And if you call me 'hen' one more time, we won't be."

The shivering figure of Greta shuffled into the living room. Mist wisped behind her. Her purpled lips parted, trembling as she wrestled out the words. "G-give her what she n-needs."

"We could test it with my van," he said to Caitlyn. "Drive over the town line. Can't stop you if you're in a vehicle, surely?"

"No," said Caitlyn. "The barrier felt so dense. It'd fold me like a tin can."

"Well, we could walk it. Has to be a gap somewhere, right?"

Caitlyn groaned and clapped her face between both of her palms, smushing up her face. "I feel so caged up, you know? Ever since Nana Dottie gave me that wee camera when I was a bairn, all I've ever wanted was to capture perfection. I knew I'd fly all over the world. No two days the same. No horizon the same. Chasing the sun, you know? Chasing the sun."

"Doing a bang-up job, lad," said Ramsay. "Bang-up job."

"Leaf."

Haider flinched at the sound of his brother's narrow voice. Jace stood in the doorway, arms folded. The sight of the purple bruise around his neck made a wave of fire churn in Haider's stomach.

"What is it?" said Caitlyn, eyes alert.

"Nothing," said Haider. "Stay with me? Please? We could work this out. You and me, gorgeous."

Caitlyn stared at the doorway. "You miss them real bad, eh?"

"They don't give me the chance."

II.

THEY'D SAT in murky silence as they drank, stacking up crinkled cans of beer on the coffee table. An hour or so later, Caitlyn stood, mumbling about needing 'time to think' before stumbling down the hall. She swore as she fumbled with the locked door. The house rocked as she slammed it shut. Despite the imploring eyes of his dead family, Haider stayed put, swapping the beers for the bite of much-loved cider.

The wind tumbled down the street as he stared out his living room window. A flash of the tree's swirling, lively skin pierced his thoughts, made him clutch the can of cider until its golden liquid tracked down the back of his hand. He sipped it up, then downed the rest.

Later, with the effects of alcohol throbbing in his earlobes, he marched toward the invisible barrier. He leaned back, expecting to collide into it as the overgrown bushes by the side of the path reached for his calves.

They'd come to the opposite end of Pitlair, right where the twisty road started its way to the better parts of Fife. The sting of barley was on his tongue from a nearby field as he passed under the yellowed sign that marked the end of town.

"See? Told you," said Caitlyn, hugging herself, running her fingers along the outside of her arm. "No need to look so chuffed."

Haider tasted the promise of rain on the air as the wind ploughed through his fringe. He turned back, pausing beneath the rusty sign that squealed in the wind.

"Maybe it'll work if I pull you through?" Haider held out his hand.

Caitlyn cast her feverish eyes up and down the empty road. She slapped and wiped her palms on her jeans like she had dirt on her hands she desperately needed to get off. He caught the scent of fresh shampoo as she stopped in front of him.

He nodded down at his outstretched hand. She took it.

It didn't work.

He willed the black stain of his wish away as they walked under the sign. Her clammy hand was in his and then it wasn't. It was as if she'd been snapped away from him. It didn't matter how much he tried to pull her through. Her hand whitened as she pressed against the barrier until she screamed in anguish.

"Was never gonna work," said Caitlyn, rubbing her palm. "Stuck here the rest of my days. You go on, though. Have a wee trot all the way to St. Andrews. Nice day out, if you fancy it? Don't let me stop you."

"I could try it with my tools."

"What good you think that's gonna do?"

"It's worth a shot, is it not? Could've brought something from my van. Smash the thing into pieces."

"No use. It's done. Final. We can't take it back."

"Take what back?"

Caitlyn gnawed at the top of her white t-shirt, eyes lost in the sway of trees that overhung the road. Her phone buzzed. She answered it. "What is it?"

Haider saw the glassy look in her eyes as she brought a hand up to cover her mouth.

"What is it?" said Haider. "What happened?"

"I-I'll be right there. Shit." She ended the call and clutched onto his outstretched arms, almost digging into the skin on his forearms. "They're dead. Both of them."

Haider marched with Caitlyn to her house, barely keeping pace. Her eyes grew more and more haunted and they neared her house.

"Knew this would happen," she said as they slunk through the crowd of gawkers, up the path and toward the officer standing guard.

He smelled the iron of it as soon as he walked through the front door. They made him wait in Caitlyn's room as PC Johnson spoke to her in private. His ear pressed to the cold door, he listened to the muffled conversation in the hall. Caitlyn's gasps and sniffles pierced his heart. He longed to throw open the door and wrap his arms around her.

She was all he had. And now he was all she had.

The tang of coppery blood stained the air as he plonked himself on her bed, eyeing her wall of pictures. He busied himself by calling his next few jobs, telling them he had a family emergency and he'd rearrange the work when he could. Word spread damn quick. They'd all heard the news, asking their sordid questions.

Caitlyn came back into the room like a ghost, her eyes gazing into the realms of the cream carpet. He went to her, folding her in his arms. She didn't cry, just lay her head against his chest.

"I knew it would come to this," she said.

"Grab a bag of your stuff. Stay at mine's. You can tell me what happened there, if you're up for it. Fine if you don't. We could just sit and get mashed if that'll help. Whatever you need, gorgeous. Whatever you need."

"I needed them gone. And now they are."

He gently held her by the shoulders, trying to meet her gaze. "You don't mean that."

"I wished for it I don't know how many times."

Her dad had tied her mum up bondage style before carving into her with a Stanley knife. She'd bled out over the bedroom carpet. It was not a quick death. Then he turned the knife on himself, opening his own wrists.

She recited this as she stayed rooted in the same spot, her voice devoid of any emotion. Haider grabbed a bag and offered it to her. When she didn't take it, he started packing clothes himself.

He was the silent helper, doing whatever she needed, knowing what it was like to have your world tipped upside-down without warning. Caitlyn's powerful and constant presence was the only thing that had kept him sane through his own dark times.

"I hated them." Caitlyn slumped onto the corner of the bed. "Shite thing to say, but I always have. There was something in the air these last few days. The thick threat of violence. More than usual, you know?" She played with a strand of hair, twirling it around her unblemished fingers. "Thought I'd be well clear of this place before anything real happened, though. Now this."

Haider stood and opened the door, looking into the hall, looking for PC Johnson. He wanted to ask what happened next so he could be there. A policeman guarding her parent's bedroom door shot him a warning glare.

Opposite the cop, Jace leaned against the wall, a smile stretching up his face. Black ooze burbled out his brother's smile and onto the floor, spattering against the policeman's boots.

"Can I help you there, young man?" said the cop in an American accent.

"Nothing, officer," said Haider, looking at the spot where Jace had been. "Just shocked, I guess."

He closed the door. It felt as if a wheel was scraping the lining from his stomach. His family had never followed him outside the confines of his own house before. What did it mean?

"You're going batshit, that's what," said Haider.

"What?"

"Nothing." He walked over and placed his hand on her shoulder. "I'll help you however I can, alright? Just say it, and it's done. I've cancelled my jobs for the next few days. I'm all yours."

"I'll move in."

"You sure?"

"Nowhere else to go, have I? I don't trust myself to be alone right now."

"I know it sounds impossible, but you'll get through this, gorgeous."

She stood, then stormed out of the room, marching into the hall. He heard the cop protest, and then the opening of a door.

"I wanna see them," he heard Caitlyn say.

He waited. The mumbles of PC Johnson buzzed through the wall to him. He fidgeted with his phone, twirling it between his thumb and forefinger, not sure what to do. Go in there? See the dead bodies? Bile touched the back of his throat at the thought. Jace had been the one for gnarly things all their life. He went all foamy in the head at the sight of his own blood.

Minutes later, Caitlyn came through clutching an armful of books and photo albums. "Taking these."

"Alright, babe. We going now?"

"Aye. The stench of death is in my skin. Don't think it'll ever come out."

As she glared at the ground, he grabbed the books from her to shove them in the bag. She yelped and tried to clutch them back off him, causing them to fall to the floor. Their pages rifled open.

"Sorry, babe," said Haider, kneeling to pick them up. "I..."

His legs turned to water and he crashed to his knees.

A black leaf peered out from a photo album.

12.

HAIDER DID the only thing that came naturally – he hit the sauce. They'd tanked most of a bottle of vodka by the time the sun fell out the sky. The thought of Caitlyn's dad taking a knife to her tied-up mum made his bones quake.

No denying it now – the tree and its leaves held sway over the ones who'd made their wishes. Liddy abandoning little Katrina beneath the floorboards, the hulking brute at the police station, and now Caitlyn's dad. They'd all made their wish, it seemed, and they'd all committed acts of gut-wrenching terror. Black liquid ran over his hand as he took a shaky drink.

"You alright?" said Caitlyn, crossing one leg beneath her on the couch. "Look like you're having a stroke or something."

Her deep blue eyes pierced into him and he felt the muscles in his arms turn to jelly. He set the drink on the coffee table before it slipped out. The burn of alcohol was thrumming in his cheeks. Now would be the time. Let her know. He closed his eyes, ready to let it out.

All that you love will be taken away.

"D-Don't," shivered Greta, standing by the window, covers hugged tight around her. "N-Nightmare."

"Aye, sure is," said Haider, raising a toast to her. The fuzz of syrupy cola clung to his teeth after he downed the rest of it.

Caitlyn followed his gaze, then stared down at the empty space between them on the couch. She scrunched up her face, wrestling tears. "Do you see them? Are they really still here?"

"Sometimes I think it's just me making them up, you know? Like some messed up coping thing. They got whipped away so fast."

He quickly poured himself another drink. The sting of vodka hit the air as the liquid glugged. He took it straight, thankful for the burn of it before the tears won him over. Caitlyn needed him to be strong.

"I hope my parents aren't kicking about my house, then," said Caitlyn. "Do you think that's what happens?"

Haider stared at the ruddy face of his father who relaxed in his big chair, then back to his mother whose teeth chattered. He heard their bony clicking inside his skull.

"I think you carry around who you want to carry, you know?" said Haider. "Like I'll always carry you, no matter where you end up."

Caitlyn lay back on the couch, staring up at the ceiling. Her eyes were half-lidded. "You wanna know what the worst of it is?"

"What?"

"I knew. I knew, damn it. That's what's eating me."

"Don't think that way, gorgeous. What were you supposed to do? Stand guard like a prison warden twenty-four seven?"

"Could've stopped it. Could've made more of a fuss with the cops when... other stuff happened."

Katrina's shrunken skull flashed in his mind and her ginger hair that would never again feel the sun. His thoughts turned to the box that lay below Jace's bed. "I'm not sure you could have. Feels like it was destined to happen, one way or the other. Just glad you weren't there."

"Destined?"

"Never mind. I'm blethering. Another? Sure I've got some absinthe crawling about here somewhere."

"Fuck no. I'm going to bed."

"Aw, you two are complete amateurs," said Ramsay, can of Guinness in hand. He'd been enjoying the company all evening, drinking his never-ending phantom brew. "Thought I was getting a decent drink in for a change."

"I can't go toe to toe with you anymore, old man," said Haider.

Caitlyn stood and stretched her arms over her head, letting a huge yawn take her. Her hands slapped to her side once she was done. "I'm going to bed before you creep me out totally."

"Sorry, gorgeous. Last few days have been mental."

He hugged her tight, savouring the way his arms seemed to fit perfectly around her. She planted a kiss on his cheek and moved to go past him but stubbed her toe on the big chair.

She fell onto the seat, blurring with the ghost of his father. The warring images caused a wave of pain to squelch through his eyes.

"Get up!" He yanked her arm, dragging her back onto her feet.

He blinked away the pain as he held onto her shoulders. Reality slowly crystalised before him.

Ramsay grinned from the big chair like it was the funniest thing in the world. "Most action I've had in decades. She's ripe."

"Get your mitts off me, Haider," said Caitlyn, wincing. "Fuck sake."

White ovals on her skin eased back to normal as he let go. "Sorry, babe. Why don't you go on through? I'll be there in a wee sec."

The heat drained from her eyes as she deflated, letting go of her anger. She muttered to herself as she stumbled down the hall, crossing her arms over her chest.

Jace appeared in the doorway, his voice scraping like jagged metal on plastic. "Sweet."

Ramsay stood from the chair, a jolly look in his eyes. His jowls shone with sweat. "She came onto me. I had nothing to do with it. Can't help that this old tiger still has his stripes, eh?"

"You two shut it," said Haider, clawing at his hair. "Be quiet, alright? Let me think."

Jace looked back into the hall, in the direction Caitlyn went. "Unhappy."

"You've sure messed up the whole thing," said Ramsay. "Didn't get your skills from me, obviously."

"S-She must stay." Greta stood by the window. Moonlight trickled over her, accenting the mist that echoed off her shoulders. "M-Make her. G-Good for you."

"You need her," said Ramsay.

Jace ran a hand over his neck, scratching out a sound like rough sandpaper. "Stay."

"If she needs to go," said Haider, "who am I to stop her?"

13.

THE AIR HELD the sting of mid-autumn as he walked. His knuckles protested as he squeezed the small box with his leaf inside. A vibration beat against his palm as if he carried a small heart. He shuffled on, feet scraping the small stones on the path as he zigzagged all over the place, the vodka still smashing its way through his blood.

He'd stood by the foot of his bed watching Caitlyn sleep. The way her hair tumbled over her face made him want to climb in and run his hand through it. He felt his family's presence over his shoulder as he continued to watch her.

"I need to make it right," he whispered, turning to face his brother. "Watch her for me?"

"Always."

"That's not creepy at all." He'd closed his eyes and squeezed the bridge of his nose. The world twisted like he stood inside a giant can of cider being spun about. He waited until it felt safe to open his eyes. "Do you have to talk like that?"

"T-Tree," said Greta, her ice-cold fingers gripping his shoulder. "You must g-go."

The wind picked up, billowing his through his open jacket as he stottered from side to side. A shadow of a figure stood outside a church. Haider did what any sensible local did about here – kept his eyes on the ground and tried to move on as silent as possible.

"You show that tree who's boss," said the man with deep, lung-scraping effort.

Haider stopped. "Dad?"

The image vanished. Something in the centre of his skull slithered about as he stood there, blinking.

"You're losing it, Haider," said Haider.

Soon, Cuttie Hill park loomed before him. He stood before the arch that once foamed with roses when he'd been a kid. The wooden frame had been left to rot. It tilted as if it were made of glued match-sticks. As he stepped forward, a puff of smoke steamed from the other side. Fear grabbed at his stomach, tugging it south. A group of lads smoking and drinking was the last thing he needed to stumble into in his state.

"It's n-not from h-here," said Greta from the other side. "It'll t-take everything."

Haider stepped under the arch. All that remained of his mother was a wisp of white that curled in the air. He groaned up at the cold stars.

The box hummed to life in his hand. What was he doing here? What was his plan?

His gaze fell upon the tree. It coiled itself at the sky. Its branches were warped, like some drug-addled painter had captured the very worst idea of a tree.

Standing before it, tremors buzzed up his calves. Despite the full bloom of the trees on either side of it, only a handful of leaves clung to its dead limbs. As he stepped closer, he caught the burned-out scent of worn batteries. The tree's skin chittered as its colony of black dots swirled and shifted around.

"I take it back." Haider's balance wavered as he followed the length of the tree to the sky. "You hear me? Whatever you are, and wherever you came from, you need to take it back. I need to let her go."

He opened the box and held the leaf by its skeletal stem, careful not to touch its sharp edges.

"I was wrong," he said. "Let her go."

The bark teemed with life as if the black dots could smell him. Their patterns held him, sapping his blood. A faintness washed over him like a cold shroud. His hand looked far away as he reached out, as if it belonged to someone else.

Before the white that sizzled at the corners of his vision took him over completely, he shot his hand forward, placing his leaf in a small grove at the base of a thick branch.

Black beads shot up his arm. A thousand pricks of pain needled his skin as the things scuttled over him.

He roared his agony at the sky. The sky had changed. His feet no longer touched ground. Free and weightless, he floated among the stars. Comets burned past him, leaving a taste of ozone on his tongue. In every direction, gas clouds of wondrous galaxies pulsed with awful life.

"Hello?" he shouted. The vast space before him ate his words. "Let me out of here."

A voice thundered through him. Its bass vibrated in the pit of his stomach. "She can't leave."

He flicked his gaze in every direction. "What are you?"

"Your dream made true."

"You can't do this. Let me go. Let Caitlyn go. She doesn't deserve this."

Haider kicked his legs, swimming through the vast ocean of space. His skin tingled all over like a crowd of ghosts watched his every move. As he clawed his way through the space, he saw that his arm looked like it had been dipped in black wax.

"She doesn't deserve this!" he screamed.

"You all deserve it."

"If you need someone, take me."

"Too late."

Something rumbled in the distant, gas cloud galaxies. Haider turned to face the sound. A black stain spread, blotting out the stars, leaving a terrible absence.

14.

COLD CRASHED over Haider's chest. He gasped in a desperate breath as he sprung awake and almost toppled off the couch. Water dripped off his chin as Caitlyn's blazing blue eyes bore into him. Her jaw trembled as if she chewed the inside of her cheek. She slammed the empty glass onto the coffee table.

"Talk," she said.

Haider sat up. A small river of water puddled in his crotch as he breathed heavy. He held his arms out to the side as if a coat-hanger was lodged between his shoulder blades. His heart galloped, pounding its choppy rhythm in his throat. The sun pouring in through the window drove a spike of pain through his eyes.

With trembling, sickly hands, he took off his sodden t-shirt and set it on the table. "Wha—"

She clapped him on the side of the head with an open fist. "Don't you ever sneak out on me like that again, got that?"

"Sorry, I—"

"I'm not done, fuck-head. Bad enough you abandoned me after my folks died, but you left me in this eery shite hole with them."

Haider ran a hand over his wet hair. The vile taste of last night's vodka began creeping its numb fingers up his gullet. He gulped away the green feeling. "You can see them?"

"What? No. Place still gives me the major creeps, though. Like they're here, somewhere. You were talking in your sleep. You know more than you're letting on. Spill."

Ramsay leaned back in his big chair, shrugging his shoulders, popping the top on a new, ever-existing beer. Jace and Greta both leaned against the wall at either side of the window. His mum clasped the top of her covers with an iron grip while Jace only smiled his callous smile.

"W-What was I saying, exactly?" said Haider, the chill rattling into his hungover bones. The room cartwheeled about him. He closed his eyes, praying his guts wouldn't shoot their way out his mouth.

"Let's start with where the fuck you went last night. And don't lie to me."

"Look, I was plastered. Went for a wee walk. Fresh air and all that. Been a weird few days."

She folded her arms. "Where did you go?"

He rubbed at the centre of his forehead. His father had been there with him when he'd walked. So, too, had his mother. What were they doing outside? Where had he gone?

The weightlessness of swimming through a black void thundered into his mind. The tree had spoken to him. Its voice had pulsed in his bones.

He opened his mouth to speak. A torrent of puke rushed out of his mouth. He turned his head just in time, sending chunks of undigested pizza rolling down the fabric of his couch. The milky scent of it as it dripped from his nostrils made him gag once more, adding to the pile.

"Pathetic arsehole," said Caitlyn as she walked to the window, standing next to Jace who grinned, looking as if he fought the urge to throw a hand around her shoulders.

"Where did you find me?" croaked Haider.

"Find you?"

"I passed out at the foot of that tree."

Caitlyn sighed and turned. The sunlight roamed over her glossy hair and smooth, angelic skin. He longed to go to her, to touch her, hold her close before she spun away. Instead, he grabbed his wet t-shirt and chucked it atop the pile of spew.

"Is that where you made a wish?" said Caitlyn.

By the window, Greta let out a stream of white smoke. Puke threatened to rise again. He closed his eyes and balanced his head on his palms.

"Time to let it out." Caitlyn turned. The sunlight made her blue eyes flame like marbles. "Do you trust me? Tell me the truth of it."

Haider stared at his brother who seemed to take it all in with his mocking smile.

"Truth," said Jace, his voice thin and scratched.

Haider took a deep breath. The stain of puke filled the air. "This is gonna sound mad, alright."

"Try me."

He told her about the leaves he'd found out about. What Liddy did to little Katrina. The shackled man in the police station. And now her dad who'd done those awful things. All three had been found with leaves that had fallen from the alien-like tree.

"You see?" he finished. "It's all connected, somehow. And that tree is at the centre of it all."

Caitlyn leaned against the windowsill and sighed. She looked down at him, trying to catch his eye. "That everything?"

He shifted under the weight of her stare. *She can't leave.* The tree, or whatever it was refused to let her go. "Evil tree not enough for you, likes? We should go to the police with this."

"Wait. You telling me my dad didn't kill my mum? The tree did it? Made him turn the knife on himself?"

"I think it takes whatever's in someone's heart and amplifies it."

"It hasn't always been there."

"What?"

"The other day when we sat up Cuttie Hill. You asked if that tree's always been there. It's not."

"How'd you know that?"

She whipped out her phone then sat next to him. The sweet aroma of her orange perfume tingled his nostrils. The nearness of her stopped his heart trip-trapping away in his chest. Their knees touched as she tapped at her phone screen.

"Look," she said, flicking between two photos she'd taken from atop the hill. "This one I took a year ago. And this one from about three months ago. See? Tree. No tree. Tree. No tree."

"What does it all mean?"

"Something mighty fucked up is going on, that's what it means. And I think it's the thing not letting me escape."

Haider gulped. His glands were swollen and harsh from the puking. "What makes you say that?"

She put the phone away and sunk back into the couch. "Think about it. My dad told me he wanted me here, always. That I'd never make it out there. Surprised you two never got along better. Maybe he wished to be in control of us and to never let me leave."

"Sounds possible. Yesterday, the man getting arrested screamed that it was the tree that did it."

"So, someone makes a wish and they're powerless to stop whatever happens next?"

Is that what would happen to him? One day, he'd wake up and try to butcher her, being able to do nothing to stop it? He felt his eyes going wide with fright as he looked to his family. They'd gone. Back into whatever part of the imagination they sprouted from.

"Why though?" said Caitlyn. "What's it all mean?"

"All I know is when I touched it..."

"What?"

"It's not from around here."

"What were you doing at the tree, Haider?"

The blackness that had crawled over his arm came to mind. It felt as if he'd stuck his fingers in a live socket. "I begged it to stop. To go back to wherever it came from. And I guess I blacked out."

A watery stream burst out his mouth. He managed to turn his head in time to add it to the patch of sick already soaking into the carpet.

Caitlyn covered her nose. "I am not cleaning that up."

15.

TWO DAYS PASSED in a flurry of vodka and takeaways. He chipped away at Caitlyn, knowing that she needed to open up about the deaths of her mum and dad. Keeping something like that locked up would eat at her the rest of her days. When he'd lost his family, Caitlyn had been there, holding his hand as he broke down in a flood of healing tears. If he kept feeding her vodka, she'd eventually let her guard down and have a good cry about it.

On the Thursday evening, when they'd spoken of the tree, he'd waited on her passing out on the couch, then snuck into Jace's shadowy room. He must've left the box at the park, but the leaf had returned to its usual spot under his brother's bed.

He left her on Saturday morning to play catch up on his paint jobs. The workman's institute asked him to paint over all the lurid remarks it had accumulated from decades of hosting sportsman's dinners and high school parties.

In the dim light of the dusty hall, he chuckled nervously as he swiped white emulsion over remarks left in crude biro.

Donald Trump is your da'.

U R gay I.D.S.T.

CFC 1888.

All that you love will be taken away.

He dropped his roller. It clattered onto the cover he'd set down. His hands shook as he covered his mouth. The scrawled writing morphed itself into a lurid invitation to the bathroom.

"Away."

He spun. Jace stood by the open double doors, his impossible shadow spilling into the hall.

"I'm losing it, eh?" said Haider. "You can't be here."

"Caitlyn."

He marched toward the spectre of his brother. "What about her?"

Jace's panic-sparkled eyes made him stop in his tracks. His brother pointed toward their home, then his image vanished.

Haider groaned and kicked a stack of metal chairs piled high against the wall. The noise of the wobbling metal filled the high-ceilinged space.

They'd had so many good drinks in here as a family. He could still taste the ghost of the warm beer they'd had during their last day out here for a charity race night.

He rushed home, slamming the front door open and sprinting down the hall to the living room. Caitlyn looked up from her stack of papers she'd laid out over the coffee table.

"Where's the fire, hot stuff?" said Caitlyn.

"I just," said Haider, sucking in lungfuls of trapped summer air. "Never mind."

"I found another leaf. Well? Don't just stand there with that dumb face on."

Despite how he'd scrubbed at it, the stale scent of puke rose up to him as he sat next to her on the couch. "Where did you find it?"

"When you... found that poor wee Katrina, did you touch the leaf?"

"I'd rather not think about it."

"They're so... warm. Made my skin feel all dotty, you know?"

A rough scratching sound filled the room as he ran his hand over his unshaven jaw. The thought of being in that woman's bedroom, looking down into the dark space made jitters dance to life inside him.

"She's well wicked," said Ramsay, raising a toast from his big chair. "Been watching her, I have. Sharp."

Haider stood and walked into the kitchen, pouring himself an overflowing glass of water. The water quenched something deep within him as he drank the whole glass. He made a mental note to stop drinking so much booze.

Caitlyn joined him, sitting up on the kitchen counter. "I think you're right."

"Right about what?

"About the tree."

Water spat off the sink as he turned the tap on full, refilling his glass. "Wish I wasn't."

"I went for a stroll. Ended up standing at the foot of that tree. Dunno how. Like it called me there, you know? It's pretty much on a straight row of trees that line the path, but if you stand there long enough, you'll see that everybody kind of swerves round it. No reason to."

"Tell me you didn't take a leaf."

"Calm down. Think I'm that daft?"

She hopped off the counter, opened the fridge, clucked her tongue for a few seconds, then pulled out two tins of cider. She popped them both open and handed him one. His tongue moistened at the sight of the beads of cold trickling down the blue can. He grabbed it and downed half of it in one go.

Caitlyn bounced back up to the counter and sipped at hers, screwing her face up. "Man, I hate cider. Tastes like a rotten whore's perfume."

Drink nearly crept out his nostril as Jace appeared beside the fridge, staring at Caitlyn. He'd hadn't seen Jace look so stressed when he'd been alive – before he'd quit on him and hung himself.

"Truth," said Jace.

"You found a leaf?" said Haider.

"Was about to turn and walk home since I can't go anywhere

fucking else since I'm stuck here for the rest of my life and everything's fucked and it's all gonna end and no one underst—"

"Woah, woah." Haider leaned over and placed a hand on her thigh. "You're alright."

She batted at a tear that flowed from her eye. "Hate you seeing me like this. Must make you sick."

"Never. I'd put up with you forever. You know that."

"Aw, shucks. I always wanted to find my shiny prince who'd swear an oath to 'put up with me forever.' Stuff fairy tales are made of."

"The leaf?"

"At the park, in front of wee bairn's and everything. There were these two kids. Right pimply and dorky, you know? Must've been no older than thirteen. Well, they jump this boy. This much bigger boy. Was like they'd waited for years on revenge. I'm sitting at the base of that damned tree watching, getting to that stage where you start thinking about stepping in. They beat him bloody, but the bigger kid gets up, all threatening. Looks as if he's gonna tear through the two of them. That's when..."

"When?"

"One of the kids brings out an axe. One of those wee ones, but still able to do the damage. Aw man, the sound it made. Thunk. Right into the boy's neck. Blood everywhere. Spouting like a fucking red fountain. Some parents are hauling their kids away by the ear, some are just pointing their phones at it while their toddlers stare."

"You went to help."

"Aye, I did. I'm not one to ogle at death. The kid dropped the axe. He had blood spattered everywhere. That's when I saw the leaf sticking out the pocket on his shirt. I took it out and he looked at me. And I knew."

"What did he say?"

"He told me he didn't want to spend his days floating through the forever. He was pleased. That was the worst of it."

"Floating..."

"Cops came, took the boy away. His chum had bolted, but the one who murdered the bigger kid got in the police car like he'd just been picked up by his dad after football or something. I could see it in his eyes. Release. Like he hadn't been in charge, but now he was free." Caitlyn set her drink to the side, then batted away another tear. "This is some fucked up mess, Haider. How'd we get into this? What do we do now?"

"We chop it down before it's too late."

"Too late for what?"

Jace stepped forward. The harsh yellow light of the day lit up his bruised, misshapen neck. "Wish."

Haider gulped down a torrent of cider until he killed the rising guilt. The fizz of the alcohol burned the back of his throat as Jace glared up at him.

"I doubt the cops will believe us," said Haider. "We need to stop it before more people die. It's got its talons sunk into the town. Lord knows how many other leaves are out there."

Caitlyn let out a long breath. The light of hope in her eyes made a fresh wave of guilt ride through him.

"If we kill it," she said, "then it'll break its hold on me. I'll be free."

16.

ALIEN SYLLABLES BUZZED through the window, thrumming up Haider's spine as he opened his eyes. The black syrup of a nightmare settled over him as the tree tapped at the glass with its spiny branches like long fingers reaching. The tree's dead leaves reflected the harsh moonlight, burning spots onto his vision.

He patted around his bed in the dark. Caitlyn's empty pillow was still warm.

Moonlit shadows danced along his wall as the tree leaned closer.

Haider punched himself in the jaw. "Come on. Wake up." He punched himself again, his teeth clattering together. "Come on."

Vibrations hummed in his calves as the tree seemed to leer at him through the window. The ground rumbled like a midnight train passed beneath him.

"I have come," roared the tree inside his mind. "She can't leave."

Black leaves twirled in the air, mesmerising him with their sparks of cold light. The leaves aimed themselves, darting through the windowpane, leaving the glass unblemished.

He twisted to the side as the leaves hovered around him like invading wasps. A line of blood screamed with heat as a leaf burned itself along his forearm. One embedded its sharp point in his earlobe.

The tree's branches snapped as it rose to its full height. It lumbered out of view, collapsing sheds and fences as it churned through the earth.

He chucked his boot at one of the leaves that thudded off the wall, leaving a black smudge like a squashed bug. The sting of coppery blood was in the roof of his mouth as he bolted for the door, slamming it shut behind him. Three leaves thunked into the wood on the other side.

The dark hallway seemed to skew in his vision as he got his breath back. "Caitlyn?"

Jace stepped out from his silent bedroom, uncoiling the noose from around his neck. The rope tumbled to the carpet. "Truth."

"Don't give me that. You think I don't know what I have to do? Who are you to push me? Quitter."

"Fuck me sideways," said Ramsay, joining them in the cold hall. "Big bastard that tree, eh?"

Beads of sweat rolled off his father's forehead. Haider reminded himself it was just a dream. No need to go ape at his brother for quitting. No need to tell his dad to sit down before he keeled over.

"Where's Caitlyn?" said Haider.

"O-Outside," said his mum, appearing in a cloud of mist. "S-Save her."

The machine-gun noise of branches sliding against the house was deafening. The floor rumbled under his feet like the house would shift off its foundations.

Despite the clear sky and the full moon, lashing rain poured over him, diluting the blood that ran down his face. He bolted to the end of the small garden, his socked feet sloshing through mud and puddle.

Caitlyn gazed up at the stars. Rain bounced off the top of her head, yet she paid no notice. Her hair clung to her shoulders. Her pyjamas were soaked through so much that they shone in the pale moonlight.

He held her by the shoulders, trying to shake her attention from the stars. "Come back to me. Caitlyn?"

"I'm trapped. Right where you want me. Caged like a good wifey. This is what you wanted, right?"

"We need to move. It's coming."

She turned to face him. Black streaks of mascara bracketed her wet cheeks. "The tree's already got me, Haider. Don't you see that? Don't you see what you've done?"

He grabbed her thin wrist and pulled her toward the house. "We'll fix it, gorgeous. I promise."

"I don't want you to. It's so wonderful inside the tree. I can see worlds no one else has. Red worlds. It shows me all."

The tree hissed at the sky as it dragged its roots through the grass. It blotted out the moon as it hunched over them. An electrical hum rose from its heart. The snapping, clicking sound interrupted his thoughts. He stood, staring helplessly up at it as it towered above them.

"You're not real," said Haider. "I'm dreaming all this up, aren't I?"

It loomed over them as large as a mountain, consuming the sky. It spoke in a thousand droning voices that made his ears ache. "All that you love will be taken away."

"No!" said Greta.

His mum threw her duvet off and ran out into the cold. She grabbed Caitlyn by the wrists, guiding her away. A spill of light shone from the house as Caitlyn was guided through the front door. Jace and Ramsay stood like sentries, ushering them inside.

The tree's bark crackled as it turned its attention on his family.

"Family," said Haider. For that's exactly what they were. Caitlyn included. And he'd give anything for her.

"Hey you, ya big alien tree bastard," he shouted. "You can't have her. You hear me?"

"She can't leave!" the tree bellowed inside his mind.

"Haider," said his dad from the front door. "For the love of fuck, get in here."

"No." Haider ran a hand slowly over his chin. His palm came away slick with watery blood. "You think you can just come here and take her away from me, eh? I—"

"You did this," the tree dragged itself forward, the earth rising in a wave of dirt before him. "Your wish."

A sound like thunder pulsed in his ears. The tree leaned back, then whipped a thick branch at him. Haider watched it coming.

Jace tackled him just as the branch tore a chunk of dirt from the ground in a wide slash. Puffs of clumped grass and earth scattered about them.

"What you doing?" said Haider, getting to his feet.

"Home," Jace strained, pushing him at the open door.

"McFarlane's don't give up like that, son," shouted his dad, joining them in the rain. "We fight."

"We?" said Haider.

"In the house. Now."

The tree screeched as Jace and Ramsay pushed him toward home. His mum reached from the doorway, touching him with shocking cold fingers and hauled him inside.

He threw his arms around Caitlyn who gazed up at the tree, a shell-shocked gleam in her eyes. He nuzzled into her neck, holding her tight.

"You will fall," the tree roared.

Haider turned. Jace, Greta and Ramsay stood before the tree, standing shoulder to shoulder. A thunderous bellow erupted from the tree. Rain glistened along its black surface. It leaned back, then aimed a large limb down to crush his family.

"No!" said Haider.

A piercing light exploded as the branch erupted into splinters when it hit the ground. An eruption of dirt and grass flew in all directions.

Caitlyn clutched at his wrist, imploring him to stay.

When he turned back around, the tree and his family were gone.

17.

. . .

A SOB WRENCHED its way through Haider's gut as he screamed himself awake. Beside him, Caitlyn yelped and sat bolt upright, kicking at the bed like a snake slithered under the covers. She slapped him. The sound reverberated in the small room as red warmth spread across his cheek.

"Prick!" said Caitlyn, clutching the covers to her chest. "Nearly made my guts fall out my arse."

"Sorry. Bad dream, I guess." Haider rubbed absently at his face while he stared out the window. The predawn sky flirted with blue as the stars clung on. The chill of nightmare still rode his blood. He traced a finger over a straight cut that ran the length of his forearm. "The leaf got me."

Caitlyn threw herself back on the bed, turning her back to him. His hand hovered above her shoulder. He lowered it, setting it in his lap as he looked at the encroaching dawn.

In his nightmare, his family had stood together, defying the tree. He remembered the brilliant flash of light as the thing had crashed into them. He chucked the covers off and pulled his legs into last night's jeans.

"Jace? Mum? Dad?" he called as he ran through the house.

Jace didn't swing from his noose. Greta didn't shiver in her bed. Ramsay didn't sit on his big chair.

"Haider?" said Caitlyn, following him down the hall. "Stop."

He stepped into his brother's stale bedroom, running a hand through his oily hair. The cold hate that usually twisted his heart was gone. All that was left was an empty space as the scent of dead dust climbed into his nose.

"Jace?" he said. "You can't quit on me now, you spineless cunt. Hear me? Get back here. Finish this with me. You can't just... just..."

Caitlyn collided into his back and wrapped her arms around him. Her dainty hands clasped at the centre of his chest. "Breathe. You need to let him go. I know it's—"

"They're gone. All of them. And it's all my fault." He placed one hand on Caitlyn's hands and wiped his nose with the other. "Now you'll leave me, too."

"Wheest your face. There's worse people I could be stuck with."

"Aw, cheers."

She let go, turned him by the shoulders and cast the full power of her blue eyes on him. He could swim in those eyes the rest of his days.

"Maybe it's alright that the tree is doing this," she said. "Maybe it was meant to be."

"Not like this. It can't."

"Rip my heart out, why don't you? Took me a lot to say that."

"The tree. It won't stop. I see that now."

"Slow down. What?"

"I'm gonna burn that bastard to the ground. It took them, Caitlyn. Jace. Mum. Dad. They were here just last night. I can feel it in my bones. They're gone."

"No, Haider. They've been gone a while now. You know that, right? The tree didn't have anything to do with that."

"But, they — In my dream."

"Just a nightmare, big guy. Just a dream."

Haider blinked away a tear as he moved past her and into his messy bedroom. He shoved on a thick hoodie and laced up his boots. "There's only one way to make sure it releases you."

"Haider? It's, like, four in the morning. Wait until it's bright out at least."

"I don't wanna see what happens if I wait any longer."

"I'm not coming with you."

The muggy stillness of the morning settled upon him as he grabbed an axe from his spider-laced shed. His van rattled as he twisted the key in the ignition. The towering tree of his nightmare scoured his mind as he drove. He remembered the way it had keeled through the ground, churning up slow waves of earth in its wake.

Cuttie Hill park rose before him. He bumped up a small kerb, almost bouncing out of his seat as he ploughed through the archway and into the park. Wood churned under his tyres as he applied the brakes, sliding to a stop in front of the tree.

The tree reached its sharp, brittle branches toward the last of the stars. The scent of dewy grass hit his nostrils as he hopped out of the van. He moved closer to the tree. Black things chittered and shifted around on its trunk.

All that—

He snapped his gaze away. "You can't have her."

A shiver rocked through him as if those swirling black beads tingled his neck. The memory of floating through a cold void attacked him. The park lay silent except for the twisting, creaking sound made by the tree's lively skin. He hefted the axe over his shoulder and moved forward.

He groaned as the heavy axe bit into the tree with a satisfying *crack*. Black splinters spat into the air as if it were charcoal. He hacked away, working up a sweat. Liquorice pus oozed from the angle he created as he aimed to bring the tree down on itself.

Orange spilled over the horizon as he wiped the running sweat from his forehead. The salt of it stung his eyes. The tree's tar-like blood clotted over his hands. He let go of the axe's handle. It thudded to the ground inches from his feet.

The tree stood whole and untouched.

"W-What are you?" said Haider.

"All you wished for," said the tree in its grating, buzzsaw voice. "This place and its reek of desperation called to me from across the great black sky."

He climbed into the back of his van and brought out a petrol can. The clear liquid sloshed over the bark. Tiny specks of black seemed to recoil from the petrol, exposing smooth, gunmetal grey beneath like it was part machine.

He scratched a match to life along the edge of a matchbox. Orange flame danced in his vision. "Let Caitlyn go."

He tossed the match.

The flame *whooshed*, leaping up the tree. The heat of it licked at his face as he sunk to his knees. He closed his eyes. "Get back to whatever alien world you came from."

The fire took on the purple, electric tint like a gas fire. He smiled as he rose to his feet, slapping dry dirt off his palms. Footsteps pounded from behind him.

"Get away from it!"

"Jace?" said Haider, turning around.

His brother tackled him, the crown of his head crashing into his sternum. The wind blew out of Haider's lungs as they fell to the ground. The flames ripped at the sky, climbing up the branches like angry fire spirits. Embers rained around them like fireflies.

"You're alright?" said Haider, getting to his feet. "I thought the tree..."

"No need to sweat it, dude," said Jace, no purple bruises around his neck. "I'm here."

Haider's vision blurred. "I knew you wouldn't quit on me."

"Think you were getting rid of me that easy?"

Haider launched himself at Jace, dragging him into a fierce hug. They slapped each other on the back, squeezing until it hurt. A recoiling stench of battery acid rose from Jace. The reek hazed out his skin until Haider could taste the burn of it on the roof of his mouth. He placed his hands on Jace's shoulders, and gently pushed him off, holding onto to him.

He stared into his brother's blackening eyes. "You're not Jace."

The image of his brother smiled. A river of black, curdled mess dribbled down his chin and onto the grass. When he spoke, the tree's voice pounded Haider's centre. "All that you love..."

The figure clomped forward. His brother's eyes reformed, becoming two empty rectangles that glowed red. The harshness of that light made a circle of heat burn in Haider's stomach. A mass of black dots writhed on the figure's skin.

"You deserve to float the ocean of nothing forever," said the entity that had mimicked Jace.

Haider knelt, picked up the axe, and swung it at the figure. The blade bit into its side. It made no difference. It smiled and moved forward, the axe handle sticking out of its gut.

As it set its hand upon the axe, black spread up the wooden handle. It coiled a hand around the axeblade and ripped it out. Its ruined skin made a moist slopping sound as the wound healed itself. It gripped the axe with two hands and punched the handle against Haider's chest.

Haider fell to the ground. Pain stabbed at his lung like the thing had cracked a rib.

"Leave Caitlyn," he wheezed, staring into the grass. "She shouldn't be part of this. Take me instead."

A figure crashed into the alien thing, wrestling it to the ground. Haider rose to his feet. Above the fighting pair, the tree crackled in unnatural hues, lighting up the grass in a rainbow of flames as if lit through a prism.

"Jace?" said Haider.

The alien was now a blackened husk with red glowing from its features as the real Jace pinned it and drove his head down, cracking its nose.

Haider stepped over and rammed the end of the axe into the alien's temple. It gave an ear-wrenching yell of pain that made Haider collapse backward. A noise like crackling static filled his brain as the thing dissolved into the grass.

"Bro," croaked Jace.

Haider stood and leaned on his knees, catching his breath. It felt as if a balloon expanded in his brain, ready to pop at any moment. "Saved my bacon. Thanks."

"Caitlyn."

"What about her?"

Haider stepped forward, but his brother's image blinked away into nothing. The cool of the dawn breezed over his face, soothing the heat that had baked into his cheeks. All lay still. No wood crackled.

The tree no longer burned.

It stood tall and proud, its chittering skin unblemished.

"Caitlyn prepares for the end," said the tree echoing inside his mind.

"What have you done?"

"Come closer."

He dropped the useless axe and stepped forward. "What did you say about—"

A tide of black things scuttled down the tree, along the dirt and the grass. They covered his boots, swarming his ankles and up his legs. Hundreds of needle points pricked his flesh.

Caitlyn blossomed in his mind's eye. She sat at his kitchen table, tears dripping off her reddened face. She grit her teeth, stabbing at a piece of paper with a pen. As if he stood over her shoulder, the tree showed him what she wrote:

... think me a bitch for adding another death to this house. Maybe that's a good thing. I'm no good, Haider. Maybe you'll find that out. I hope you don't. All you wanted was your family around you. Maybe this way I'll be included in that? Maybe I can grant you that last wish? Hate me for being a coward, but I see no other way. I really am sorry.

"No," said Haider, coming back to himself. He shook off the army of blackness on his skin. It drifted into the air like black snow.

He got in his van and drove.

18.

HAIDER'S ARSE hit the doorframe as he skidded into the kitchen. Caitlyn sat at the table, cupping a folded paper funnel in front of her open mouth. White powder as fine as sand spilled from the funnel and onto the table as she paused. Her puffy eyes held a screaming, private note of pain he'd never seen before.

He stretched over and batted her hand. A puff of white misted the air as the folded paper unfurled itself and landed on the table. The taste of bitter painkiller swirled about his tongue as he stared at the rows of empty blue pill casings.

"I can't be this cooked-up version of me," said Caitlyn, her hand still held before her mouth. "If I can't see the world, the world isn't getting to see me."

"You can't leave me, gorgeous." Haider cupped her vacant face in his hands. "Got that?"

"Just let me go. I'd rather die than be stuck here. That's the truth. I wish it weren't, but there you go." She jerked her watery eyes up at him. Hope ballooned in those big blues. "Were you able to rip that tree up?"

"No." He dropped his hands. "No, it's impossible."

"Well. That's that, then. Some knight in shining armour you turned out to be, eh?"

"Don't be like that. I'll try again. There has to be a way to—"

Caitlyn slapped her hand on the table. A dry scratch sounded as she wiped the powder, scooping it into her hand. She almost slammed her nose off the table as she leaned down to take the mound of crushed death into her mouth. He gripped her shoulders, wrestling her away from it.

"Stop it." Haider pinned her hands by her side to stop her licking at her whitened fingers. She kicked over a table as he hauled her through the living room.

"Let me go, prick."

"I wish I could."

She went limp in his arms. "Maybe now's the time when you share whatever it is you need to tell me."

"What you mean?"

"I found it, Haider." She stabbed a finger toward the coffee table. "How long, eh? How long?"

His leaf lay flat on the tabletop. Its midnight surface glimmered in the soft sunrise that hazed through the window. "How did you—"

"Never mind how, you lying cunt-face. How long? How long did you sit there and let me think I was losing my mind, when it was you who did this to me? Well? Go on. Man up about it at least."

Ramsay appeared in his big chair, clutching his can of Guinness and slurping away. A rivulet of sweat traced down a vein on his father's temple as he stared out the window, looking like a kid ignoring his arguing parents.

Caitlyn let out a rising groan, then rifled a hand through her frazzled hair. "You were pretty sleek when we found my dad's leaf, weren't you? All loving and caring. What next, Haider? If I don't do as you bid are you gonna cut me up?"

"Don't be daft."

"Daft? Daft? Lucky I'm not the one doing the carving right now."

He bit down on the searing words willing themselves to erupt. The bloodlust cast to her eyes made him take a step back. There was something in her stance that made him think she really would stick him right now if she had a knife.

"The leaf came to me about a week ago," said Haider. "After I visited the tree. You have to listen to me. I didn't mean for any of this to happen. It called to me one night. I was hammered and before I knew what I was doing, I told the tree what I wanted."

"And just what was that, exactly?"

As he closed his eyes, a tear tickled its way down the side of his nose. "That you can't leave."

She held her tense fists by her side. The orange of her perfume stung him as she turned to face the window. He savoured the fruity scent, knowing this might be the last time he could.

"Let me get this the right way round," she said, her back to him. "Just so I know what lengths of sheer cuntery you went to."

"I didn't mean for this, gorgeous. Honest, I—"

"You made your wish. Then I got that call saying my place had been taken away. That lassie was killed and shoved down that hole. The guy at the station screamed about his bloody murder. I got trapped here by some alien dome thingy. Then what my father did before he offed himself. You sat there knowing what was going on and you stayed quiet."

"Hey, come on. That's a bit unfair. I didn't do all that."

"But you knew. And you could've done something about it."

"I don't know if that's true."

She turned her fiery eyes on him. "What?"

"That tree isn't a tree. It's some kind of alien, I think. I know that sounds well daft, but it showed me things. I-I tried chopping it down, but it magically healed itself. Fire doesn't do the trick, either."

As Caitlyn shook with rage, his mother appeared beside her. The hurt in Greta's eyes made a fresh tear fall down his cheek. Greta's skeletal hand smoked out from the folds of her duvet. She reached over and stroked Caitlyn's shoulder.

Caitlyn flinched and turned round. Her eyes darted about the room like she'd just been stung.

"Forgive her," said Haider. "She just misses you, is all."

"Who?" said Caitlyn.

"My mum. Who else?"

"God, this is fucked." Some of the anger seemed to dissolve out of her. "What do we do then, hotshot? Any bright ideas? Or is this us?

Stuck in this house with the ghosts of your family watching as I try not to kill myself day after boring day."

"Why can't I be enough for you?" Haider reached and took her hand. "You dream about being away in the big wide world, but I dream about you. About us. Sad as that sounds, it's true. I look at you and my belly still goes flipsy-daisy. So, aye, I found myself at the base of that tree. And I made my wish. And I'd do anything to take it back if I could."

"Do it."

"I tried taking the leaf back, but it just reappeared."

Caitlyn turned and kicked the base of the couch. Ramsay flinched, still trying to ignore their conversation. Haider heard him slurping excess beer from the top of the can that had spilled over with thick, black liquid.

"Right," said Caitlyn, running the knuckle of her thumbs below each running eye. "My head's been well and truly grated. I'm going to bed. Maybe when it's a decent hour we'll work a way through this."

On the couch, Jace and Greta sat. Each clutched a glass as they laughed at something his dad said.

"I'll be through in a wee bit, gorgeous," said Haider.

Caitlyn stared at the couch, squinting her eyes. "Don't bother, sunshine. I need to be alone."

She stomped down the hallway and slammed the bedroom door closed. The sound drove fresh pain around his skull.

He took a can of cider from the fridge and sat next to his jolly family. As he leaned back on the couch, the drift of pleasant conversation humming in his ears, he drifted off.

19.

ALL THAT YOU love will be taken away.

A wail whimpered its way out of Haider's mouth. The iron reverberations of the tree's voice still rung between his ears as the early morning sun burned windowpane shapes in his vision.

He stared up at the ceiling from his spot on the couch, his family crowding around him. They seemed so far away, like he lay at the bottom of a grave as they said their final farewells. They stared down at him with solemn, hollow eyes. Dizziness touched its cold way over him.

"Mess," croaked Jace. From this angle, his purpled bruise looked like a torn smile up his neck.

"Would you all stop looking at me like that?" said Haider. "Feel like I pissed myself, or something."

"Had ourselves a good drink without you," said Ramsay, his ruddy cheeks slick with sweat. "Missed yourself, ya wet blanket."

"C-Caitlyn," said Greta.

"What about her?" said Haider.

"N-Needs you."

Haider stood, the world tipping about him. His brain felt as if it'd been dipped in wax. He rubbed at the centre of his forehead and waited for the world to right itself.

"She's still here, son," said Ramsay. "Don't you sweat it."

"Did you see her try to kill herself?" said Haider.

"Aye. We saw. Poor lassie's been through the ringer."

Haider rubbed at his eyes. His frazzled mind tried to claw itself from the fuzz of sleep. "What do I do?"

"Stay," said Jace.

"I didn't ask you, ya quitting bastard."

"D-Don't," said Greta, mist curling off the top of her head. "P-Peace. No fighting. F-Family."

Haider sighed and looked out at the promise of a sunny day. "I thought if I could make her stay, she'd see how happy I could make her, you know? Sounds daft now, but I believed that we could make a proper go of it."

"N-Nothing is lost."

Jace sprung to life, jabbing a finger at the open door. "Caitlyn."

Haider stared at the empty doorway. He leaned forward, listening. "What?"

They'd vanished. Cold loneliness settled on his skin like a fine rain.

He walked over to the window and set his forehead against the cool glass. There had to be a way out of this – a way to chop down that tree. He needed some heavy-duty machinery.

A mirthless, sour laugh puffed out of his mouth. "Needs more than a prick with an axe."

A black leaf danced outside the window. He stepped back, bumping into the couch. His world toppled as he fell. The coffee table made a wooden slap noise as he leaned against it. The leaf wasn't there.

He peered out the window again, examining the leaf as it hovered like a hummingbird picking a target. It was his leaf. He'd recognise its contours and its map of veins anywhere.

"What are—"

It zipped through the window. Hot pain sliced along the side of his neck. He fell to one knee and clamped a hand over the cut. The taste of iron curled at the back of his throat as the hot blood moistened his palm.

He twisted round and prepared for the buzzing, vibrating leaf to come at him again. Nothing but silence came for him. He seethed in a long breath through clenched teeth as the pain ripped to life along his neck. The ground seemed to quiver as he stood and removed his hand. The air attacked the wound, sending fresh pain zigzagging its way up his jaw. His hand was covered in thick, black blood.

He raced to the corner of the living room, to the mirror that lay in a spot lit alcove surrounded by family photos and framed pictures Caitlyn had taken. His hand shook as he lifted the small, oval mirror.

Along his neck, black ink spread under his skin with searching, smoky tendrils.

The tree was inside him. A surge of thick heat rolled in his stomach, climbing up his spine. He dropped the mirror. It smashed into shards beside his foot. The clamping pain in his chest made him double over. As his heart beat harder, blood swelled in his ears.

"Argh!"

The pain ascended to blinding heights. His legs folded under him. Keening, animal noises erupted from somewhere deep as he set his forehead against the scratchy carpet.

Darkness spread down his wrists like spilled ink in water. It blossomed, claiming his pale skin inch by inch with its oily black.

A shard of mirrored glass twinkled beside his knee. In its small reflection, he caught the scream captured in his wide eyes. The urge to dig that glass into his wrists rose within him. He willed his hand to grab the glass, but it stayed where it was, clutched around his stomach.

"Caitlyn?" he shouted. "Caitlyn, help—"

The pressure behind his eyeballs built. It felt as if he were having a seizure. Spit steamed out the corner of his mouth, spattering on the carpet as the pain made him shuffle his legs beneath him.

"What happened?" said Caitlyn, bursting into the room.

"It's got me. The tree..."

He lifted a trembling hand. Blood ran cold under his flesh where the darkness claimed his skin. He rose to his feet as if tugged by some invisible string. The muscles in his leg tensed.

"Run!" said Haider.

She turned and fled. Haider followed in a stilted, jerking trot. As she looked back at him, she tripped over her own foot. Her palms slapped the carpet as she saved herself from head-butting the floor.

He threw every bit of his inner being at trying to escape the tree's grasp, but his legs pistoned on. It felt as if he were trapped in the predestined moves of a nightmare.

Caitlyn kicked at the ground, scuttling back, her face a picture of icy panic. She yelped as he grabbed an ankle and hauled her back onto the floor.

"Don't," she said, trying to kick her way out of his grip.

"I'm sorry, gorgeous."

His charred, blackened hands grabbed an ankle each and pulled Caitlyn below him. Her top rolled up as she slid, exposing a stomach so flat her ribcage looked almost caved in.

She held him with a pleading, agonised gaze as he sat on her stomach. Her hand reached into her pocket. A blade glinted silver as it skimmed his cheek.

He slid off of her, his back hitting the wall. She whimpered as she got to her feet, clutching the small knife in her hand. With her jaw set, Haider saw the look of murder in her fevered eyes.

She jerked her hand forward like a striking snake. He chucked himself to the side. The knife scraped the wall. Caitlyn came for him again. Metal sliced through his thin t-shirt as he leapt back.

He held his palms up. "Wait."

"I'm gonna watch you bleed out for what you did to me."

"This ain't you."

"I wouldn't be so sure about that, sunshine."

Haider felt his muscles bracing, waiting for the strike. He tried to instruct his body to relax, to give up the fight, but he waited, one foot in front of the other, ready.

"We'll beat it," said Haider. "We'll find a way. But listen to me. You need to get away, alright? I can't stop it."

"Too little, too late."

She swung her knife hand at his stomach, groaning with the effort. Haider bounced back on his toes, letting the blade go under him. His black fingers clutched her hand. With a strength he didn't know he was capable of, he crushed her hand until knuckles and bone popped. With his other hand, he took the knife.

She dropped to one knee, holding her mangled hand close to her chest.

He flipped the knife around in his hand, then held it above his head. Sweat dropped down his face with the useless effort of trying to stop the tree using his body. He was going to murder the one good thing left in his life.

"I'm so sorry, gorgeous," he said. "It wasn't supposed to be this way. We were supposed to be happy."

"Do it. Come on. What you waiting for? I'm done." She set her other knee on the ground and bowed her head. A single tear fell to the carpet. "I'm done."

His arm tensed and he felt his body give all his strength to the thrust.

A hand gripped his wrist, stopping the blow.

"Jace?" said Haider. "How?"

Through the knots of blond hair covering his brother's face, he saw the determined set to Jace's features. He could see the risen burns along his brother's neck where the rope as scorned him.

"Family," said Jace.

Haider closed his eyes and thought of the times they'd spent crashing through the forest. The times when he'd thought he'd lost Jace in the unending trees and how panicked he'd been when he'd find him atop a tree stump with that stupid grin on his face.

A rush like cold water cleansed its way through Haider's muscles. He lowered his hand. The knife clattered to the floor.

Caitlyn chuffed ragged breaths, looking up at him and then at the spot where Jace stood. She leaned on a palm and hauled herself up to her feet. He longed to go to her, to wrap his arms around her. His palms were as black as charred wood.

"So, what do we do now?" said Caitlyn, reaching a hand over her midriff, clutching at her arm. "Is that to be our life now? Waiting for the moment you kill me?"

"It's best you go."

"Go? Go where?"

"I-I don't know. I wish it didn't have to be like this. I wish you'd have chosen to stay on your own. After all we've been through, for you to just vanish and leave me here."

"That makes it alright, does it?"

"I can feel it building again."

Caitlyn breathed in an uneven breath. "I won't lay down and die."

She turned and ran out of the house, slamming the door behind her.

Jace moved in front of him. "Stay."

20.

PULSING violence spread through Haider's chest like freezing water. His socked feet slapped the pavement as red-eyed onlookers gawked at him chasing a woman in distress. The tree's energy still thrummed inside him, baying for Caitlyn's blood.

She leapt over the crumpled archway of Cuttie Hill park, watching over her shoulder as he gained on her. The silver look of fear in her eyes curdled his gut. No matter how he willed himself to stop, his feet churned on. He caught up to her at the base of the glimmering tree.

"Don't just stand there. Find a way. Fight it," said Caitlyn, catching her breath.

He hardly recognised the voice that garbled out his mouth. "You must not leave. Ever. He willed it so."

Caitlyn straightened. "Go fuck yourself, ya alien bastards. Leave us alone. Fight it, Haider!"

He clamped his jaw shut, struggling against the fiery words that rumbled from somewhere deep inside. "What made you believe that someone of your breeding deserved to see this Earth?"

"What?"

Haider punched his chin as hard as he could. "Get out of me. You can't... You were always a street trash whore. The sticky stuff at the bottom of the bin. Why'd you think he chose you? Such an easy, desperate wife you'd have made."

The dewy grass seeped through the bottom of his socks as he was pulled closer.

"No. No, that's not it. You're lying," said Caitlyn, stepping into the shadow of the tree.

Haider tasted the high burning scent of used machinery as he moved forward. He darted his blackened hand out, grabbed her wrist, then drove his fist into her stomach. Spit flew from her mouth as she doubled over, struggling to draw a breath. Behind them, the skin of the tree danced like black fire.

He grabbed a fistful of her hair and yanked her head up. Strands of her hair snapped between his fingers as the alien force inside made him pull her closer.

"You said the tree amplifies what's already inside someone." Caitlyn's voice strained through the unnatural angle of her neck. "Is this what's been inside you all this time?"

"I'm sorry."

Haider raised his clenched fist. The morning sun lit up her freckles and those wondrous blue eyes. In his countless dreams of their wedding, he'd spun her around and around in her white dress, holding her close.

He summoned every piece of internal strength he could muster and let her go. She stumbled, then stood straighter. The tree let out a bellow like approaching thunder. He marched up to it, craning his neck.

"What you gonna do?" said Caitlyn.

"I've absolutely no idea."

He heard the distant noise of people starting their day. Soon, there would be families here, if the blue sky was anything to go by – families who could fall prey to the tree's clutches.

Jace appeared next to him. "Champs."

"We'll never quit," said Haider, nodding at his brother.

The ground rumbled, vibrating up his calves. Haider remembered how the thing had unrooted itself in his nightmare.

"You can't have her," said Haider.

A chittering of black dots piled over each other. Crackling shapes joined together, forming the words.

All that you love will be taken away.

"All that I had, I've already lost," said Haider. "You picked on the wrong person. Show me what you really are."

He felt a hot cold sensation ride up the back of his legs. The tree was reaching for control again. He turned and waved at Caitlyn, urging her to leave.

He stood shoulder to shoulder with his brother as the alien thing reached into in. Jace took his hand. It felt strong and true, just as calloused as it had been in real life.

"Champs," said Jace.

Jace dropped his hand and ran for the tree. He knelt in the dirt and flung himself at it, raising his fist as if to strike a mighty blow.

"No!" shouted Haider.

His brother hit the tree. Instead of bouncing off, he clung to the bark as if he were a fly on honey. The tree's black army covered his body, consuming him. The tree's surface seemed to melt as it absorbed Jace into its dark depths.

Haider clutched at the collar of his t-shirt. Where Jace had been eaten, a dull, metallic grey shone under the skin like a wound. On its smooth surface, two red eyes burned at him.

A branch snapped off the tree, falling to the ground by his foot. Its dead leaves shook from the impact, exploding into ash.

"What happened?" said Caitlyn, beside him.

"You have to go. Go now."

"You hurt it."

"Jace hurt it. Jace..."

A burst of electric pain shot through his skull. He fell to his knees and lay his head against the cool grass. The sour taste of the ashen leaves was on his tongue as he fought to stay in control of himself.

"No more," roared the tree.

"Haider, get up," said Caitlyn. "You can do it. You—"

He shoved her as hard as he could. She stumbled back, struggling to stay on her feet. "I'm begging you, gorgeous. Go. For me."

Another branch snapped off the tree. As it hit the ground, puffs of ashy dust burst into the air like angry gnats.

"T-Time," said his mother, appearing at his side.

She placed a frigid hand on his shoulder. A defiant smile rose through a plume of winter breath as she nodded at him.

"We'll have ourselves a right good drink on the other side, my big guy," said his dad, appearing at his other side. "Time for us to get out of that house. Time for you to get on with living."

"Mum? Dad? No."

"Aye, son." Ramsay slapped him on the back. "We can fight it. Picked on the wrong family, that bastard tree."

"I can't lose you."

"You never will."

"Don't. Please? Don't go with Jace. You don't know what—"

"Ssh," said Greta, holding a cold finger on his lips. "G-Going. Won't be c-cold no more."

"Don't."

Haider pawed at the tear running down his face. A smear of black came off the back of his hand. The tree sent a wave of power smashing into him. The alien grip made him turn and face Caitlyn who'd retreated to the mangled entrance.

"Love you, son," said his dad.

"No," said Haider. "No, you can't."

His muscles protested as he fought to turn his neck. His parents stood hand in hand before the failing tree. Ramsay leaned over and gave Greta a gentle peck on the cheek. She smiled like a smitten schoolgirl. As two, they walked into the tree.

"No!" roared Haider.

The tree released its hold on him. The earth vibrated below the soles of his wet feet. The tree's bark split as bigger branches rained onto the ground. He marched over, just outside the range of the tree's dead limbs.

A high-pitched screech filled his world. He covered his ears and fell to his knees. The small black dots that writhed along the tree's surface fell away, tumbling into a mound of dead, black things. He felt the pain of each creature as it perished, dissolving into the earth.

"Is it over?" said Caitlyn, throwing an arm around him.

He slowly released his clamped hands from his ears. "I think so."

The tree looked like a chopped mess, just the way he'd fantasised when he'd been foolish enough to try take it down with just his axe. Its bark was cracked and dead. Under the skin, the metal glinted with no life.

He looked up into Caitlyn's reddened face. "I should never have tried to keep you here. You should've been free to live your dreams. I should've been the one to die. Not them. They're gone, Caitlyn. Because of me. And now you."

"Maybe this way you can start to live a life again. And me? Dreams are made for changing, babes. Nothing left to stop me now, is there?" She kissed the top of his head. "Is there?"

"I..."

A being stood behind her. Its skin was made of tough, rubbery darkness. Two red eyes danced with malice as the creature stalked forward. Where its mouth should've been, a row of four jagged squares burned with the same alien light as its eyes. He felt its life pulse in that awful glow.

Haider squeezed Caitlyn's hand. "Take some pictures for me, alright?"

He pulled her down into a kiss and then shoved her away from the nightmare apparition. The thing walked in a limping, injured gait. Haider felt static buzz inside his brain as the creature examined him.

"Haider? What—" Caitlyn stopped. An animal wail blew out of her as she fell to the ground.

"I won't let you have her," said Haider.

The alien thing grunted as he bolted for the tree. It held a shaking hand toward him. The last of its power tried to take him over again, to stop him from going to the dying tree, but he wouldn't be denied.

He closed his eyes and leapt into the metallic centre of the tree.

21.

WEIGHTLESS AND UNTETHERED, Haider spun in the void. It had sucked him into its cold, dark dream of stars. Each time the alien let out a deafening roar, it felt like his brain would bleed out of his ears. The galaxies and distant gas clouds vibrated, blurring in his vision like overcharged atoms.

His family floated with him. No matter how hard he tried to swim to them, to touch them, they spun in slow rotations, maddeningly just out of reach. They hovered together in the vast emptiness like four edges of an unseen square.

They'd saved Caitlyn – sacrificed themselves so she could leave Pitlair and live her life. It was only right that he had delivered the final blow. After he felt himself sucked into this void, whatever it was, he felt something in his brain pop. His wish to have Caitlyn stay was finished, its hold on her severed.

Now, he could be with his family forever. He'd pay the price for what he'd done. He hated that he'd dragged his family into the same fate.

His mother kicked at space as if lithely changing directions underwater. A smile tugged at the corner of her mouth as she reached out her hand. He saw a stream of excited chatter run from her mouth.

"Mum?" said Haider. "Mum? I can't hear you."

It had been so long since he'd seen her without her covers wrapped tight over her shoulders. He forgot how small she was. He forgot how tall she seemed when she glared at you.

She took in a deep breath then shouted, but still no sound came to him.

"Jace?" said Haider, shifting to look at his brother who leaned back as if he treaded water. "Jace, you hear me?"

His tag team partner didn't budge. Directly across from him, Ramsay's panicked eyes flared. His dad's mouth bobbed up and down as a tear dropped off his face.

Haider swallowed the dry lump in his throat. "I'm sorry. I'm sorry, okay? This was all my fault. I shouldn't have dragged you all into this. What am I saying? You can't even hear me. Will you ever hear me again? God, what is this place?"

The passage of time was an impossible thing to mark. He watched Jace's languid rotations, hoping to catch his brother's attention, but he always seemed to be able to steer his face away from him.

Greta stretched herself, her tongue sticking out with the effort of trying to reach her husband. Ramsay did the same thing, clawing at the space between them as if he could dig his way to her. Haider's sight blurred and he turned away, staring out into the cold abyss.

Despite the vast space, he felt as if he were trapped in a small box, the walls shifting ever closer. He caught a distant hint of Caitlyn's orangey perfume from somewhere on him. He sniffed himself all over. He lost the scent.

"Fly for me," he said, knuckling a tear from his cheek.

And they floated.

And floated.

The stars never changed.

A rumbling laughter filled the space. It shook the pit of his stomach as he looked around him, searching for the source of the gut-wrenching noise. His family searched desperately for it, too.

A leaf zipped from the darkness, stopping just before his eyes. Upon its liquorice surface, two red squares glowed with a light that made bile creep up his gullet. He gagged and covered his mouth.

The laughter melted away into the distance. Around the leaf, the fabric of existence seemed to rip open. He blinked rapidly at what he was seeing. Before him, a square-shaped window showed images of the world beyond this void-place – images of Pitlair.

His eyes grew dry as he watched the footage cast before him like a TV. It skipped like a programme on rewind, showing his family sacrificing themselves, Caitlyn fleeing as the leaf controlled him, her squeezing pills and emptying their white contents onto the paper funnel, his useless attempts to chop the tree down and further back in time.

It froze on an image of Caitlyn.

He reached out to touch her face. His hand buzzed through the image. Murder was in her blue eyes. Clutched in her fist, a knife. Along her top, slashes of crimson blood shone in dim light.

He placed a hand over his mouth. Cold flushed over his skin. "No."

The vision played. Caitlyn moved toward her tied up mother. Her mum's eyes looked as if they'd pop out of her skull. She held her tied hands up toward her daughter, mumbling a prayer through the rope that was tied across her mouth.

The smile that split Caitlyn's gorgeous face was something he'd never seen before. It carried such heat, such wanting. She strode forward and punched the knife into her mother over and over until she was nothing more than a slumped-over corpse. Blood dotted Caitlyn's face as she lit up in ecstasy.

"No!" yelled Haider.

Caitlyn walked out of the vision. Haider was left with a view of Caitlyn's mum's lifeless body as a stain of red seeped around her on the carpet.

Caitlyn appeared again, hunched over. She dragged her father's body into the room. Her dad's shirt was matted with blood, and yet she drove the knife into his chest.

"Don't!" Haider cried. A tear rolled off his cheek, floating in mid-air before him like a small bubble.

He watched Caitlyn hold her stomach, chortling with glee.

She reached into her pocket.

A black leaf.

She bent down and smeared the leaf into her dad's chest, smothering it in his blood.

He tore himself away from the vision, but the window moved before his eyes no matter where he focused. It wouldn't let him look away. He closed his eyes, but the sound of her laughter pierced him.

"She knew I had my leaf because she had her own," said Haider. A sharp taste of ozone needled up his nostril and into his sinuses as he breathed in a sharp, shaky breath. "All this time. You knew. What did you wish for?"

The sound rumbled from everywhere around him and inside his skull. It mimicked Caitlyn's summery voice. "Give me freedom from everything that holds me back."

"Everything that holds me back."

She had her freedom now. He would hold her back no more.

The vision before him snowed out like a dodgy telly.

"Why?" he asked the void. "Why do all this?"

Its laughter buzzed between his ears, making his teeth clack together.

The window appeared again.

The images rolled.

Caitlyn tied up her mother. She smiled her dimple-creasing smile. She stuck the knife in her mother over and over.

Haider screamed into the void.

AFTERWORD

Did you make it to the end without discovering your own black leaf? If you end up at the foot that gnarled, nightmare tree, what would you wish for? What is in your deepest heart?

Apart from making time stop going by so damn fast, I'd wish for short stories to be as famous as novels. You can be transported to magical places, be awed by the stories punch, all within half an hour or so. It's a crying shame that most people don't know short stories exist.

A collection of stories is like a music album – if you don't like one story, just skip to the next. And if a story gets in your bones, you can come back to it forever.

In today's Netflixian world, I think bitesize stories are perfect for those who don't have the time, or the desire, to read a chunky novel.

Along with the masters (Ray Bradbury, Shirley Jackson, John Collier, Harlan Ellison, Mark Twain, Joyce Carol Oates, to name a small few), I'd recommend Black Static magazine, the NoSleep podcast, Nightmare magazine and KZine if you need a short story fix.

All the tales in this collection are diary entries with some coming close to being non-fiction. *In a Jar of Spiders* will always hold a special place in my writerly heart as it was the first time I enjoyed what I'd written. Took me a few years, and it's far from perfect, but it is *me.*

And yes, we did go around hedges collecting spiders in jam jars. Not something I'd recommend, but a strong memory all the same.

There have been many helpful editors and writer chums along the way that helped me with each of these stories. Tim Major and Christa Angelios were editors that I found at the right time in my career. They both went above and beyond, almost coaching me into the writer I am today. Jaime Powell helped give each of the stories the polish they needed – any remaining mistakes are all me! Timea from Fantastical-Ink.com did a cracking job on the cover. A special thank you goes to my critique chums at sff.onlinewritingworkshop.com.

Of course, I owe my biggest thanks to my glorious wife who watches me escape into my stories, giving me the space to spread my dream-wings.

And thanks to you, dear reader. Perhaps next time you'll join me for a Midnight Walk?

May your shadow never grow less,
Paul O'Neill
September 2021

ABOUT THE AUTHOR

Paul O'Neill is a short fiction writer from Fife, Scotland. He is an Internal Communications professional who battles the demon of corporate speak on a daily basis.

His stories have appeared in Eerie River's It Calls from the Doors anthology, Scare Street's Night Terrors series, Purple Wall stories and many more. He also placed second in Teleport Magazine's 2020 short story competition.

Outside of reading and writing, his favourite pastimes include laughing with his family, the Green Bay Packers, and repeating how to pronounce his sons' names over and over until people actually get it.

You can find him at pauloneillwriter.com or on Twitter @PaulOn1984.

Printed in Great Britain
by Amazon